Anna's
Adventure

Anna's Adventure

A Tale of Crime, Disasters and Mystery.

A. P. BAZELEY

Ordering Information:

BookTrail Agency
8838 Sleepy Hollow Rd.
Kansas City, MO 64114

Printed in the United States of America

DEDICATION

This book is dedicated to my children. Whether I actually gave birth to you or not, you know who you are and how much you are loved, appreciated and in my thoughts and prayers daily.

Acknowledgements

To the ones who have inspired, teased, pushed me and encouraged me to keep going. You have made me have some fun and to laugh a lot! You have given me work, rest and play and for all that I thank you.

I consider the fact that my world now includes grandchildren and great- grandchildren as a bonus or is it buy one get one free I mean? All I know that there seem to be quite a few of you now and I love that we all can have good times together now that we no longer have such stringent lockdown measures in place. So, see you all soon.

However, a special mention must be given for the sheer courage it took for my daughter to edit my previous book, Jeni and tell me to keep going and get myself even more experienced advice to follow, Gina, you are a star! For my new editorial advice I have to thank accomplished writer Fay Sampson. Without you I would not have finished this book. To Rachael Schilling-Payne for her copy writing advice, Tania Ashdown for her proof reading skills, I owe a big debt of gratitude for your kindness, support and friendship. Due to you, I was encouraged to carry on with the next book, a new venture for me, into the world of murder. However, when it came to this book's title, I was left to dig into the past and remember an old friend, Anna. Anna, as you were the quiet one who surprised us all with how your life turned out, I felt this book had to carry your name on its cover. I hope that if you ever read this book you will remember me as your friend and flatmate up in Newcastle-Upon-Tyne during our happy student days.

As always, I have to give a mention to my husband. The man who has read, critiqued, encouraged and generally kept me on track. Thank you dear, is never enough. However, it is always sincerely meant. You know that there is no one quite like you as far as I am concerned. As another singer too once sang, "You're the best, better than all the rest."

Finally, to those you have taken the time to read both Tilly and Jeni, I thank you too. I hope that here you will find that their adventures have come to a conclusion; with your questions answered and a sigh of contentment as you lay this book down. For that, dear readers, would make me happier than anything. Enjoy!

Character List

ANNA LEWIS – A Purchasing and Marketing executive for a large London department store.

LEON LEWIS– Anna's husband. A Librarian.

TILLY BROWN - Old friend of Anna. Co-owner of GT BUSINESS SERVICES.

CRAIG RYMAN – Police Officer. Boyfriend of Tilly.

JENI DURHAM – Close friend of Anna. An author. Real name Jeni Marr.

PLOCKTON – A village in the West of Scotland. Temporary home of Jeni.

GLORIA - Housekeeper to Jeni.

JACKSON REDMAN – Jeni's boyfriend. Best friend of Fernando Alverez.

JO LAWSON – An artist in glass. Close friend.

CRAIGLOCKHART CREATIVE CRAFTS – Jo's business named after the village to where she lives.

FERNANDO ALVEREZ – Boyfriend of Jo. Has a Yacht Charter Business at **KYLE OF DRUMCRAE**.

CATHY GILLMAN – Tilly's Godmother and good friend to Anna, Jeni and Jo.

LORD PERCIVAL MARMADUKE GREYSTOKE – PERCY, Cathy's husband to be.

GEORGE CROWTHER – Old friend and Best Man to Lord Greystoke.

SHONA ADAMS – Jo's right hand at CRAIGLOCKHART CREATIVE CRAFTS.

DREW ADAMS – Shona's husband and also a driver for Jo's business.

XANDER SMITH – Jo's new driver for her business.

CANDICE "CANDY"- The mysterious woman party gate-crasher.

MARGARITA CONSUELA FORTUNATA – known as Maggie - a Spanish Wedding Dress Designer.

DON JUAN MANUEL DE FORTUNATA CRISTOBEL – Maggie's grandfather and proprietor of the House of Fortunata Fashion House.

DEVON CHANCE – A debt collection agent not averse to crossing the line.

ANGUS GUTHRIE – Station Commander of the Police Station at Kyle of Drumcrae.

MICHAEL GRAEME – The plainclothes police officer allocated to Jackson Redman as his aide.

TOM BRUCE – Subordinate of Jackson Redman.

Chapter One

ANNA LEWIS STOOD day dreaming. It was her favourite occupation of late. Not the best hobby to have if you are an up and coming Purchasing Executive for one of the leading department stores on Oxford Street. It had all started when she had received an unexpected present from her old friend, Jeni Durham, two weeks ago. She had come home from work that day to find a notice from the postman telling her that she would need to go to the Sorting Office to pick up her parcel as he hadn't been able to catch her in. The following day was Saturday; so she got up early and went there first thing on the way to do her weekly shop. It was only eight o'clock and there was already a queue in the tiny cubicle at the Sorting Office! The woman at the front of it was well organised and out in no time. The next, unfortunately, was not so rapidly dealt with. By the time it was her turn Anna was getting fidgety and so was the queue behind her; it stretched out of the door and onto the path and she was anxious to get off to make a start on her day. She had claimed the small lightweight box marked fragile and was turning to get out of the door when her arm was tugged sharply, and she was, effectively halted in her tracks.

The young man who had been behind her in the queue was speaking. "I don't think that you'll get very far without this today." He said as he gave her a shy smile. Anna looked down. He held out to her the wallet in which she kept the I.D. documents she had used to claim her parcel. In her haste and in the noise of too many people in too small a space, she had forgotten to put them back in her handbag and had left them on the counter. As she looked up again into his face properly, she saw the kindness in this man's dark brown eyes and the thought that he would be a lovely person to get to know just popped into her head. She thanked him prettily for returning the wallet to her but, because of the press of bodies, had headed out the door to the relative peace outside the building swiftly afterwards. Drawn by her gentle smile, the man had followed her out, totally forgetting about the package he had come to pick up!

Anna noticed at once that he had followed her out and wondered why he hadn't stayed to conduct his business. As they both continued along the narrow path out of the premises, he engaged her attention by making a couple of general comments on the conditions of the sorting office and in no time they had reached the High Street before either had even noticed where they were. As Anna and the gentleman had come to a halt, the aroma of freshly brewed coffee floated towards them from an open door.

They had looked at each other and together come out with, "Shall we?"

Chapter Two

DURING THE RESULTING half hour Anna had learnt that he was single, a librarian and very interested in her. She had been meeting up with Leon Lewis for coffee, then lunch and even dinner regularly ever since. When she was not with Leon she found herself, like today, staring into space, daydreaming. Last night she had even dreamt of marriage and children. Now that was a first. However, daydreaming does not accomplish much in the workplace! Hence, Anna told herself that she had better get down to doing some actual work. It wasn't that she didn't like her job. It was all that parcel's fault!

Inside it had been a surprise. Jeni had sent her a delightfully wrapped box containing a beautifully crafted Christmas tree ornament made of delicately pretty coloured glass. A sprig of mistletoe, in shades of pale greens and white that could be hung by the rich red satin ribbon. It was an exquisite little treasure and Anna loved it on sight. When she had rung Jeni to thank her for it, she had asked her where she had found it. Jeni had known that she would want to learn more and told her that she had already sent her a link to her friend Jo's website. Jeni knew her so well! As a buyer for a large, exclusive department store, Anna was always on the lookout for exciting and interesting items with which to stock it.

Jo's unusual and attractive glasswork certainly met her criteria and Anna was eager to get in touch.

Now she had made contact with Jo Lawson at her Highland workshop, but what she really needed was to pay her a visit to discuss her business in more detail before committing herself to placing an order. All that remained was when? Anna thought of her diary and realised that it was quite full until later on in the month. She would have to just try and pencil something in for then and firm it up later. So far so good.

It was the thought that she might be able to combine it with a catch up with Jeni that had made it seem like the only bright spot in her busy but dull life. Work and everything was running quite smoothly but every week seemed the same. She loved her time with Leon and had filled all her spare time with him because it just was so easy to be with him. Otherwise nothing seemed to be going on in her life.

Perhaps it was just a touch of envy? Her two dearest friends, Jeni and Tilly, seemed to lead such exciting lives in comparison. Full of daily challenges and even adventures. Hers seemed so ordinary. Even her dreams were of ordinary things like love, marriage, children. Her long term plan to set up on her own as a consultant buyer and agent had not progressed since she had met Leon. With that thought, she spent the rest of the day ploughing through the paperwork and calls that awaited her and when it was done shut the office door with a bang behind her. She was fully determined that her bad mood would not follow her home to spoil her time with Leon that evening, Anna mentally shook herself and told herself to get a grip on things. After all, she was lucky to have a lovely man in her life, good friends and a good job. Surely there was nothing more she should be craving?

Chapter Three

MR. BIG SAT. He stared straight ahead. His eyes looked blank, as if no-one was there. However, his mind was in overdrive. He was contemplating how he had arrived in his current situation. Banged up!

Now, he was nothing if he wasn't honest ...... with himself. It had been his own vanity that had led him to this sorry state. His driving need to aggressively pursue anyone who got the better of him, however slight, had led to the abduction of Fernando Alverez and Jo Lawson. The fact that they were innocent parties was irrelevant. They were the key to getting his own back on Jackson Redman; the man whose single-minded pursuit of him had brought about his downfall. He was sure of that now. He would not make the same mistake twice! His mind raced as he coldly calculated his revenge; not only would he exact vengeance on Jackson Redman but he would also make sure that the pay-back would gain him his freedom too. It didn't matter how long it took him. Time. It was the one thing he wasn't short of. He had thirty five years to spend behind bars at Her Majesty's pleasure and all because of meddlers. He recalled their names in a slow litany. Jackson Redman, Fernando Alverez, Tilly Brown, Craig Ryan, Jeni Durham, Jo Lawson. They had all played their part and he would make them pay.

Just how that could be done would take careful planning. As he looked round his cell, he was aware of how that skill had got him the best cell on the wing and the cushiest job assignment too. No crappy cleaning toilets and showers for him. He was an aide in the two bed medical bay. Only really called upon if someone was confined there due to injury or illness. Easy. Better food too as sick people need good food to get better. Eaten in the medical bay so as to be on hand when needed, privacy; priceless in a busy place like this prison. Through his contacts he had already got the lowdown on who could arrange what and was able to wear his own clothes now and have his own barber come and do his hair. Perhaps not as frequently as before but still, when he looked in the mirror he looked like his old self once more. He firmly intended to put all that knowledge to good use in future when he planned to leave and take up his former occupation once more. In the meantime, he had arranged to be informed of anything pertaining to his targets his men on the outside could get their hands on. In fact, he had heard only that morning of a friend of theirs getting married. Could that be an opportunity to spring a trap? He wondered.

Chapter Four

As Anna looked over at her husband's smiling face she found it hard to believe that they had already been married for four whole weeks! Her Saturdays were now very different. In fact, her whole life was different! Otherwise how would she be sitting in a soft play centre at 10 o'clock on a Saturday morning having such a strange debate with a man she'd only known three months baby-sitting his twin niece and nephew?

She recalled. Her quick answer "Yes!" had both delighted and reassured him. Next, he had thought a moment and then come out with, "Why not just do it?" He had then asked Anna if there was any reason that they shouldn't get married as soon as he could arrange it. She had answered him with, "None that I know of."

They had spent the rest of the evening searching the internet for how to do just that. The more they found out that it was possible, the more they just wanted to do it. Both of them were shy about large crowds and being in the spotlight. A *fait accompli*, would save all that and a small fortune too they had discovered. It was settled; they were going to get married!

Three days later Leon had obtained a special licence. Anna's minister, Reverend Clive Jenkins, when consulted, was very happy to carry out a very simple wedding ceremony for the young couple he had seen every weekend at his Sunday Service since they first met. He had followed their growing love for each other and felt confident that although this wedding was a hurried affair, their marriage would be a long and happy one. They always seemed to be so good at putting the other person first. Naturally thoughtful and considerate, but also aware of the needs of others. Not so wrapped up in their own world that they didn't see if another person needed help. Anna and Leon seemed to instinctively work as a team. He had seen all this for himself as he had watched them one Sunday morning helping an elderly gentleman up the church steps and into his pew. Anna had charmed him into letting her take his arm by tucking his under hers and leaning in towards him to exchange a whispered aside. Meanwhile, Leon had come on his other side putting a gentle arm there for him to lean on for stability and direction that enabled Old Mr. Hendry to reach his usual seat with dignity and a confident smile on his face. They had gently asked if they could join him in his pew and throughout the service had shared hymn books, when he hadn't been able to find the number quickly enough or handed him his glasses when he had misplaced them. All done with the minimum of fuss and a lot of kindly grace. Reverend Jenkins hadn't seen anything more than a look pass between them to accomplish it all. Communication skills that were well-honed so early on boded well indeed for their relationship, he had thought to himself.

When he had been asked, he had said that he would have to speak with them privately first but he saw no reason to say no to their request to be married. After all, so many young folk nowadays just didn't bother with marriage let alone understand what it actually means.

It was a refreshing change to see two people value each other and their future together so much that they had put the spiritual side of it before having the 'big day'.

They had done it! They were actually married now. Anna recalled all the details of their special day; from how she had looked in the pretty long white dress that she had bought only the previous afternoon. It was gorgeous. A dream dress. Floaty and lacy and she would always treasure it. Her hair had just seemed to know that it was a special day and done exactly what she asked of it, her curls had waved rather than frizzed and her pretty pale ballet shoe pink nails hadn't smudged despite her haste. She knew she had looked as near to perfect as she would ever look. She had kept it simple with a small hand tied bouquet of pink roses, with the white and green lily of the valley and the dainty little florets of baby's breath from the florists she had often used to send flowers to her friend Cathy. It had gone perfectly with her perfect outfit, Leon, her perfect man and her perfect wedding day.

Just then it dawned on her that Leon's mouth was moving, he was actually talking to her. Oh dear what had she been saying before she had drifted off?

"Nature or nurture? Which one do you think it is, Leon?" Anna remembered asking her husband while looking at his cheeks with their slight pink flush. She had felt hers glowing too. Their debate, over what made the twins like they were, during the past hour had been lively. At one point she thought that they might have had to break open their belated wedding present from Jeni and Tilly. Fortunately or unfortunately, they had left their gift of two pairs of colourful blow up boxing gloves behind.

Coming back to the present, Anna, realised that Leon had gone. Vanished!

Anna immediately scanned the other three sections of the very large building beyond the café area that they had been sharing a table in. Then a smile broke out across her unconventionally beautiful face. There he was. His height was a dead giveaway. Just as well, as it was very busy in the Play Pen soft play zone this morning. He held in each of his hands a small hand belonging to Anya and Archie; his niece and nephew.

The two were cherubic looking twins. Both were dressed in blue jeans and matching red long sleeved t-shirts; one sporting spotty dinosaurs and the other colourful unicorns. The outfits a gift from their new adopted auntie, her friend Jeni. It certainly came in handy having a famous author as an auntie when birthdays came around! They looked so cute in their designer outfits. As Leon and the twins drew closer Anna thought how fortunate she was to have these three in her life.

"I think a five minute time-out is due, to let these two cool off a bit!" He said as he seated them in the spare seats at their table.

Anna was already getting the wet wipes out from the mini rucksack of essentials; that she now knew never to go anywhere without and was busily wiping their hands. A mini box of raisins and a small banana each and a good drink of water and they were desperate to get back into the climbing zone to catch up with their friends again.

"Now, where were we before those hooligans took my attention?" Leon asked her, giving her a big grin. "Round 14 or was it 15?" Anna chuckled and said that she would rather just have a fresh latte instead, if that was alright with him?

"As you wish." He told her as he wound his way through the tables to the service counter to order her a latte and a mug of tea for himself. Returning with the drinks and seated once more, they watched the children at play and gave them a wave every now and again.

"I do love our monthly Saturday brunches here, Anna." He told her.

"I enjoy them too! It means that I actually get to eat breakfast with you in relative peace, if not quiet. In addition we get to hold a conversation with minimal interruptions. I never thought that you would hear me say that bliss is the Play Pen", she had continued.

"Me neither!" Leon exclaimed. "Do you ever wish that we would have children?" He asked her.

"Do you?" Anna said.

Anna's counter reply had made him think before answering.

"Yes. I think that it's good if we were to have them soon, while we are young enough to enjoy growing up with them and then when they are off our hands, we'll still have the energy to do all those things we've dreamt of and maybe even have some money to do them with!" He answered her.

"It's as well you like children, as we have our hands full right now with these two. Just look at what they are up to now!" Anna called as she raced towards the twins.

It wasn't until later that evening when the twins were asleep and they had finally sat down again that he asked Anna why she hadn't answered "no way" to his question earlier. Anna smiled at him and told him that she had just been thinking that life had settled into a very comfortable routine for the two of them and now that the 'terrible two' were in bed she could give it more serious consideration. Leon decided to let her think and picked up the paper to read until she was ready to engage in conversation again.

Anna thought of what her week had been like. It had all been getting up and off to work, coming home afterwards to eat a hurried dinner and then spending her time off with Leon. Which had all seemed a bit bland when she compared her life with the adventures of her university friends Jeni and Tilly.

Leon had wondered himself if reading about Jeni's escapades in the newspapers last month had perhaps unsettled Anna a little. He knew how close the three girls were. As he sat quietly, he remembered wondering too was Anna was ready to move on from that part of her life to one with him? It had been on the spur of that moment he had asked Anna to marry him, rather than as he had planned, to wait for her birthday the following month. Then he remembered a special wedding gift and how they had both enjoyed a good laugh about her girlfriends' idea of a good wedding present, and its lack of use, it gave him a little smile. He still had a couple of questions though; had he rushed her into it and was their quiet life filling Anna with regrets?

Chapter Five

Jackson Redman was sitting in his girlfriend Jeni's kitchen. Shamelessly he was listening in on her telephone conversation with Anna. A habit that he had picked up in his line of work. The shriek that Jeni let out next could have shattered his eardrums. "You're what?" Jeni had exclaimed. "I just can't believe it!" "It's really happening tomorrow morning?" "That's fabulous, amazing and absolutely wonderful news, Anna." Jeni went on. Then came an anguished, "At nine o'clock!" It was a while before Jeni came out with "How am I going to be able to get a flight down in time?"

"I know it's too much to ask you to make the trip down," continued Anna, "so I'm not asking you to be there. I just couldn't face my big day without you and Tilly knowing about it and your blessings too."

"Of course you have that," Jeni told her, "I couldn't be happier for you than if I had planned it all myself!" There was some crackling on the line and a while longer again before Jeni's next response of, "If you are sure it's alright; but it does seem strange that I won't be there for you on your special day." It was to be another twenty minutes before Jeni finally put down the phone and turned to Jackson with tears in her eyes.

"Are you going to be alright? He asked her gently.

Dabbing her beautiful bluey green eyes she had smiled up at him. The big giant of a man, with his flaming head of red gold hair was looking very concerned and she hastened to assure him that they were in fact happy tears. He was her very own hero. He had helped to rescue her from a very close call, a brush with death, you could say. Her mind drifted back to the damp dark cell she had been held in and she shuddered.

Seeing this Jackson sought to take her mind away from the past. "Well what's the good news?"

Jeni went on to explain that she was very happy because her friend Anna was getting married.

"Then why on earth are you crying woman?" Jackson asked.

"Because I won't be at her wedding." Jeni stated baldly. Jackson looked confused and Jeni realised that she would have to explain properly.

"You know that Anna is one of my best friends and that we met while she, Tilly and I were still teenagers?" Jeni had continued.

Jackson just nodded, not wishing to interrupt her flow of words.

"Well, she is getting married tomorrow at nine o'clock in the morning." Jeni told him.

Jackson frowned and said, "Now I see why you cannot be at the wedding."

He knew the logistics of getting from a small place on the west coast of Scotland to London at short notice and realised instantly, as had Jeni, that it was virtually impossible. Such short notice did seem rather unusual and so he asked why the wedding had to be tomorrow. Jeni had told him previously that her friend Anna had been dating a new man for only a few weeks, which was one of the reasons Jackson had not met Anna yet. Now she told him that Anna was a somewhat shyer person than Jeni and Tilly. Also, that she had been told that Leon too was of a quiet disposition and rather than having a big affair the couple had decided that they would do things their way, quietly slipping away to get married and catch their friends up with their happy news after the deed was done. "Are they off to Gretna Green then?" He asked.

"No, no, it's a special licence and the minister at her local church is marrying them." Jeni stated.

"It's not a hole in the corner or a shotgun affair then," he joked; raising a watery smile from Jeni. "Actually, it sounds just right for them," Jeni responded. "I just wonder what Tilly will make of it all? I'll have to give her a call later to find out, when Anna has had a chance to speak to her."

"That sounds like a good idea," Jackson told her; "but right now I'm starving. It was a long drive to here from my flat!"

Jeni chuckled. If there was one thing that the past weeks had taught her about Jackson it was that he was always hungry. At almost every part of their time together he had raised this issue. She presumed that it was a by-product of his erratic way of life, constantly on call and moving from one scenario to another as the situation developed meant that he wasn't able to keep regular hours, or easily find somewhere to eat if he was in a strange place. Jeni had assumed that he was some kind of a policeman like Tilly's boyfriend, Craig. On reflection she had come to realise that perhaps he was something more. It was not that he didn't share with her, just that he was very selective in what he did tell her. He was secretive and an open book and all at the same time.

She knew that he was honest as the day is long and she trusted him implicitly, but what he did for a living was another matter entirely.

Tilly wailed down the telephone she was clutching tightly in her hand. "There's just no way that I will be able to get hold of my client to change our meeting time tomorrow; I don't have a mobile contact number for him. I can't come to your wedding, Anna!" when Anna had phoned her straight after putting the phone down on Jeni. "You must take pictures. Lots of selfies and get someone else to take some too. Please Anna." She pleaded, knowing Anna's reluctance to have her photo taken. "You want to have something to remember it all by and share with your children." There was a sudden flurry of crackles and strange noises on the line. However it cleared, and Anna continued to tell Tilly of their hastily hatched wedding plans. The line went funny again though as they rang off but Tilly just assumed that Leon had been listening too and had put down the extension to let them say their goodbyes. She made a mental note to self to get the line checked out.

As Tilly's boyfriend, Craig Ryan, knew all about Anna and her new boyfriend and also of the big meeting with the client who could potentially double their business. He was very sympathetic; as for Tilly and her business partner, Georgie, it was a really big deal. The meeting was to take place the next day. It had taken Tilly weeks to pin the man down to a meeting and she couldn't just not turn up for it, or leave Georgie to cope with it on her own.

When Tilly had finally returned the telephone to its stand, he just held out his arms and she ran into them for a big hug. With all that had happened over the past few weeks, Craig was not surprised when the tears began to flow too. He knew that she would be happy for Anna and Leon and their plan to marry the following morning but, right now she was too emotional to cope without a good cry. After a few minutes the tempest had passed and she gave him a squeeze to thank him for the comfort he had given her, before he finally released her to go and wash away the tearstains on her cheeks. Craig consoled himself with the thought that releasing all that pent-up tension from all the emotional highs and lows of recent weeks, could do her nothing but good. In his role as her rescuer from the clutches of her abductor, Craig well knew how fragile she was. He was constantly amazed at how well she had coped in the aftermath of her abduction. He was used to dealing with press interviews and the antics of newspaper photojournalists. She was both plucky and selfless; qualities that he admired greatly. However, right now his arms missed holding her. The more time he spent with Tilly the more he realised that she was becoming very dear to him. His mind started wandering to weddings and marriage next. Could she be his Mrs. Right?

"I must think of something special to give Anna and Leon for a wedding present and ring Jeni to find out what she thinks about it all," Tilly told Craig as she set out some plates and cutlery ready to have their evening meal.

Craig popped their takeaway dessert into the microwave to warm it up a bit more. While Tilly filled him in on the details she had gleaned from Anna. They continued to mull it all over as they ate the mound of delicious salads, meats and the scrumptious melting chocolate pudding that their local Sweet Tomatoes restaurant had put together. Sweet Tomatoes was their favourite place to eat or grab some takeaway food from on those evenings when they hadn't found time to shop or prepare a meal. It was a restaurant that specialised in healthy simple foods that were served really fresh. You could watch them busily preparing food all day. They only did small quantities at a time and even the bread was freshly baked every hour. It did a roaring trade at any time of the day and so it was sometimes actually quite nice to bring home a takeaway and enjoy eating their scrummy food in the quiet of Tilly's flat for a change. While Craig cleared the washing up and restored Tilly's small kitchen to its usual orderly state, Tilly phoned Jeni to learn her views on Anna's news. He was very happy to hear her ringing laughter a short while later when he entered the lounge. She would be alright now he felt sure. When told what the girls had hatched by way of a belated wedding present surprise he too chuckled. The thought of two pairs of bright red and blue enormous inflatable boxing gloves scheduled to appear on Anna and Leon's wedding night with a label that read,

Not to be opened until you have your first argument, with love for you both from Jeni and Tilly.

Chapter Six

LEON'S QUIET CALM nature was so peaceful. No, he wasn't handsome like most of her previous boyfriends, but he would talk to and with her about anything and everything, Anna thought. They found the same things funny and often laughed together. Even a look between them while watching a television programme could set them off. It was true that they hadn't known each other a long time. However, it was also true that she had never felt so comfortable with anyone else in her entire life. She was looking forward to sharing the rest of her life with this man. Growing a family with this man. Even growing old with Leon seemed somehow safe and filled with possibilities. She, Mrs. Leon Lewis, was a very lucky woman indeed; she had found her Mr. Right. Leon had even encouraged Anna to continue her friendship with Jeni and Tilly. Telling her that she should plan that they would meet up once a month for girl time. He had insisted that it was important that she shouldn't neglect her friends.

It had only been since Jeni had decided to rent the house in Scotland for a few months serious writing time that they hadn't had their regular weekly girls' nights out. When Anna had phoned the girls to let them know that she was getting married the next day they had been both shocked and very happy for her. It was such short notice that Jeni couldn't get a flight back down to London and Tilly was committed to meeting a highly influential prospective client. No, she hadn't wanted them to change their plans but she had wanted them to know about the wedding. Anna would have hated for them to find out about such an important event in her life from a third party. But, it was no wonder she was feeling a bit low now all the excitement of getting married was long over, even Tilly's life had been adventurous lately. Not that Leon wanted Anna to have quite that sort of excitement.

"I know what you need" he told Anna, "a little break."

"Oh, don't be silly; I'm fine", she told him, "Anyway we're going to have one next month when we finally get away for our belated honeymoon."

"No, you're not fine. When your friends are out there doing the exciting things in life, here you are spending your first free weekend of married life babysitting two little monsters." Leon told her.

"I'll have you know that those children are not monsters, they're absolute cherubs." Was Anna's instant response. "They're gorgeous little cherubs."

"Well, that's not what you called them when they were still calling down to you for a drink of water at half past nine tonight." Leon shot back at her.

"But they are asleep now," said Anna, "and so should we be."

With that, Leon switched off the table lamp and pulled her up out of the sofa, "Time for bed." He said, with a twist of pretend mustachios and a look that would have done a lecherous villain in an old black and white film proud.

Later, after Leon had rolled over in bed to give her a final kiss goodnight just as Anna began to drift off to sleep, her last thought was; maybe a few days away might do me good. Perhaps Tilly would join her. They could pop up to visit Jeni and Jo. That way they could see for themselves that there was no aftermath from all that they had been through when Mr. Big had entered their lives just weeks before. Now, that was a thought to cheer her up!

That might have been all it was destined to be if, Mr. Big hadn't taken a hand in the matter once again.

Chapter Seven

WHILE ANNA WAS busy making the last of the Sunday roast preparations for their parents and Leon's brother, Janus and wife Lucy, who were joining them for their first hosting of a family lunch. The twins were fully absorbed with their pretend campsite in the garden room. Janus had put up a small two man tent and they were all kept amused by their antics as the twins pretended to camp out. Sneaking out of the room, Leon took the opportunity to phone Tilly and suggest the reinstatement of the monthly girly get together, perhaps it could take the form of a long weekend? Sooner, rather than later he further suggested.

"Why? What's up with Anna?" Tilly fired at him. Without giving him time to answer, she asked half-jokingly, "Have you two lovebirds had a falling out?"

"No, no," he was quick to assure her. "She's just feeling a bit left out, what with all the excitement you and Jeni have been experiencing lately and our wedding being such a quiet affair."

"Yes," said Tilly, "it certainly hasn't been boring round here or in Scotland, for that matter. I think a little jolly north of the border is a great idea. Just leave it with me and I'll get back to you when I've spoken to Jeni about it."

With his, "will do," it was time to get off the phone before Anna wondered who he was talking to.

It was this conversation, when reported to him, which had fired up Mr. Big and made his cell the centre of attention for the next few days.

On Thursday morning that week, Leon's secretary, Angie, told him that there was a young lady on the phone for him. He was both surprised and pleased that it was Tilly. "Not like you to ring me at the office," Tilly, he remarked. Tilly responded that she had thought that he might want to make the trip a bit of a surprise for Anna, and she hadn't wanted to give the game away by asking specially to speak to him if Anna had answered their home phone before him. He complimented her on her wise move and then followed it up with asking her if she had managed to speak with Jeni yet? "That's why I'm ringing today." Tilly stated. "If I can arrange it for this weekend, could Anna get away?"

"Yes, and I'll be able to use the time to catch up on some things that have been on hold for a while. No problem in fact, as I can always get Mum to give me a meal on Sunday if I am feeling too lazy to cook. She's always saying she'd love to spend more time with me. Since I met up with Anna she tells me she hardly sees me anymore." Leon told her.

"Well, I'll pop round this afternoon while Anna is at work to pack a bag for her, if you will loan me your house key. Then I will swing by and pick her up on the way to the airport at eight tomorrow morning." Tilly said.

"The airport? Leon queried.

"Yes, Anna won't need her passport, if that's what you're thinking. We're going to get a hop up to Scotland with a friend I used to work with, Martin Jamieson. He has a small four seater plane and he happens to be visiting family up that way this weekend and offered me, or should I say us, a ride."

"Sounds great to me," Leon told her. "I'll leave my key to the front door with Angie for you to collect when you're ready, as I have a meeting now and may not be around when you come by."

Tilly finished with. "Thanks Leon, see you in the morning."

One o'clock found Tilly letting herself into Anna and Leon's modern town house. Running lightly up the curved staircase from the entrance hall to the next floor's master suite, Tilly quickly found Anna's weekend wheelie suitcase in the cupboard on the top of the wardrobe. After twenty minutes she had assembled a selection of suitable clothing on the bed and began to quickly fold, roll and pack it into the suitcase. She even remembered that Anna had always kept an extra wash bag for herself packed ready for emergencies and she had eventually found it in the cupboard of the ensuite. It was a habit formed by Anna's sudden trips to France for her previous job. Tilly checked, it even had a new toothbrush in it. Good to go, so into the suitcase that went too. All done, she zipped the case round and placed it on the floor while she straightened up the bed. Looking round and seeing no trace of her presence was left behind, she trotted back down the stairs and out of the front door. She locked it behind her and then placed the wheelie suitcase in the boot of her car. Two minutes later she had left the driveway and was on her way back to her office to finish up her latest assignment and Anna was none the wiser.

Leon could hardly contain his excitement that evening, it was fortunate that he was a naturally deep sleeper and had done his usual thing of snoring the night through. Otherwise, he may well have given the game away! As it was he had to pretend that he was going into the office an hour later that morning as he had to stay in town for a meeting that evening. Anna, seeing a chance for some extra time with Leon had cooked him a special breakfast. She was just dishing her own up when the doorbell rang its cheerful chime. Leon let Anna go to answer it and, quietly followed her, to stand at the back of the hall and see her reaction to Tilly's surprise.

It was all that he could have hoped for. Her amazement at Tilly's early morning appearance was eclipsed by her joy at learning that she was being whisked away for a girly long weekend.

"How? When? Where?" All came flying out one after the other.

However, Tilly was prepared and answered only, "Blame your husband and hurry and get your coat on."

Anna's "But, but, but", was soon wafted away as she was handed her coat and her shoes by Leon and told to get a move on by Tilly. Once she had kissed and cuddled and bid her wonderful husband a fond farewell, she was pushed out of the front door and into the passenger seat of Tilly's bright turquoise run around. They were off!

Tilly told Anna that she would have to wait to have her questions answered, as she needed to concentrate on the road for a while, not being familiar with the route. Anna duly closed her mouth and contented herself with the view from her window.

She let her thoughts drift for a moment to her friend Tilly and their mutual friend, Jeni. The three of them had met when they were just students looking for somewhere to live in London. It was so expensive that independently they had decided that they would have to share if they were to afford anywhere even vaguely decent; so, each had taken their carefully written advert to place in the local newspaper and turned up at its office simultaneously. Whilst waiting to be attended to, the three girls had sat down and started chatting generally about the expense of living away from home and on realising that they had all come with the same purpose that day, elected to give sharing together a try. They had left the newspaper office that day without placing their ads but had bought a copy of the paper, adjourned to the nearby coffee shop and spent the rest of their time searching its "For Rent" pages for a suitable place for them all to live.

They were lucky enough to find one and even a landlady who was willing to let them have the flat at a ridiculously low rent. That evening they had all gone out to dinner together to celebrate their good fortune. It had been the beginning of their friendship and that was still there all these years later. Anna considered her friends and knew that she was blessed with two of the very best. No matter what, Tilly and Jeni had been there for her. When she had broken up with her boyfriend from home they had come home to the flat armed with ice-cream, tissues and a movie designed to transport her elsewhere for a few hours while she came to terms with the initial shock. They had celebrated the highs and lows of dating, exams and finding jobs, birthdays and throughout it all had shared lots of fun and laughter. She then realised for herself, that she had been feeling low because she had felt that she had in some way let them down. She hadn't been there for either of them in their time of need. She had been too busy falling in love.

Not that Anna regretted meeting her wonderful husband for one minute. Merely that she wished that she had been able to be of more use in the search when Jeni had gone missing and earlier when Tilly's life had been imperilled by her abduction. She had been quite shaken to think that one of her closest friends could have died and been lost to her forever. They could never be replaced and she would have been very lost without them. Thank goodness both episodes had ended well. She had thanked God for taking care of the girls and hoped that they could all be back together very soon.

When Anna had finished her musing, she noticed that the landscape outside her car window had changed. They were turning into an entrance to what appeared to be a private airfield. What on earth were they doing there? She wondered. Tilly having negotiated the parking area and neatly put her car in a slot close to a small prefabricated building sporting a bright orange windsock like a pointy hat atop, turned off her engine.

"We've arrived!" Tilly announced. As Anna still looked bemused, Tilly added, "Grab your bag, Anna, we need to get going."

"Going where?" Anna asked her.

Tilly pointed up to the bright blue cloudless sky, "Up there!", then she tugged Anna out of the car and into the airport office.

Tilly soon spotted Martin across the room. He was leaning on the counter chatting to the girl standing behind the reception desk. Martin quickly excused himself, then strode over to Tilly and Anna. He gave Tilly a big bear hug lifting her right off her feet, whilst telling her how good it was to see her in the flesh. Tilly was laughing when he finally put her down.

"You only saw me last Friday, Martin, when we went to see that movie together with the gang." She reminded him.

"Yes," he agreed. "Only to find that you chose to sit next to that Craig fellow instead of me". This and the doleful facial expression similar to a hound with long floppy ears, had Tilly chuckling.

"Well," she told them both, "you can't really expect me to invite my boyfriend to meet you all and then abandon him to sit with another guy all night, can you!"

Anna smiled at this and noted that this was the first time Tilly had publicly acknowledged that she was seriously going out with Craig Ryan; the policeman she had bumped into when buying a book for her godmother Cathy's birthday. A big step forward for Tilly, she thought to herself. In the meantime, Martin was being introduced to Anna by Tilly and she was also told that Martin would be flying them to their destination, as it was on his way home for the weekend. Just to keep Anna in suspense a little longer, Tilly had asked Martin to refrain from mentioning where he was taking them by name. Ever game for a laugh, Martin had agreed, and so, when Anna looked as though she was about to ask him where that might be to, he quickly told the receptionist that they would be getting off now. He ushered them both quickly out of another door that lead onto the tarmac aircraft park. He explained as he walked them over towards the planes that they would need to get on their way quickly, as the young lady had already logged them as leaving at 9am and it was only a few minutes before that now. Then, with a wave of his free hand he encouraged them to admire his pride and joy "Esmerelda".

To Anna the little plane didn't look anywhere near big enough to carry three people aloft. It looked more like a toy aeroplane that might be operated by a remote control. Dismay must have shown on her face. Both Martin and Tilly were quick to reassure her that it was entirely airworthy and safe for the three of them to fly off in. However, it was with trepidation that Anna climbed aboard and buckled herself in. "Don't I have to wear a parachute or something?" She had asked anxiously.

"No, no, you'll be fine. It's just like getting into a car for a commuter journey," Martin had told her. "We'll be there before you know it this way," Tilly had piped up and gave Anna's arm a quick squeeze for good measure. Then she buckled up and gave Martin the all clear to go thumbs up, before fitting Anna and then herself with headsets to enable them to hear each other clearly over the engine noise.

Meanwhile, Martin had started the plane's engine and contacted the tower to request permission to advance to the runway. The tower responded that he was now cleared for immediate take-off along runway one. "Thank you, tower" Martin replied before turning to give the girls in the back a big smile and announcing, "We're off!" But where to? Anna wondered.

It was no sooner said than done as Anna tried not to let the sheer terror of going aloft in such a tiny craft show on her face. They taxied down to the start of the runway and then swiftly gathered speed as they pounded down it. The lights across the end of the runway seemed to be flying towards them when suddenly they lurched up into the air. As the ground fell away below them, Anna ventured a look through the window beside her head. Promptly wishing she hadn't, when she saw the countryside around the airfield appear and then the houses of the surrounding suburb looking far too small for her liking. Then the plane seemed to give a lurch and Anna's stomach rolled over as they banked to turn north and head away from all that she knew and held dear. For a moment she felt totally bereft. Down below her somewhere, her beloved Leon was on his way to work in the library as usual, just like every other working day. Whereas she, Anna, was flying in a tiny tin can to an unknown destination. A vast difference from her normal Friday routine. She thought to herself, what adventures might lie ahead?

Chapter Eight

IT WAS MAIL call and Mr. Big had received a post card. It showed a lovely beach scene and a voluptuous brunette sunbathing whilst reading a book. The contents of the post card read,

Wish you could enjoy this too! I'm reading Tilly Meets Her Match! Get it in an audiobook and see if you like it as much as I do. Love and kisses.

The signature was an illegible scrawl and the postmark equally indistinct. However, it brought a very rare smile to the reader's face. Later that day he requested a library visit. When the time came the Librarian was a little surprised by his choice of an audio book and a very up to date one at that! From the picture on the front of it not a likely choice for a man like Mr. Big at all. When given the explanation that it had been recommended to him as light relief, the Librarian checked it out and watched him leave with a smile to himself, that reflected his thought that Mr. Big may well get more than he bargained for!

Once alone in his cell and unlikely to be interrupted by the routine of the prison day, Mr. Big inserted his earbuds and listened intently whilst trying to look relaxed. The more he listened the more interested he became. Then he got excited when the possibilities for action were presented to him. It wouldn't be just Tilly who met her match, it would be Jackson Redman and all his friends. Even better! The transcription of the phone calls between Jeni and Jo were nothing much; but those between Jeni, Tilly and Anna were definitely more interesting listening. The money that he had had to spend to get the services of his lawyer and the taps put on certain phones were paying off. Now all he had to do was figure out a way to put all this information to good use.

The next twenty-four hours had the cogs of his brain whizzing round as he grappled with devising a plan to take Jackson and his friends down. Following this up by utilising his pre-arranged communication system would enable it to be enacted. Once he was sure he had thought of any and every possible thing that could prevent its successful conclusion.

When he returned his audiobook to the library promptly after only three days, the Librarian's face once again registered surprise. He asked Mr. Big," Did you enjoy your book?"

The man turned to him and replied, "Much more than I had expected to!"

"Recommend it?" He continued intrigued.

Mr. Big said, "It was more of a mystery than the romance I thought it looked like on the cover. It was well worth starting on as it drew me in and I couldn't stop listening until I'd got to the end." Then he hot-footed it back to his cell; leaving a very bewildered librarian to ponder on the strangeness of life in prison.

With his plans hatched, Mr. Big went on with the job of establishing himself as the man to be reckoned with. Money talked in prison and he was soon running an effective operation to service the unofficial needs of the inmates. He carefully selected his henchmen and put them to work quelling any opposition from the current top dogs, smoothly taking over the reins himself. The excellent report he had received in the Man Management section of his Business Studies course as a student had certainly proved to be a true observation. If only the latter part of his mid-term report had been in the same vein. Instead, it had continued with the hope expressed that the rough edges and harshness noted during observation of practical sessions would be resolved quickly, as he gained further experience in life. Otherwise, the mentor of Mr. Big had forecast, he would become a bully and very much disliked by his employees. However, the bully was now flexing his muscles and the prisoners were feeling his power and on the run from it. He may not be here much longer, he thought, but they'll not forget me when I'm gone!

The little Cessna 501 flew on through the bright morning skies. With only a few white cotton wool ball clouds to contend with, the view from the plane's small windows were amazing. Anna still wasn't sure which direction they were heading in. The traffic on the motorway below appeared like toy cars on a child's play-mat. Towns seemed jumbles of housing with larger spaces, perhaps car parks, in between. Even when some hills appeared they didn't seem as awe inspiring as when seen from the road or on foot. It was only when she suddenly she recognised a jetty sticking out into a lake that had appeared in the green below she knew the hills were mountains. She noted a couple of places from a long-ago holiday in the Lake District and appreciated that they were now travelling northwards. Then they banked once more to change direction, her stomach seemed to be left behind this time and it took a few moments before she felt brave enough to look out once more. Her attention was then dragged from the view to the coffee mug that Tilly was handing her and engaged by the offer of her favourites from university days, bourbon biscuits. Tilly's carefully timed distraction had done its job. When Anna looked out again, she had no idea where they were; she had lost her bearings again. There was no major motorway or even a big road in sight but with the lovely sunshine pouring in the window, what did Anna care!

Another thirty minutes and even less going on below on the ground and Martin announced that they would be landing shortly, could they please stow away bags etc. and tighten their seatbelts. Swiftly the girls complied, while Martin spoke into his headset mike to request permission to land his plane. All was safe and ready for their descent. It was then her stomach flip flopped reminding her that she was still in a tin can high up in the sky. When Anna dared a peek out of the window, it was with a gasp of dismay. Were they going to land in a field? Not quite. The single line of landing strip came into view. A quick sharp drop, that left her tummy behind somewhere in the blue sky, a couple of bumps and the wheels of the tiny plane had touched down. The brakes applied and a neat turn at the end of the runway, enabled Martin to bring them to a halt outside the nearest small building. Engine switched off and headsets removed he invited them to descend to terra firma once more. Anna couldn't believe that they had made it intact.

Once he had unloaded their luggage, Martin carried it into the building. On asking Anna if she had enjoyed her first flight in a Cessna, He was told in no uncertain terms that it was amazing, delightful and would not be forgotten for many a long day. Both girls were profuse in their thanks and assured Martin of their happiness at being offered a similar trip home when their stay was over.

As Martin had still further to go to his final destination they made do with a quick hug before waving him off again up into the wide blue yonder.

At the loud cry of joy from the now open doorway behind them, Anna finally knew just where she was to spend her mystery weekend. Jeni flung herself at her friends almost bowling them over like an eager puppy in her happiness at being reunited. Tilly and Anna were no less enthusiastic. The three jumped up and down in a little circle laughing with joy. Much as they had done in their student days. Excitement momentarily dissipated a little, they separated to give each other a good look up and down.

Anna's "You'll do Jeni." Was one of relief that both her friends looked fit and shone with well-being. Tilly and Jeni had not suffered physically during their recent adventures; but, Anna had been concerned for their emotional states. However, right now they looked happy and she would content herself with that any day.

Jeni was soon getting them organised and their luggage loaded in the boot of her car. It was not the most glamorous of vehicles, but it did have four wheel drive and comfy seats. The very efficient heater had also come in handy on colder days. However, the Gulfstream kept the weather there on the west coast relatively mild and so it hadn't been needed much so far. Before Anna knew it they were bowling along the road through beautiful scenery with glimpses of the sea or swathes of what appeared to be almost tropical vegetation. It was lush; and when Anna began to see palm trees she thought she must be dreaming. "Was that a palm tree that we just passed?" She asked Jeni.

Jeni's response was a casual, "Oh yes, you see quite a few of those round here."

"Surely it gets too cold in Scotland to grow palm trees outside." Anna exclaimed.

"Not here on the west coast. The coconuts arrive with the warm waters of the Gulfstream and get washed up on the beaches. They plant themselves and hey presto we have coconut palms. The folk round here often end up with them in their gardens and they look healthy enough there, don't they?" Jeni said.

"They certainly do." Anna replied. "It was just such a surprise to see them."

"Oh you'll find this place full of surprises Anna. Did you know that the village of Plockton has its own harbour and train station as well the airport? I'll just give you a very quick drive round before we go home to give you a flavour of the place. It's delightful." Jeni enthused, as she turned to follow the road into the village proper.

It led them through a tunnel of greenery. The large lush dark green shiny leaves nearly met overhead and cast a faintly green light over the road making it look mysterious. It was surprisingly bright when the car exited the tunnel and the scene that opened out before Anna and Tilly's eyes seemed to float in a light mist.

Tilly's exclamation of "It's like in that old film! What was it called, Anna? We watched it one night at the flat. I know. Brigadoon!"

It didn't seem at all exaggerated, for Anna thought that it looked absolutely magical. White painted, turf thatched cottages, a village green or common land reached by driving through a ford, highland cattle roaming free and munching the top of a garden hedge for lunch; at each turn of the wheel a new enchantment appeared. "No wonder you wanted to spend some time living here, Jeni." She gasped.

Their wide-eyed reaction was all that she could have hoped for, Jeni thought. They had grasped for themselves what had captured her heart. She pulled into a parking spot that overlooked the small but perfectly formed harbour to let them admire the colourful scene. Small boats bobbed up and down on the sparkling water.

"It looks so clean and fresh," enthused Tilly, "it could almost be the perfect painting of boats at rest you could ever wish for."

Anna gazed round in wonder. Her surprise trip was certainly proving to be an eye-opener. Jeni gave her watch a quick glance and told them that it was about time they were making tracks as she had a full itinerary for them over the next few days and she didn't want them to miss out on anything the area had to offer. Though reluctant to leave such an idyllic spot, Anna and Tilly were happy to fall in with Jeni's plans when she promised to bring them back to Plockton for a lovely lunch on the Sunday before they had to go home again.

With so much of interest to look at through their windows the girls were amazed to find themselves drawing up before Jeni's house minutes later. They were quickly out of the car to help Jeni unload their suitcases from the boot. As they reached the front door it was opened from within. Jeni introduced them to her housekeeper with a cheery, "This is Gloria. She who must be obeyed." At the astonished looks on their faces, both Jeni and Gloria, burst out laughing. "You do look funny," She continued. "I mean that she is my fabulous housekeeper who keeps me on track and my house in tip top order."

Gloria ushered them in with her graceful welcome and "It's a pleasure to meet you both at last. Jeni talks about you all the time; so it is good to put faces to the names."

Tilly and Anna warmed to this smiling warm hearted woman that they had spoken to over the past few weeks.

Looking round, Anna turned to her to say, "The house looks beautiful, Gloria, you're doing a wonderful job, no wonder Jeni always sings your praises to us."

Gloria turned a rosy red with the compliment and swiftly brushed it away with a "Whishtay, that's enough of such nonsense, just drop your bags there and away in with you now." She directed them on and into a lovely room with an enormous window that had a panoramic view to die for.

Anna and Tilly could scarcely drag their eyes away from it long enough to see where they were walking and avoid tripping up and landing on the large squashy sofa set directly opposite. Instead they plonked themselves down on it and just carried on enjoying the view. Jeni and Gloria quite used to new guests' reactions to the vista just continued to settle the matter of the disposal of the luggage by Gloria to the allotted bedrooms and the pouring of tea from the delicate china teapot on the prepared tea tray that Gloria had placed on a handy table. Knowing their preferences so well it was soon done and Jeni brought them back to their surrounding as she placed their drinks in their hands. Then Jeni seated, they all started chatting at once. The girls told her about their trip up and congratulated Jeni on her luck in finding such a lovely place to do her writing.

Gradually over the next hours they filled each other in on the details of the weeks they had spent apart. Anna's rings and photos were admired and the sincerity of their joy in her happiness was patent. Jeni and Tilly were content to see their friend so profoundly happy in her newly married state that they both decided that Leon would be welcomed into their circle anyway, but now with ease because of his consideration and concern for their Anna; he obviously loved her just as much.

Having caught up fairly well, they were happy to be given a tour of the rest of the house and be shown their bedrooms and left to freshen up before dinner at eight o'clock. Jeni had told them that she had invited a couple of extra guests for dinner and that Jackson would be joining them too. Anna and Tilly were quick on the uptake and asked would her guests be Jo and Fernando by any chance? If so, it would be quite a party. "Yes," Jeni agreed, "I wanted all my dearest friends to meet as soon as possible and this was sooner than I expected but too good an opportunity to miss. It's just a shame that Craig and Leon can't be here too."

As Tilly hung up the contents of her suitcase, Anna rang Leon to let him know that she had arrived safely at Jeni's and was very grateful for her lovely surprise trip. She filled him in on all the new facts she had learnt, he was very happy to know that she had lost that underlying tone of weariness from her voice. She was back to herself once more. A few more minutes and she replaced the phone knowing that he was coping without her but missing her just as much as she was missing him.

Jeni's introductions over pre-dinner aperitifs were formal but hardly necessary. The word pictures she had given Anna over the telephone had enabled Anna to easily distinguish the sculptured cheeks, dark curling hair and body of a Greek god as Fernando Alverez from the rugged, flame haired giant standing next to him. Boy, was Jackson Redman huge! Jeni almost looked like a midget next to such a man. Then her eyes had turned to Jo Lawson, Jeni's new friend and Anna's potential supplier.

Her healthy tanned skin gave Jo the look of an outdoors type despite her more delicate appearance. It was her hands that gave her strength away. Instead of pale and finely fashioned they were far more workman like and crisscrossing her fingers were several fine lines of scars. Presumably they were from her work with glass, Anna thought to herself. Jo's artistic nature was displayed in her choice of wonderfully simple clothes in deep jewel colours. As a whole she was a feast for the eyes. And Anna could tell that Fernando thought so too.

Dinner that evening was a real success Anna thought, as she looked around the table at her friends new and old. Though she had only met Jackson, Fernando and Jo a mere three hours ago, she felt that they had already become good friends. Such was the harmony in the room, it was as if they had grown up together. She could say with certainty that Leon would feel the same way. The two seated men seemed to share all the values that the girls had recognised in each other when they had first met years ago. The small attentions that they paid to Jeni and Jo without being asked or even seeming to think about it, showed how focussed and in tune they were with them. The love just shone from them. Anna felt sure that Tilly had met her match in Craig and now saw that Jeni may well have met hers too. Fernando and Jo also appeared to be well on the way to an understanding; so, all was well with the world as far as Anna was concerned. For another hour or so they sat finding out more about each other over coffee and it was Tilly's escaping yawn that reminded them all that the night was far advanced, they needed to let the travellers get some well-earned rest.

Goodbye hugs given all round and plans for the rest of the weekend, to start with a visit to Jo's studio in the morning, were made before the door was shut behind the three visitors. Jeni then shepherded Anna and Tilly up the stairs with the assurance that the dinner dishes were already being dealt with by the dishwasher and Gloria would do the coffee tray in the morning when she came in. Anna reflected that it must be nice to be able to go to bed knowing that you had help to clear away in the morning. She wasn't about to swop Leon for Gloria any time soon; but she could appreciate that it must make it a lot easier for Jeni to concentrate on her writing if she didn't have to deal with all the domestic chores as well. It was with funny visions of dozens of housemaids in frilly French maid costumes flicking dusters while they bumped into and fell over each other in her tiny London home that Anna finally fell asleep with a satisfied smile on her lips looking forward to a quiet few days in a beautiful place in the company of good friends.

Not quite what someone else had in mind!

Chapter Nine

His next communication from his minions came via his barber. Along with a short back and sides, Mr. Big received the news that the wedding of Anna had already taken place before anything could be done. For that alone, she and her new husband were added to his mental list of people to exact his revenge upon. The more the merrier. It was welcome news, however, that most of the party were now together in Scotland for a few days. He could arrange for better surveillance there and hopefully another opportunity would open up soon.

In the meantime, his mind raced with possibilities. A car crash? Food poisoning? Financial ruin? They all played out as he sat in the upright, ancient chair. Its highly polished chrome and Art Deco design padded comfort were totally wasted on such a Philistine. Never the less he enjoyed the attention he was accorded and reluctantly made way for the next customer of the day. On his casual stroll back to his cell Mr. Big stopped several times to pass the day with useful allies, ensuring that his commands were being carried out with alacrity. The deference with which he was treated by them being noted by various prison warders and reported up the line at the next daily briefing session. All changes in the informal prison hierarchy were always of grave concern in the smooth running of the prison, hence treated as vital intelligence information. The Governor noted it in his records and made a future note to check on progress for a week later in his diary.

What was Mr. Big up to?

Chapter Ten

Everyone was up bright and early the next morning and breakfast eaten with sunshine streaming in through the morning room window. The freshly smoked kippers were succulent and very tasty served with hot buttered toast and washed down with a fragrant cup of steaming hot coffee. With a good breakfast inside them the girls were ready to face the day. After letting Gloria know that they would be out for lunch and saying their goodbyes, it was time to head off to visit Jo and the promised tour of her glass studio.

A short drive through ever more verdant countryside and they had reached the next village of Tillymurie. Tilly exclaimed as they turned down a little lane. "Look Anna, what a fabulous garden!" Anna turned her head to look out the window on the other side of the car as Jeni slowed to a halt. The front garden of the cottage that they had just pulled up at was an amazing blaze of colour. With flowers and plants crammed into every corner and climbing over each other in their effort to claim the attention they so richly deserved. No wonder Tilly, renowned for her ability to kill off the hardiest of spider plants, sounded so enthusiastic in her admiration; Anna thought. It was a worthy contender for a gold award at The Chelsea Flower Show.

"I can understand why you had to stop here to let us see this," Jeni", Anna told her friend. Jeni turned to them and with the suspicion of a twinkle in her eye, asked if they would like to see the back garden too, as it was even better.

"Of course" Tilly and Anna chorused. Jeni had soon shepherded her charges up the path and loudly rung the bell. When it was opened wide by Jo, the girls were laughing.

"You tricked us, Jeni!" Tilly said. While Anna was quietly telling Jo that her garden was simply the best cottage garden she had ever seen and she would love to go straight outside to see the rear one too. Jo was only too happy to delay their trip round the studio and workshop to show off her pride and joy. With her ears ringing with their lavish praise, she finally brought them back into her cottage for a drink. After all the talking they had needed a cuppa. Once that was done, Jo led them by a secret gate out from her garden off to her workshop.

The quiet efficiency of the workshop was a sharp contrast to the riotous colour of the garden. The muted soft tones of the sage green and cream décor were calming and a great foil for the colours of the pieces in the display cabinet in the reception area. Jo called in her assistant and delivery man to be introduced. Shona Adams reminded Anna of the cheeky robin in her parent's garden. With her brown hair, twinkling dark eyes, ruddy red cheeks and beautifully clear pale skin she had only needed to produce her flashing shy smile to complete the picture. Her plain nut brown dress was functional but added a quiet elegance to her short stature. Her firm handshake instilled an assurance of competence. The welcome to Jo Lawson Designs she gave was such that Anna could see why Jo had talked about her being, a treasure and her right- hand woman.

The unassuming quiet man in his late thirties who came out from behind a pile of boxes for his turn in the limelight also had an air of confidence and capability. Shona introduced him as her husband and co-worker. When Tilly had asked Drew Adams what his role involved he was not at all awkward about explaining that he was something of a jack of all trades. He told them he could pack orders for dispatch and deliver them or do any maintenance needed and ensured that the workshop was kept clean and well stocked to enable Jo to be free to create her designs. He appeared to take a pride in keeping things in order and in the work produced. He too was a great asset to Jo's business, Anna could tell. After walking round the various areas of the workshop they ended up at what was obviously Jo's drawing board and design development area. With sketches and photographs and shelves full of cameras and interesting natural items, it was bursting with the creative vibe. Anna, though used to creative spaces and their chaos, found that Jo's showed an organised side too; with a load of National Geographic and wild life magazines neatly stacked on shelves next to her work in progress pieces.

It didn't take much encouragement for Jo to show them her the creative process through its various stages. In fact, Jo chose as her example the lovely mistletoe tree ornament familiar to Anna and Jeni. First there was the rough sketch that she had drawn from a photograph taken late the previous autumn when she had been in a friend's garden admiring her apple tree. This had led to a sketch of the mistletoe close up. Then a scale drawing with colour references. This was followed by photographs of trial examples and finally the real thing. Tilly was full of compliments for the delightful sprig when handed it to examine. While Anna was happily getting close up with other examples from Jo's range of goods and as the two of them continued to discuss production capabilities and costing figures, Jeni and Tilly discretely took themselves back to the cottage.

Jeni had arranged for Gloria to make up a picnic hamper to bring along with them to ensure that they would have lunch wherever they had found a nice spot to stop and enjoy the view. Now she told Tilly that in view of Anna's eagerness to develop a business connection between her employer and Jo Lawson Designs it looked like the two of them had better just get it out of the boot and set it up right there in Jo's kitchen. Tilly agreed that it looked as though it would be a working lunch for them, but wondered if they couldn't have it outside as it was such a sunny day? That way they could make the most of the wonderful garden too. Jeni leapt up at her suggestion and told her that Jo had a table and chairs tucked away somewhere and she would just pop and ask Drew if he could get them out and set them up in a sheltered sunny spot.

Drew was more than happy to oblige. When he stopped after putting the chairs out, Jeni asked him to add a couple more round the table. She felt sure that Jo would want her co-workers to come and join them for their impromptu alfresco meal. Jeni returned to the kitchen and asked Tilly to raid Jo's fridge to see if she could find anything there to augment the contents of the picnic basket that Drew had kindly carried in from the car for her. Half an hour later there was a veritable feast for them to carry out and place on the table. While Jeni laid it with the required cutlery and plates etc., Tilly returned to the workshop to encourage Jo and Anna to join them for lunch. When she saw Jo's quick glance towards the back room where Shona and Drew were busy packing up an airmail consignment, Tilly assured her that there was more than enough for six and she went over to them to invite them to clean up and come and have some lunch.

It was a happy affair as they made inroads into the wide selection of delicious cheeses with homemade pickles or smoked salmon and cucumber on morning rolls with farm fresh butter and followed up with generous hunks of a huge game pie, all washed down with homemade ginger beer. Though there was still some talk of the future of Jo's business, the topics of conversation were rich and varied to accompany the selection of sweet items to follow. A strawberry shortcake, millionaires shortbread and a wickedly sinful ginger and plain chocolate mousse. As they licked their spoons between mouthfuls Anna, Tilly and Jeni learnt about the wild life, flora and fauna that inhabited the locale. In addition, they learned that a lot of the photographs they had seen had come from Drew.

Jo had discovered his secret talent when he had brought into work a photo of a very cuddly looking rabbit taken early one morning. On Jo's complimentary comments about the quality of the shot and the detail revealed, when asked he had admitted that photography was a passion. When she enquired if he had any other shots he thought she might like, Drew had brought in a portfolio of his best work and Jo had asked if she could use some for inspiration for her own work and offered to pay him for the ones that she felt she could use. Now, they had worked out a good arrangement whereby he would submit any shots that he felt were interesting enough to warrant a look and Jo had first dibs at buying them. She had even displayed a couple of them mounted in the reception area and as a result he had sold a few to interested clients. It was proving to be quite a lucrative side-line for him, Drew told them. Anna at this, made a mental note to ask to see that portfolio for herself. Perhaps she could help Drew market his work to a larger audience? No sooner had she had the thought than Jeni voiced it for her.

Anna looked at her friends as they told Jo, Drew and Shona that she was always saying that one day she would go freelance and set up her own business, a public relations development consultancy. Jo was quick to say that she would love to be able to put that side of her own business in Anna's very capable hands and Drew followed suit with his own enquiry as to whether she felt she could do the same for him.

"There you are," said Tilly, "you have your first clients, Anna."

Anna looked round the picnic table at the remains of their scrumptious lunch and their eager faces and the company name came into her mind. "I'll call it Phoenix" she told them with her next breath.

"Why Phoenix?" Jeni asked her.

"Because it has come out of the remains of our lunch!" Anna said. This provoked some laughter and the decision that it was time to clear away.

While the others packed up the picnic basket, Jo took Anna aside and asked her if she would consider promoting her business for her on a professional basis and advise her on the next stage of its development. Anna told Jo that she would be happy to do that anyway, whether she set up a consultancy in her own right or not, as she considered Jo a friend now. Jo thanked her and promised that she would be in touch again soon to pursue the matter further. Then it was time for goodbyes, as Jeni had a packed itinerary for them and wanted to get started on it. Tilly and Anna thanked their hostess and her staff for a wonderful visit and promised to come again before they hopped back into the car to wend their way down more of the winding roads to see some of the local sights.

The outstanding beauty of the coastline and mountains was a revelation to Anna who had never been north of the border before. She was constantly pointing out something to Tilly and Jeni, much like a child let loose in a toy shop for the first time. By the end of the afternoon that had involved taking in the places where some of their favourite movies had been filmed. A visit to a local smokehouse to see round and buy some more kippers for their breakfast on Sunday morning. A sheep farm, where the wife had her own knitwear cottage industry and the girls bought some gorgeous accessories to take home as gifts for friends and family. Anna had even found a felted trilby hat that she was sure Leon would fall in love with. They had chattered all the way and just generally enjoyed being together again. It was almost seven o'clock before they had turned onto the road to Kyle of Drumcrae and Jeni told them they were now heading towards their dinner engagement. Tilly and Anna looked a little dismayed. Its ok, Jeni told them. We're going to Jackson's apartment first to freshen up before we meet Fernando and Jo at the restaurant. That gained a smile almost as big as the ones they later displayed on seeing where Jackson lived.

His apartment was rather nice! The views across the bay were wonderful and the layout very practical and elegant. It was both spacious and stylish without being over the top. It was just a comfortable bachelor pad that was both enjoyed and loved by its owner. While Tilly used the sleek, shiny bathroom and Jeni the hi-tech ensuite facility, Anna wandered around with her cup of tea in hand admiring the couple of seascapes she had spotted in the entrance hall and lounge. She turned to Jackson and asked if they had been done by local artists as she hadn't recognised the signatures displayed on them despite them being very finely executed. Jackson then gave her a potted history of how he had met the artists purely by accident whilst out walking the local coastal path one day. He had loved the sketches they were making, they had got chatting. After an invitation to their studio and he had seen these particular examples and so he had bought for himself.

"Well, said Anna, they look like a very good investment to me. I'd love to have one myself."

Jackson told her that he would try to find out if they could fit in a visit to the studio before they had to fly home again. Happy with that thought, it was now Anna's turn to freshen up for the evening ahead.

While Anna was out of earshot, Jeni and Tilly swopped notes and decided that Anna appeared to be past her bout of the blues and back to her usual self. However, they both agreed that she ought not to be wasting her talents working for the store as a buyer for much longer. They were going to make her think more seriously about her future and not put off her consultancy dreams any longer. With at least two potential customers in the offing, the ideal time for taking the plunge into independence was upon her and Anna needed to grasp and run with it. With that decided to their satisfaction, Anna and Jackson walked into the room and then they were all being firmly ushered out of the flat, down the stairs, to be seated in his very nice car. Sinking into the smart leather seats the girls enjoyed being chauffer driven down the hill to arrive in style outside "The Mango Tree" where Fernando and Jo stood waiting for them.

Anna and Tilly were eagerly looking round at the restaurant that had played such an important role in their friends' recent adventures. Once ordering had been dealt with, the girls they were quick to fire off questions about which table etc. they had been sitting at and who had served them when the four had first met. Then, it was time to eat and so they had put that episode to bed. Although, from the flurry of interest shown in their arrival, they were obviously still a topic of local interest! Instead, Anna and Tilly were encouraged to share their day which they were more than happy to do.

Anna waxed lyrical about the potential for growth she could see in Jo's wonderful products and those of the artisans that they had met on their travels. Anna said that she felt sure that she could place even the kippers into the delicatessens of the major London department stores like Harrods, as they were all of such a high standard. She even felt that Jackson's seascape finds deserved to reach a wider market. Jeni and Tilly couldn't help themselves. Their grins were so big that even the men noticed and commented.

Tilly said it all when she responded with, "It's so good to see you've got your mojo back Anna."

Jeni echoed with, "We'll be able to give Leon a good report and give him his sparkling bride back again."

Anna beamed her beautiful smile around her circle of friends and thanked them for the wonderful time she was having and made a mental note to thank Leon for being so perceptive as to realise that she had been subconsciously fretting over their well-being, and for finding a way to deal with it. She had married a gem in Leon. To deflect attention from herself, Anna, asked Tilly if she was seeing Craig now that the case was officially over, having had its day in court.

Tilly's blush gave the game away. Tilly now backed into a corner, had to come clean and admit that she was dating a certain police officer.

The girls all eagerly chorused, "Spill the beans and tell us more juicy details."

Giving into their demands she began to fill them in on her budding romance. The way her eyes softened when she said Craig's name convinced Anna that Tilly was quite serious about this one. Maybe this one is the keeper, she thought. Jackson and Fernando took a bit of a back seat at this turn in the conversation, but were listening to the ebb and flow of what Jackson, considered to be, an excellent interrogation. They would make good policemen! Poor Tilly hadn't stood a chance. They had all the details of their meetings down pat in no time. Even Fernando was impressed how skilfully they had drawn her out and played her, until they had exactly what they wanted from her. Tilly didn't even know how much she had given away of her true feelings. For despite her assurances that they were still meeting casually, all at the table knew that she was in this relationship for the long haul. She positively glowed with luminosity when she spoke of Craig's daring part in her adventures and subsequent rescue. There was a lot of silent speculation going on as the meal continued with conversation which ebbed and flowed easily between them all and it was closing time before they realised it. They said their last farewells outside on the pavement and separated to go home with cheery waves.

Once back at Jackson's apartment block the girls had elected not to go back upstairs as they were now feeling tired from their busy day; thanking him for lovely time and the ride back, they got into Jeni's car to return to her house. The drive back was a quieter one. The chatter died down to a companionable silence as they drove through the darkness. When they got out at the end of their homeward journey Anna looked up into the night sky and with amazement saw it was covered in twinkling stars. She gasped loud enough for Jeni and Tilly to wonder what could be amiss. Seeing her upward stare they gazed heavenward too and joined her in appreciating the wonder of the firmament displayed there. "Isn't it amazing?" Anna exclaimed.

Tilly and Jeni nodded their agreement. It was a beautiful sight. Jeni quietly pointed out Orion and a few of the other constellations she recognised from her time as a Girl Guide. After a few moments the chill of the clear night began to take hold and reluctantly they went indoors and up to bed. It was the end of a long, happy day for them and a very frustrating one for Mr. Big. He still had no way to bring about his revenge, but "where there's a will, there's a way" was his motto.

Chapter Eleven

OVER BREAKFAST THE following morning Anna outlined her plans for promoting Jo's business and her own one too. Both Jeni and Tilly were enthusiastic in their praise and encouragement for this new step in her life. Now, she couldn't wait to get back home to London to share them with her Leon. She knew that he would be supportive; but would the family finances run to launching a new business? They would have to do some number crunching together to see what would be involved and how they could enable it all to happen. She couldn't, realistically, see having any free time together or double dating with their friends for a while. Life would be very frenetic while she got it all up and functioning well. Sad, but it would have to be done. In the meantime, there were wonderful kippers to demolish before the girls could get on with their day. However, it was all change when the phone rang only minutes later.

It was Jackson and Fernando. Rather than talk over the phone, they had said that they would be along shortly to share the girl's pot of coffee. Meanwhile, the girls carried on discussing various suggestions for Anna's new business venture. When the two guys joined them, they were at the naming stage and so they too soon joined in and contributed their share of silly ideas.

Anna and Tilly had the opportunity to see the lighter side of their characters and how their minds worked as the suggestions became more and more ridiculous until they were almost crying with laughter as Fernando described vividly his vision for the name "Handy Anna" as giant hands grabbing at passing "innocent bystanders" in Anna's pursuit of their business.

Anna went quiet a moment as she gave this new direction a bit of thought. What did she want to do? Help people to promote their business in better ways. In other words be a helping hand. Hands were an easy symbol to make into a logo and it could be a catchy strap line for the business too; with a bit of work, she thought. To try it out she threw "A Helping Hand" into the conversation and found that the others liked it and when she had expanded on how she thought it could be used as a logo, strap line and translated into media advertising; they were excited for her.

By the time the pot of coffee and its successor had been drained, Fernando, had revealed his hidden skill and drawn her a very usable logo, Jackson had created a credible strap line for her advertising campaign and the girls had drawn a cartoon type storyboard for a very short multi-media advert for the fledgling business.

Anna looked round the breakfast table at her friends new and old and thought to herself how fortunate she was to have such a supportive and creative bunch in her life. She felt very blessed. If Jackson and Fernando did become permanent fixtures, the girls would be very lucky indeed. She could see a happy future for them all. She was enthusiastic in her praise of all her "Think Tank's" efforts on her behalf and assured them that she would have them implemented in no time. However, the breakfast washing up still needed doing, as it was gone eleven o'clock and Gloria was having some time off. With this reminder, it was a case of no sooner said than done. Jackson volunteered his services as Washer-Upper in Chief and Fernando as Drier-Upper. Jeni said that she would put away. After all, it was her kitchen. Tilly and Anna were soon made redundant and left to go upstairs and ready themselves for the day ahead.

Fernando had nipped off to pick up Jo and when reunited they all piled into the two cars and drove off to the beach a bit further south for a walk, to give them an appetite for lunch. The walk along the sandy strand, which was empty of people and rubbish, was very refreshing. The salty breath of the onshore breeze and the cries of the swooping, swirling gulls and occasional colourfully beaked visiting puffins made it magical. They were walking along chatting quietly when Fernando accidently scuffed some sand up over the top of Tilly's shoe. With a mischievous twinkle in her eye she bent down pretended to brush it off, while she swiftly grabbed a small handful and flung it at him. Most of it misfired and landed on Jeni. Before they knew it they had "sand balls" flying and bodies dodging about everywhere. The laughter rang out as they ducked and dived celebrating direct hits with air punches and dances direct from football pitches. When things had calmed down a little, their stroll continued with wide smiles and wild threats of sudden retribution for imaginary foul plays, which settled down into hunting for unusual shells and other treasures.

They all managed to find something of interest to pick up and share with the others, before it all went into the rapidly growing collection being held in the biggest pocket to be found in Jackson's gilet. When Tilly insisted that they must take home with them the somewhat large piece of driftwood that she had discovered half hidden under some sand, Jackson put his foot down, declared that his pocket was not Mary Poppins' carpet bag and that they had better be making their way back to the car if that monstrosity was to go with them. With Tilly's protests that it was a wonderful piece of sea art falling on deaf ears, it was a reluctant band of beachcombers that made their way back to the vehicles parked in the layby close to the shore. Tilly's driftwood being pulled by Fernando and leaving a deep gouge in the sand trailing like a tail behind them. A quick dusting down to shake off as much sand as possible and the treasures of their seashore ramble safely cached in the boot of Jackson's car and they were off once more.

No-one noticed the flash as the sun bounced off the lens of a pair of high-powered binoculars that had been trained on them the whole time they had been walking. The observer calmly removed his notebook from his light coloured camouflage jacket and after making a few careful notations, returned it to its pocket and left his hide amidst the dunes as silently as he had arrived.

Chapter Twelve

THANKFULLY THE RESTAURANT that Jeni had booked
them into for Sunday lunch was not at all formal.
The background music was muted easy listening and
the diners' dress code ranged from chinos to jeans or
shorts with t-shirts to open necked shirts for both
sexes, all sprinkled throughout with some colourful
summer dresses. The clients also appeared to speak
several different languages from Gaelic and French to a
smattering of other European languages and a distinctly
Texan twang. Anna was fascinated by the lively scene.
When they had all been seated and drinks brought to
them she was free to ask the questions that had sprung
to mind while she had surreptitiously looked around.

Jeni told them that it was her first time there too
but Gloria, her housekeeper, had assured her that the
food was good and the atmosphere lively. Both assertions
turned out to be severely understated.

The food was amazing! So fresh and bursting with
interesting flavours. As they had all elected to have
different main dishes from a good but not extensive
menu, they ended up tasting mouthfuls of each dish.
The ample, if not downright generous helpings allowing
them to do so. The platter of freshly caught mackerel
stuffed with gooseberries and herbs and served with an

artisan horseradish sauce being a particular hit with them all. When the waiter asked would they like desserts they were all feeling a bit too full to follow such sumptuousness with a pudding. However, the waiter told them there were only two choices for the dessert menu. Intrigued by such a meagre choice after such splendour before, Jeni asked why and what they were.

The, by now widely smiling, waiter replied, "Well that would be the Chef's Special or the Chef's Platter, Miss." Now he had everyone's undivided attention.

This was Jackson's turn to question him. "And what might the Chef's Special be?" He asked politely.

"Why? Don't you know that he's famous for his Caledonian Cream?" The waiter fired backed, the twinkle in his eye, belying his shocked facial expression.

Tilly then jumped in with "And the Chef's Platter, please?"

"A little of what he fancies, of course!" The waiter rapidly replied. He had them in the palm of his hand and he knew it. Fernando thought that he would get him by asking for his personal recommendation and received the response that if they were to choose the dessert platter it would have some Caledonian Cream on it and so they would know what that tasted like anyway. They had to have one but agreed with the waiter's suggestion of one to share and six spoons as a good solution for their rather full tummies.

No sooner ordered than MacManus, the waiter, was back carrying a slate platter that bore a closer resemblance to a large tray. It was artfully arranged with a selection of small hand thrown pots, colourful artisan glass bowls and beautiful turned wood mini trays. Each containing colourful and temptingly scrumptious array.

It was almost criminal to have to dip their spoons into such artistry. However, the temptation was too great to delay their breaching for long. At Jackson's suggestion, Jeni was encouraged to get out her ever present notebook and pen, the better to make notes about what they were about to consume and for which they were all truly thankful. Helpfully, there was attached to the base of each container a number. Using this as her guide, Jeni recorded their comments as they shared one delightful explosion of deliciousness after another, cleansing their palates in between with the glasses of water so thoughtfully provided by the ever attentive, MacManus. The Caledonian Cream was indeed the piece de resistance of the epicurean wonders but the Tayberry Delight more than lived up to its name. Sunset Tango was a tangibly different tangy concoction of sorbets to finish with. None could be faulted, was the groups conclusion. They each did have their own particular favourites; that were duly noted for future reference, as they were bound to come again on their next visit to the wilds of Scotland for Leon and Craig to meet everyone.

MacManus was happy to drag a rather shy Chef from his kitchen haven to accept their overflowing praises and both were fascinated to read the comments they had made on their taste bud journey through the dessert platter. The Chef saying, that he found them most helpful and had been given idea for a new chocolate based dessert: one that he would be able to pursue to perfection before their next visit. After they left the table the gang rounded off their delicious meal with coffees in the comfortable sofas and chairs of the bar area and it was a very satisfied lot that left the restaurant some twenty minutes later. The discussion in the cars on the return journey to Jeni's house was of when they would be able to return and visit the wonderful establishment again?

Anna piped up that she would have the perfect excuse as she had to visit her new client to make sure that all her ideas were functioning to Jo's satisfaction. Tilly then claimed that she would have to return soon as she knew Craig was eager to meet her friend Jeni and get to know her. Now he would have to meet Jackson, Fernando and Jo too, the urgency would be even greater. Jeni was most happy to encourage them as she had missed them while she had been up North and added her piece with an open invitation to visit any time they liked. It was smiles all round as they followed their own lines of thought on the subject for the few minutes left of their journey.

Once back at Jeni's lovely abode the time had come for saying goodbyes as the two girls were to be packed and ready to be picked up shortly to fly back south. With hugs all round and promises to return soon the three girls waved Jackson, Fernando and Jo off before turning round to go into the house to finish off their bags. It was then that the telephone rang and Jeni answered it. To the enquiry, "Is that Miss Durham's residence?"

Jeni answered, "Yes, indeed it is." "Can I help you?"

The man went on to explain that he was just checking that Mrs. Lewis and Miss Brown would still be accompanying Martin on his scheduled flight south.

Jeni quickly replied, "Yes, they would," only to hear the phone click as the man cut her off from saying more. Strange! She told herself. In her experience, the Scots were generally such polite people.

The odds and ends were quickly packed away and baggage placed in the hall by the front door, Tilly and

Anna were just in time to catch Jeni shrugging her shoulders with a bemused look on her face.

"Anything amiss?" Asked Anna.

"Not really, just a rather odd phone call." Jeni told them.

"What about?" Anna queried.

Jeni explained, both the girls nodded their agreement, it was a funny way for Martin to check that they were expecting to be picked up to be taken to the airport and then flown home.

"He should have just phoned us himself on my mobile." Tilly said before the matter was dismissed, in favour of a last cuppa before they set of for the airport. Tilly and Anna made their way along to the kitchen to help Jeni carry tea things into the lounge for that final look out on the panoramic view of the Kyle and open sea beyond.

"I'm going to miss this wonderful view of yours, Jeni" said Tilly.

"Me too" echoed Anna, "it's simply fabulous!"

They thanked their kind hostess for making it such a lovely trip; with Anna adding her own special thanks for helping her out of her doldrums and on into a new exciting business venture.

"So you're going to make the idea of setting up on your own work for you, Anna!" Jeni enthused.

"Yes I am." Said Anna. "I really feel led to make a go of it as soon as possible and all the work you have all put in on it for me has practically got me to the point of execution already. All that remains is to run it by Leon and see how the costs work out before I hand in my notice at work."

Tilly suggested that perhaps she could start up and run it alongside her regular job, for a few months at least, before taking the final step of severing her ties with a regular income. However, Anna told them, as they had been driven back to Jeni's house the previous evening, she felt that she would need to put in lots of hours to build up the new business quickly. That she would not be able to give of her best to either work, if she ran the two jobs in tandem. No, no. It would be far better to just bite the bullet and commit herself to where she now believed her future lay. That decision made, it was with a much less careworn face that she had turned to face the waiting lounge door, just as it flew open and heralded the entrance of Martin Jamieson, acting chauffeur, being shown through by Gloria.

"Hello girls" he chirruped, "had a nice break, have you?"

"Yes thanks, it was lovely and we're only sorry it has flown by so quickly."

"Well, I'm sorry too, but if we are to get back in time for work bright and early tomorrow we must be off now girls. Let's get your bags stowed and we'll get airborne before you know it." Martin told them picking up their suitcases with ease to walk them out to his plane and stow them away.

On the driveway, Jeni had given them a picnic bag for their journey and a hug each and extracted a promise of a phone call from each to let her know when they would be returning again. As Anna and Tilly looked down on her now below them, they could see Jeni's rapidly diminishing figure waving and sadly acknowledged that their lovely stay was now over.

All was quiet in the cockpit while Martin sorted out his route and signed off from the control tower at the airport. However, he soon had himself organised. It was then that Anna remembered the strange phone call and asked Martin why he hadn't just phoned Tilly on her mobile? The look on his face told her, that he clearly had no idea what she was talking about. She just filed it under weird one and pushed it to the back of her mind as they shared the highlights of their visit with him and asked after his family. Martin too had spent an enjoyable visit and felt happy to catch up with all the family news and views. After all that chatter they needed their flask of hot tea and the lovely pile of salmon sandwiches and dainties that Gloria had packed up for them for their supposedly, light tea. Martin, however, managed to ensure that nothing was wasted of her scrumptious spread. Each girl made a mental note to drop a line or two of thanks for Gloria's kindness in the next couple of days.

The following wind being quite strong, the journey south ended up being some forty five minutes shorter than their journey north. Martin had them safely landed and cleared of the formalities of air travel in no time and after their thanks had been expressed the girls picked up their car and Tilly began the drive to Anna's home. They were almost there, when a stupid idiot of a driver cut across her lane at minimal distance from her front bumper to exit the road they were travelling on. Tilly had no choice but to slam on her brakes and skid to an abrupt halt a mere inch before hitting the crash barrier at the juncture of the two roads. Badly shaken, the two girls didn't speak. They just nodded to acknowledge the unspoken question, are you alright? Once she had taken a deep breath, Anna realised the danger their position had left them in and asked urgently if Tilly felt able to drive them out of the main flow and onto the emergency hard shoulder. Tilly merely nodded when she saw how precariously situated they were and turned on the engine, once more putting the car into a low gear she carefully manoeuvred them to temporary safety. All the while the flowing vehicles screeched, skidded and parted to get around them and continue their journeys. Their car rocking with the buffeting wind of these movements. With the engine stilled again, in the relative safety of the emergency lane, they sat just holding each other's hands and silently thanking God for his protection over them.

It was when Tilly gently undid her seatbelt and felt her chest that Anna became aware of her own discomfort. When she looked down to the bare patch of neck where her shirt was open it was to see the start of what would be some spectacular bruising. Her slam into the seatbelt had indubitably saved her from flying forwards and an even more severe injury, but it had left its mark on her that would last for at least two or three weeks. Tilly affirmed that she too was badly bruised.

"Should we call an ambulance?" Tilly asked Anna.

"I don't think I need one," said Anna as she refastened her seatbelt. "All I want to do is get home as quickly as possible. I just want to hug my husband." She continued in a very subdued tone.

It was this that made Tilly pull herself together. There was no injury and no damage to her car or any other vehicle involved to worry about; just some rubber burnt off her tyres and brake pads that she would get checked sooner rather than later. Anna and Leon's was only five minutes away, she could make it that far. Firing up the engine she got herself back into the flow of heavy traffic that had appeared from nowhere and cautiously drove Anna home. Tilly was trembling but she had made it intact when she pulled up on the driveway.

Chapter Thirteen

LEON WAS VERY happily surprised to find his wife on the doorstep when he answered the doorbell. Her shaky appearance wasn't what he expected. He drew Anna into his arms and enveloped her in a warm hug as she let her head droop onto his shoulder. No words were said. The mere warmth of his body giving her all that she needed. As Tilly came up the path all she saw was them surrounded by the golden glow of the hall light above their heads and felt herself turning green with envy. What wouldn't she give for a big hug from Craig right now! Her deep sigh that accompanied the thought drew Leon's attention and he gently tugged Anna further into the hall and motioned Tilly to enter. She shut the door behind her and they all gravitated towards the lounge and comfy seats. Once seated and his arm around her to support her, Anna told him of their scary incident. His ashen face told its own tale and Anna, not wanting to worry him further, changed tack to telling him about their time in the Highlands.

Their broad smiles, as Tilly joined in assured him that Anna had enjoyed her trip and would be full of her joys to relate when they were alone. However, right now they were hosts and the late supper he had thoughtfully purchased from the local Marks and Sparks was greeted with enthusiasm by both girls as shock had given way to hunger. Hearing their chatter about Martin's flying skills and the joy of travelling so low that you actually enjoy viewing the landscape over which you were travelling reminding him of how quiet the house had seemed while Anna had been absent. He had missed her. Was he really such a married man already? He rather thought that he was.

The meal demolished and the evidence of its demise was cleared way. Assured of Tilly's confidence in being able to drive herself home; Anna and Leon gave Tilly warm hugs and thanks for all her help with the surprise weekend away. They stood and waved a fond farewell as she took off to find her own bed, before the morning would all too easily bring reality of working life crashing in.

After carefully locking up, Leon turned and gently took his wife in his arms and quietly told her that he wasn't sure if he could ever let her go away without him again. Looking very worried, Anna, had immediately asked him why?

His rapid "I missed you far too much."

This brought a little smile of satisfaction to her lips, as she sought to reassure him how much he had been missed despite all the fun she had shared with her friends. As they switched off the lights downstairs and wound their way up to their bedroom, she told him that she was more than happy to accept his decree, but perhaps he should hold fire a bit longer before making it an absolute. After all, he might get a bit bored with having her around all day every day……. In about fifty or sixty years. Leon was still chuckling at that thought as he climbed into bed beside her.

It was at the early hour of six in the morning, Anna had filled him in on all the fun she had in Scotland and told him about her proposal for her new business. As she had expected, Leon was as always, very supportive. He suggested that she put together a business plan as soon as possible in order to work out how they could fund it. In the meantime, he suggested that she pursue the expansion of Jo Lawson's glass working firm in principal and make it an actual when she was up and running. Happy that they were both on board, it was time to get some work done.

Chapter Fourteen

WHEN MR. BIG next obtained a library book it contained news that suffused his face with a purplish red and you could almost see the steam venting from his ears. The fact that he was not actually breathing fire from his mouth was considered a miracle by his companion. He had fairly stormed down the walkway to his cell like a steam train through a tunnel. The other prisoners falling back into their cells or leaping out of his way. No-one wanted to be the one on the receiving end of whatever had woken the sleeping volcano.

He banged the cell door open, marched in and flung himself down on his bunk. As he stared up at the underside of the upper bunk his mind whirred round and round with the news that "the accident" had failed to happen. Who knew that Tilly would be such a proficient driver and manage to evade the efforts of his own, professional stunt driver? It seemed unbelievable, but never the less it was true. Gradually, as his mind had accepted this fact his body had quietened down and the colour in his face had calmed to a flush of pink. His disappointment at not having dealt with two of his meddlers was deep but it only served to make him more determined than ever. He would succeed.

It would take a lot more planning than he had thought. That would take time. But, "revenge is a dish best served cold" and his would be practically frozen, but certainly deadly. This time he would make sure of that personally.

Chapter Fifteen

THE NEXT TWO weeks disappeared in a puff of smoke as Anna burnt the midnight oil putting together a development plan for Jo, a business plan to show to the financial sector and still managed to fit in her full-time job. She was kept fuelled for all this effort by the quiet man who shopped, cooked and cleaned. He just did everything to keep their home life running smoothly while she got her thoughts about her business down on the laptop and into presentation format.

Leon knew that Anna was a very capable woman; but he was impressed by how well she thought matters through and in almost microscopic detail. She had occasionally asked him for some help to track down a particular bit of information from the internet but mainly he had kept his attention on the practical things of life, while she waded her way through it all. When she declared that she had done all that she could and could do no more, late on a Saturday afternoon, he suggested that he take her out for dinner to celebrate. She countered with a proposal of her own. That she get showered and go out to get a take way from their favourite Chinese restaurant while he read her frantic efforts. He asked her if she was she sure that she wouldn't rather go out and be waited on? To a very firm yes, he agreed with her alternative plan for their evening.

Making himself comfortable with the laptop on his knees and his favourite pottery pint mug full of builder's tea to await her return. When Anna came downstairs ready to go and get their meal he was quick to wave her away with a cheery I'll eat whatever you fetch home, as he resumed his study of what was on the screen before him.

Anna collected her jacket, car keys and purse and drove swiftly to "Oh Nose", as they called it. The On Ho, was a popular place. Even though it was only six o'clock and its doors were newly opened, the queue was already formed inside all the way back to the outer door. Anna realised that it would be a while before her order was taken, let alone filled so. Resigning herself to the wait, she sat down on the seats so thoughtfully provided for the first dozen or so clients and got out her phone. I might as well catch up on my emails, she thought to herself. By the time she had whittled them down to those she had to answer it was time to place her order. Feeling very generous she ordered a banquet menu for two. Leon had been so good he deserved a treat and she found that her lack of interest in food, while she was working so hard, had now left her feeling absolutely ravenous. Salivating at the thought of the delights ahead, Anna went back to dealing with her emails. She had just manged to fire the last one off; the one to Jo to tell her that a business development plan should be with her on Monday morning, when a voice announced that her meal was ready for collection. Anna was quick to and leap up to grasp the well packed, brown paper carrier bags but not before she had checked if they contained her beloved prawn crackers. With Mr. Ho's beaming assurance that he had not forgotten to put some in, she made her way to the till to pay.

Mrs. Ho was always happy to see her young friend Anna. She was also quick to notice, what her husband had not. "You are married Anna?" she queried. Anna blushed a rosy hue as she told Mrs. Ho that she and Leon had just decided they couldn't wait and had a quiet wedding to avoid all the fuss that their families would have wanted for them. Mrs. Ho called her husband over to express their congratulations and then sent him back into the restaurant to bring forth a lovely bottle of wine as a belated wedding gift to take home to Leon and enjoy with their meal. Mr. Ho knowing that Leon was partial to a Tiger beer had also put a couple into the bag he provided for her to carry them out to the car. With their warm wishes for a future full of happiness ringing in her ears Anna drove home.

Calling out, "Honey I'm home," in a parody of the movie greeting, she went into the kitchen to fetch plates, forks, spoons and a pair of well-worn chopsticks. Suitably laden, she walked into the lounge. Only to find that Leon had torn himself away from the laptop long enough to move their infamous coffee table nearer in front of the sofa and fully extended it to accommodate the carrier bags that Anna was swiftly emptying out onto its heat-resistant central area. The coffee table had played a memorable part in Anna's childhood and when she had begged her parents to let her give it a permanent home in her new house Leon had entered into some serious bartering for this " family heirloom". It was finally resolved when he beat her mother all the way down from five pence to four! Leon helped open up the recyclable packages and release the tempting aromas of Anna's choice of dishes.

"Wow, Anna, this looks amazing," he said. "It's a good job I'm as hungry as a horse," came next.

"Hey, hey Leon, half this lot is mine," Anna exclaimed.

"Well, I suppose you have been on a sort of self-inflicted diet for the past two weeks and need to make up for lost time," Leon continued reluctantly, "so, I guess we can share."

After a short break to clean hands and say grace they were quick to start loading their plates, making inroads into the special fried rice and sweet and sour pork balls before adding in sticky ribs and a couple of chicken satay sticks too. For some time the food dominated and happy munching went on. However, once the initial hunger pangs were appeased, the need to congratulate Anna on the quality of her business plan had to be expressed. Leon told her, between mouthfuls, how well she had constructed her plan and provided the evidence that he would need to convince the money men of her ability to carry such a plan forward.

Anna had kept it very simple; but had built a sensible growth expansion pattern for the future that would make the business self-sustaining. Her wealth of data to showed that this service would fill a current gap in the market but also assist others in the creation of wealth. This area, was quite cleverly used and very up to the minute: proving further that she had a good grasp of the current market trends and where they might be going. Leon was more than happy to back her as his wife, but also assured her that she was a fine business woman too.

He then went on to her development plan for Jo Lawson Glass. She had, he acknowledged, not only a good grasp of the nature of the business Jo ran, but also how it could function more efficiently and cope with the increase her new business ideas would generate. He told Anna that he loved the money-saving packaging idea that she had dreamt up which would gain Jo's goods even more attention in the marketplace.

"You're a veritable whizz kid, Anna," he told her, "and I had the good sense to marry you. I'm going to be rich in no time!"

Anna laughed out loud at that suggestion but blushed at all the compliments he was paying her. She knew that even though he loved her dearly, Leon was not one to over-egg anything. He was naturally reticent and must really have liked her plans to be so enthusiastic about them. His next suggestion was to surprise her even more.

"I'd like to pop over and see Mum and Dad tomorrow and run these past them, if you have no objections, Anna?" he asked.

Anna thought a moment as she finished a particularly nice mouthful of Szechwan beef and then gave her consent. "Perhaps you had better give them a call now to see if it would be convenient." She told him.

No sooner said, than Leon had picked up the telephone. It took a minute to get a proper dialling tone. The line clicked a couple of times before engaging. For a second he thought, how odd, but when his mother answered his mind went straight into the present and the need to see his parents about Anna's plans.

Edward and Marian Lewis were delighted to receive a call from their son and even more to learn that he and his new wife were hoping to visit them the following day. Marian invited them to come and have Sunday lunch with them to give them more time to talk about this urgent matter Leon and Anna wanted to discuss with them.

While Leon was more than happy to learn his mother's opinion on the plans, it was his father's professional view that he was eager to hear. A bank manager of some twenty five years standing made him an ideal sounding board and financial advisor for Anna's fledgling business. The man had been assessing and authorising loans for the major part of his financial career and Leon knew him to be very well thought of in banking circles. If Edward Lewis thought that Anna's ideas were sound, they should have no trouble finding the right sort of financial backing to get her off to a flying start.

With the timing sorted, Leon rang off and filled Anna in. They then continued to eat their supper in a more leisurely fashion while watching an old movie called *Keeping Mum* for a couple of hours. The food got left as their need for it had been sated and the hilarious antics of Maggie Smith, Rowan Atkinson and Patrick Swayze had them chuckling and then belly laughing. "What a good laugh that film was" Leon told Anna as the final credits rolled.

"I'll never be able to look at a big trunk or a village pond without suspicion again," declared Anna.

"Time to clear up this mess," Anna told her husband, as she encouraged him to stack the empties ready for disposal in their appropriate recycling bags fetched from the kitchen cupboard.

"Wasn't it kind of Mr. and Mrs. Ho to send you home with a belated wedding gift" Leon said, "we mustn't forget to drop them a thank you note."

"Yes, I'll try and find a nice card to write it in during my lunch break on Monday, but right now I'm for bed." Anna replied.

"Did you say something about bed?" Leon asked, giving her the benefit of his best leer and twisting of fake mustachios, as he chased her up the narrow staircase and caught her just in time to throw her bodily onto the marital bed.

"Careful Tiger." Anna admonished. "We can't afford a new bed as well as a new business!"

At one o'clock sharp Leon and Anna pulled into the Lewis driveway. It didn't do to be late for one of his mum's

Sunday roast dinners. Always timed to perfection and simply delicious, they were not to be missed. Anna thought to herself that she was quite pleased to get out of doing a meal today. She knew that there was no way she could produce such a wonderful repast without spending days preparing for the event. Her own mother had such a varied menu that Sunday roasts were just as likely to turn up on a Friday night, when her mother finally realised that they hadn't partaken of one for six months or so, and felt that she ought to make the effort again. With the result, Anna's opportunities to learn such skills were few and far between. No doubt she would get the hang of it eventually; but in the meantime, she was more than happy to enjoy sharing one with her in-laws and put off that particular hurdle for a while longer.

They were soon ensconced in the comfortable armchairs that littered his parents' living room and enjoying their traditional aperitif and pre-lunch nibbles. Anna noted that the cheese straws were as usual, homemade and absolutely scrumptious. She could have happily eaten them for lunch; with perhaps a side salad. Leon was eagerly reaching for his third very large one, taking his mother's abilities in the kitchen very much for granted. Anna, however, would give credit where credit was due and was full of praise for Marian's offering. Marian was her normal dismissive self, but Anna had noted the brief flush of pleasure her compliment had brought to her hostess' cheeks and resolved to make sure she didn't forget to do so again at the end of her meal, along with her offer to wash up. On discovering that Marian Lewis' kitchen did not run to a dishwasher on an early visit to Leon's home, she had since always tried to help with clearing up after a meal and knew that it was one of the reasons that she and Marian had been able to forge their own friendship so quickly. When they had broken the news of their marriage, it was that friendship that had enabled Marian to accept that a quiet affair was more suited to who they were as a couple; and put aside any regrets she may have had to rejoice with them on their good news that they had tied the knot.

Pulling her thoughts back into the present, Anna realised that Leon was showing his father her business plan. He had even managed to print off a copy for both his parents to be able to follow it while Anna would be presenting it to them after their meal. She could see that Leon had dug out a couple of rather smart folders to bind them in and roughed a better version of the drawing of her logo to front them with. What a star! However, all that was put aside as the serious business of the carving of the roast beef was upon them. A full two hours later and Yorkshire pudding, at least five different roasted vegetables, greens with mint sauce and a side dish of horseradish sauce had been disposed of. Swiftly followed by a gorgeous sticky date and toffee pudding with homemade vanilla ice cream.

"Just to help it slide down better." Marian had claimed outrageously. Compliments paid to her and graciously received, they were instructed to leave the dishes in soak as there were much more important matters to attend to. They all trooped back into the living room and over cups of fragrantly steaming coffee, Anna was given the go ahead by Edward to make her pitch. Leon gave her a surreptitious thumbs up and she was off.

Anna had carefully tailored her proposal to last precisely one hour. Her previous experience telling her that any longer could allow attention to begin to wander, anything less would be deemed not worth bothering with. However, after the first twenty minutes, she felt pretty confident that she had her in-laws' full attention. Edward hadn't interrupted her to ask any questions and appeared to be listening very carefully to her step by step assessment of how her proposed business would develop. While Marion was giving her encouraging smiles throughout. When she had finally come to an end, she found herself being clapped by all three Lewis family members. She plonked herself down rapidly in the chair she had vacated earlier and felt the tension leave her neck and shoulders, as she left Leon to ask what his father and mother thought of her ideas. Anna listened as she drank some of the still piping hot coffee from the insulated serving jug her mother-in-law had so thoughtfully placed on the low table in front of her.

With the exception of one or two minor financial safeguards that Edward would like to see put in place prior to another pitch, he was very complimentary about the skill and sound business sense that she had brought to her proposal. He even went so far as to say, that he thought he might know someone willing to back her financially.

Leon's excited, "Do you hear that, Darling?" Would, Anna felt, have been heard half way down the street. It was followed by "I'm so proud of you, Anna". Then rounded off with. "It takes a lot for someone to impress Dad, you know!" Just in case she was in the slightest doubt as to how well she had done. However, it was Marian's quiet words that made the most impact on Anna that afternoon. As they washed, dried and put away all the lunchtime clutter she had told Anna that she felt that she was onto a winner and wold be a great success. If she, Marian, had needed a business developer she would be top of her list for sure. Anna thanked her with an impulsive hug and it would told her that when she made her first profit she would be taking Marian out for a slap up girlie lunch to celebrate her success in style. If only

Anna could have been a fly on the wall at Edward and Marian's home after she and Leon had returned home.

Edward and Marian had continued to discuss Anna's new business plan and come up with one of their own. Instead of letting the young couple go into the world of finance and search for backing, they decided that they would be Anna's sponsor and provide her with the financial backing she would need in order to go forward with all her plans. It would be done properly. In fact, it would be done how they always went about their financial matters; quietly. Edward would arrange it all through his bank and the couple would never know who the benefactor was, only that their rate would be too good to refuse! The contract would run at no interest repayments until the business was financially solvent and then the loan could be repaid in such a way as to allow the company still to grow securely. Leon may not have been aware of his parent's magnanimity personally but he did know that they practiced their Christian faith daily and would quietly help others where and whenever they could. There was never any fuss and it was always referred to as lending a helping hand, no more than that , so that when they had heard her name for her new business they saw it as a sign of God's approval. When he was younger Leon had asked his father why he did things that way and Edward's reply had stuck with him.

"Well son, you never know it might be me in his shoes one day, and in that case, I would like to be treated with respect and kindness." Edward had said.

It had made Leon realise that he was very fortunate to have such a wise man as his father. It had also coloured how he lived his own life and had been something that had drawn the attention of his wife to want to know him better.

Chapter Sixteen

TILLY HAD RESUMED her normal routine. Well, almost. She found herself having to make. No. Wanting to make. Needing to make, more and more time in it for a certain person. Craig Ryan. He had gone from haunting her dreams, to demanding her free hours. The more time she gave him, the more time she wanted to give him. They were now starting their days exercising together, whenever his shift work allowed. Grabbing a lunchtime break on days when they could and making supper together either at her place or his. He was scrupulous about her having her regular time out with her other friends. He never asked to come too or moped or tried to blackmail her into not going. He would ask kindly about how they all were and leave it at that. Since they had been seeing so much of each other Tilly found that she missed Craig when she was out elsewhere without him by her side. She found herself turning to tell him things and being disappointed when he wasn't there to share them with. She missed his sense of humour and easy laughter. He was the only one who made her laugh out loud at things. He would often know what she would like before she had even realised it for herself. He seemed to be able to read her mind. If she dared to let herself dwell on the matter, she might even think that she was falling in love with Mr. Craig Ryan.

She shared this startling revelation with Anna late that evening, in an impulsive call, just to let someone know what she had just found out about herself. Anna was eager to learn what had made her realise that Craig was special and may well be "The One!"? Willingly, Tilly, elaborated on all Craig's good qualities. His kind ways, thoughtfulness, willingness to share everything… including the chores!

After an hour, with Tilly barely stopping for breath, Anna felt that she could interrupt the flow. "Yes. Yes, I think I get the picture Tilly!" "He sounds an absolute saint and absolutely the perfect man for you." Anna told her.

That made Tilly laugh. "Did I really make him sound that goodie, goodie?" She asked Anna.

"Actually, I think that you just can't help yourself, you're besotted and it's wonderful." Anna replied.

"Yes, it is wonderful." Tilly agreed. By the time that had been done it was nearly midnight and Anna reminded her gently that they both needed to get some beauty sleep. However, Anna was too fired up to settle to sleep quickly and knowing that Jeni often stayed up late writing her novels, she decided to give her a ring. Jeni was up. She was also in need of a break from writing. Jeni was more than happy to be filled in on the latest development in Tilly's romance.

It was after Anna had put the phone down, that Tilly's revelation had made Jeni think about her own love life. Her whole world had turned upside down when Jackson had entered it. All the drama that had arisen through her online dating idea for finding Jo a new man, had been the catalyst that brought them together. Now, it was months later and they were still seeing each other. At first, with Fernando and Jo to "talk out their adventures" as part of the therapy homework, that the police counsellor had given them, to help them get their traumatic time into perspective. Lately, this had gradually changed, as Jeni had realised that she wanted to spend more time just getting to know more. More about Jackson Redman, the man; what it was that made him tick, his likes, dislikes, etc. The more time that they spent together, the more Jeni was fascinated by the complexity of his life and yet somehow he managed to keep it so simple.

That very evening they had been discussing a future dinner date with Fernando and Jo. They had both acknowledged a desire to see their friends soon; but made acknowledgement of how much they had enjoyed spending time alone with each other. To hear Jackson tell her how much he loved her company, made Jeni feel very special. She knew that Jackson was not given to bandying compliments around. His, were the rare sort and meant all the more when they came along unexpectedly. It was in the aftermath of this one, that she had the thought; that she hoped, that he might just have some special words to say to her. She loved the way his compliments made her feel so deeply appreciated. No man had ever made her feel that way before and she rather liked it. It was when she eventually switched into sleep mode that she had "her dream".

She'd had the same dream off and on throughout her life. She remembered that once, she and a school friend had tried to tell each other's future in the tealeaves in the bottom of their teacups. Her friend had flung a tea towel over her head and got Jeni to cross her palm with a twenty pence piece before predicting that her true love would be a giant of a man with flaming hair and a gentle smile. Jeni had reciprocated with an outrageous suggestion of her own and that had set off a fit of the giggles that had Jeni's mother making their two ten year old selves, do all the washing up and drying up after supper. That night had been the first time that she had dreamt about her giant with his flaming hair and got so agitated that she had woken her parents with her noise. A milky drink and she had gone back to sleep easily enough. However, this strange dream was to become a feature over the passing years and had never gone away for too long. This time it was different. Her giant had Jackson Redman's face! When she woke next morning and realised what had happened she had a gentle smile on her own face. Perhaps independent Miss Jeni Durham's mind had found her a real giant to spend her life with, who knows?

Chapter Seventeen

ANNA HAD SENT Jo her business development proposal for the glassworks, as soon as she had tidied it into a presentation format, for Jo's comments on her work by overnight courier. She thought that she should give Jo a least a week to study them before speaking to her about them. Instead, a bare two days later and Jo was in touch. Anna's package hadn't arrived.

Anna had just walked in from work when Leon told her that Jo had phoned her and would appreciate a call back as soon as she had a minute to spare. Leon also added his own observation, that Jo sounded very agitated. He suggested that she phoned Jo back from the phone in the lounge right away. He would make dinner for them while she did so. Anna flung her arms round her husband and gave him a loving kiss and told him that she was sure that she had the best husband in the world and she would be his dutiful wife and do just what he had suggested immediately! Leon had left the room chuckling at that thought.

She kicked off her shoes and curled her legs up under her on the sofa as she dialled Jo's number, that Leon had thoughtfully placed on the pad they kept right by the phone. It only rang a couple of rings before Jo picked it up.

"Jo Lawson speaking, can I help you?" Came Jo's bright voice down the line.

"Not really," Anna answered pertly, "But perhaps I can do something for you Jo?"

Jo said that she certainly hoped so and went on to explain that Anna's presentation of the business development plan had simply not been delivered. Anna had no light to shed on the matter but assured Jo that she would be getting another copy made and sent by express the next morning. She would be calling her to let her know when to expect it and would be happy to know if it arrived safely this time. Jo chuckled and assured Anna that she very much hoped so. Before eight o'clock and barely twenty four hours since she had received them, she was assuring her that she had loved the ideas that Anna had put together to develop and market her business. Then they had spent the next thirty minutes going over them, before Jo asked Anna how soon she thought that they could go ahead with them.

Anna had let out a little sigh of relief at that; then answered, "As soon as you and I can get a contract signed you can implement them."

Jo told her to get the contract to her for her approval and signature as soon as possible regardless of whether she had seen the presentation in its final form for financial backing approval. She trusted Anna and was sure that when her bank saw it they would be confident enough to loan her the monies that she would need for making it all happen. Anna promised to get right on the case just as soon as she had eaten the delicious looking meal that Leon had put down on the table nearby. Jo agreed that would be just fine with her.

After placing the phone in its cradle, Anna leapt up to give Leon a big hug and dance him round the room whilst singing "I've got my first client" to a random tune, before they both flopped down onto the sofa to eat.

When she had finally come down to earth, Anna was able to fill in all the details of her conversation with Jo and at last, do justice to the dinner that Leon had so lovingly cooked for her. He told her that her new business venture was already proving to be a successful one and that she ought to think seriously about making it full-time as soon as possible.

Jo was realising that she would need to raise more capital for her business than she had first thought, if she was to cope with the increased orders she foresaw the new marketing plan would bring in. She knew that she would have to employ either more staff or pay for more hours for her existing staff. She might even need more deliveries to be made. Another man and van? There was a lot to think about and plan for, but it would all take hard cash and right now she didn't have any more resources. What she really needed was either a fairy godmother or a sleeping partner; one to put up the cash and let her get on with running her business the way she wanted to. Pigs might fly, she thought to herself! However, she would have to talk the bank manager, with the help of Anna's presentation, of course, if she was to reap the reward for all of her hard labour.

When Mr. Big learnt of Jo's need for cash to expand her business, after her telephone call to Fernando about it the previous evening while they had arranged their next date, he positively rubbed his hands with glee. If he had the copy of the presentation of the new development plan, he would have a chance to get his own back by bringing down Jo's business. There would be a way to hurt them all through it. They were all so close now that what hurt one would hurt them all. He felt sure of his revenge already! Perhaps he could arrange for Jo to receive an offer of a business loan on very favourable terms and then foreclose on it. After, arranging for her bank manager to refuse to give her a loan when she applied for the extra funding, of course.

When later that week Jo did turn to her local bank manager for an extension to her business funding, she got turned down with regret. She was astounded. However, her bank manager, went on to tell her, he did know of some private investors who might be willing to loan her the necessary monies. If, they liked her expansion plans and if she was interested. He could arrange a loan with one of them. Jo immediately brightened up at the prospect of another way forward and agreed. He promised to send her some contact details very soon and they shook hands cordially before Jo went on her way.

Jo filled Fernando in with all the details of her meeting at the bank as they sat having lunch on the harbour wall. Fish and chips always tastes better eaten outdoors and from the paper wrapping they had agreed. Fernando also agreed that economies were needed if Jo was to be able to afford to pay off another loan. The rate would probably not be as favourable as her one from the bank, he told her. Private investors often expect a better rate of return. However he wondered if he and maybe even their other friends, could come up with some of the money and thereby make the loan a bit easier to cope with. Jo thought about it swiftly; but thought, she would rather be as financially independent as possible. She would hate to let her friends down and lose their savings, if her business should fail in any way. She tried to explain this to Fernando, but he assured her that he had every confidence in her future success and was sure her friends would feel the same way. Jo insisted that she still wanted to go with an outside loan but told him that she would keep this offer in mind for future reference.

The rest of their weekend was spent busily getting some tidying and re-organising of her workshop stock holding area done to make room for all the extra products that Jo would be creating, and placing orders for the extra deliveries of the materials needed to make them. By the time Sunday afternoon was over they were both grubby and worn out. However, it was with a sigh of contentment that came when they looked around at their handiwork. All the moving and re-labelling to organise it all had been so worthwhile. The storage now should flow a lot better and as a clear workspace always made her feel more creative, Jo was anticipating a burst of productivity when Monday morning came around. In the meantime, she thanked Fernando for all his efforts on her behalf with a big kiss, a promise of a hot shower to freshen up and a generous helping of the hearty chicken stew that she had put in the slow cooker prior to them starting work that day.

"Are there any dumplings in the stew?" Fernando was quick to ask. Jo simply beamed.

"Of course; I know they're your favourites by now as you always ask for second helpings whenever I make them." She told him.

It was a very contented, if very tired Fernando who left her to return to his apartment for an early night shortly after nine o'clock. Jo teased him as she saw him off with her parting shot.

"The neighbours will think you are going off me if you leave so early! "

"Not a chance!" He called out as he sat in the driver's seat of his car. "I love you and you'll never get rid of me."

As she closed her door to turn in for the night, Jo hoped that was a promise, as she thought that he was the most wonderful man she could ever want to meet.

Monday morning shone bright and clear. A perfect day to start her new work, Jo thought, as she hurried along the path to the glass workshop to open up before her helpers arrived and clutching her usual half-finished mug of tea. Once everyone had got in she told them to follow her and prepare to be amazed. She flung open the stock room storage door and was pleasantly surprised at their encouraging words of approval. She went on to explain that this had been done to allow them to expand their output. She took Shona and Drew back into the reception area to elaborate on the new marketing plans and how they would affect the business. When anxious looks began to pass between her co-workers, Jo was quick to ask for their input. However, the anxiety was soon put to flight with the assurance that extra hours or provision for new staff members or extra transport had all been thought about too and would be forthcoming as and when they were needed. It was with happy smiles that all three got down to the morning's work.

It was not until after the post arrived and Shona brought in a large envelope from the bank with her coffee, that Jo had to put on her business hat again. Shona gently picked up the beautiful little gilded cage that Jo had fashioned.

"Ooh this is lovely, Jo" she exclaimed. "Is it a new design?" she asked.

Jo was quick to tell her that she rather thought that it might be. Perhaps it could come as a set with birds of different coloured glass in each one. Shona was fulsome with her approval and went to fetch the camera they used to photograph each new piece for catalogue purposes, while Jo quickly inserted a cute little bluebird to sit within the cage. That done, Shona left her to have her coffee in peace.

Jo turned to the envelope and opened it. The bank manager had come through for her. When Jo went through the terms of the loan she was amazed at how reasonable it seemed. It could even work out cheaper than her existing bank loan. She was so happy with the proposal that she felt no qualms about signing the paperwork and getting Shona to send it off straight away. Shona when called in so soon was amazed that she was to rush this one through and write a letter of thanks for Jo to sign that day; but she was happy to do so and with her usual efficiency photocopied all the documentation for their records and had it all signed, sealed and in the post before home time. It was a good days work all round.

Jo reflected on the way her life was going that night while she wallowed in her lovely hot bath. She was counting her blessings. She had a wonderful boyfriend, who might even become a lot more. Great friends who she knew supported her in everything. A job she loved and people that she loved to work with. Her own business which was taking off into a new future. A cosy home to live in. What more could she possibly need? She already had everything. Then she thought a moment more. Well, the desire of her heart would be the cherry on this particular cake. Her dreams that night were full of weddings, flowers and cakes and the faces of those she loved surrounding her. The husband of her dreams?

Chapter Eighteen

THE PRISONER ASSIGNED library duty was relieved. The last time Mr. Big had come in he had smashed up a chair and table in his rage and that duty prisoner had ended up in the sick bay. In fact, he was still there! As no one had wanted to take over the library job after that, he had got press-ganged into it. Today was a new day but all he could hope for was to survive it. Mr. Big was smiling as he listened to his new audiobook through the old fashioned headphones supplied by the prison library.

Later, in his cell he was looking pleased as punch and the Wing Officer at Her Majesty's Prison got a distinctly nasty feeling in the pit of his stomach. The hairs rose on the back of his neck giving him a decidedly shivery feeling. "I wouldn't be surprised if that one is plotting some mischief." He told the Governor when he made his final status report during handover that evening. "He just looked too pleased with the world not to be up to something!"

The Governor took Mr. Skelton's feelings very seriously. They had often led to the prevention of some potentially nasty incidents in the past. He too found this particular prisoner one that made your blood run cold. Hence, he immediately gave instructions for a surprise cell search and the taking of another look at all of the phone recordings and mail relating to Mr. Big. If Mr. Big was about to pull something off, he for one, wanted to be prepared to counter it. He would have been even more concerned, if he had been able to be privy to the conversation Mr. Big had with his barber.

The arrangement to have the prison officer on duty at the prison barber's shop distracted for his appointment duration had involved some decisive measures and cost one inmate a lot of pain and some blood loss for which he had been well compensated with a supply of drugs for a week. Confident that no-one would be interrupting him, Mr. Big was able to give full vent and assure the poor man waiting to trim his locks in exquisite detail precisely what would happen to him, should he fail to convey his instructions accurately. Also, that the penalty enforced if they did not succeed was one that the poor man did not want to even think about failure. His hands were shaking so much while he carried out the required trim, that the returning officer was convinced that he was ill. Did he have a fever, he was asked? Perhaps he was coming down with flu. Whatever, it was the concern raised led to him being taken away and sent home to recover. He was still pale and shaky when he had delivered his instructions to his contact to pass on up the chain. His terror, went with them to the top.

Chapter Nineteen

ANNA WAS DELIGHTED to learn all about Jo's exciting week when she phoned her that evening for her usual weekly catch up. So much so that she almost forgot to share her own work news! Just as they were about to ring off she remembered and started with, "By the way I got offered a new job today."

Jo spluttered out, "And you forgot to tell me such amazing news until now."

"Well, I'm telling you now, aren't I?" For another hour Anna filled Jo in with her unexpected call into the Managing Directors office, all about the bombshell he dropped on her and the resultant job offer.

Apparently her boss had been caught trying to pass off another of Anna's efforts as her own and it was not being allowed to pass un-noticed this time. It was time to call time out, on someone who had no moral compass, the M.D. had declared and she would be advised to look for employment elsewhere and expected to take gardening leave immediately. Anna was shocked and said so. She had then been re-assured that this decision was nothing to do with her directly. Her only part had been as a catalyst for the shake-up. Hence, he was now in a position to offer Anna, not her boss' job but one as Purchasing and Marketing Director. The Board had met and unanimously decided, Anna was so valuable to them that they wanted to offer her a decent incentive to trust them with her future.

"Wow Anna. That's amazing." Jo told her. "A Company Directorship at your age is phenomenal!" Anna modestly said that she was quite astonished that they should place so much trust in her abilities; but Jo was equally full of praise for her friend's abilities. "Of course you'll make an amazing Purchasing and Marketing Director. Well done, Anna." She told her.

Then Anna went quiet, and it dawned on Jo that this could mean Anna might not wish to continue to provide the marketing support for her own business. Reluctant to spoil Anna's moment of glory, she stopped herself from expressing her own fears.

Anna's quiet voice saying, "I've asked them to give me until the end of the week to make up my mind what I should do," almost went unheard in the clamour of Jo's thoughts. However, Anna repeated herself and Jo cleared her wild mind to listen.

"What! Are you mad? You can't be thinking of turning them down, surely?" Jo fired out next. Anna looked down into the mouthpiece of the phone as if she thought that she would see Jo's face there. "Well, I've also had another offer from an unexpected source." Anna told Jo.

"Another job, well that's just being plain greedy?" Jo spluttered.

"Not exactly, Anna replied. "I have an offer to bankroll me setting up on my own. It means that I can go ahead with my plans that you all helped me to hash out, to set up my own consultancy firm."

"Lucky you" Jo told her, "but a tough choice." Jo told her. "On the one hand the security of regular pay and almost being your own boss running your department. Or on the other, stepping out into the unknown if you set up your own business. Scary! I'm glad that you are going to have time to think it all through and hope that you know that whatever you choose, you'll have my full support and I'm sure I speak for Fernando on this too. He's sure to want to wish all the best for your future, as I do."

Anna was overwhelmed at her friend's generosity and blessing. Her friends brought so much support and joy into her life. "Thank you Jo; that really means a lot." She told her. It was not long after that they said their final goodnights and Anna was able to put the phone down.

Leon entered the kitchen after his late night at work and caught the tail end of Anna's words and demanded to know what all the excitement was about. When told of his wife's possible rise through the ranks to director.

His comment was, "About time they recognised what a gem they have in you, Anna."

"Oh, no wonder I fell for you Darling. You're my hero." Anna said as she pulled him into her arms for a well-deserved kiss.

In due course, over their delayed evening meal, Anna filled Leon in on her astounding day at work and Jo's news too. When she had given her explanations, he had looked over the empty plates and asked his wife how she felt about the job offer.

"Well, half excited and half reluctant," Anna went on to tell him.

"Why?" Leon wanted to know.

"Don't get me wrong, I love the idea of having my say in what goes on instead of just having my brains picked all the time but, and it's a big but, I was so looking forward to the challenge of running my own consultancy, that I'm almost disappointed if I don't do it. What do you think I should do?" She asked.

Leon spent a moment or too ruminating and then spoke. "Sweetheart, you know that I will support you no matter what the outcome, but have you thought that there might be another way forward?" He asked.

"What do you mean? Anna queried.

"Well, you could set up on your own and offer to act as Consultant Director of Purchasing and Marketing until a replacement for you is found. That way they become your first big clients." He told her with a flourish.

"Well, I would never have thought of looking at it that way," exclaimed Anna.

"You could pull it off, Anna?" Leon persisted.

"Perhaps I could. The more I think about doing it, the more I like the idea. I would have to have a concrete proposal to present to the board prepared before I am due to give the M.D. my answer at the end of the week. It will take some hard work." She told him, her face brightening with every word.

Leon smiled at her and rose from his seat. "I guess I am on washing up and cook duty this week while you sort yourself out and I might as well get used to it right now." Proving as good as his word, he collected up the dishes and shooed Anna off to do the deed. Blowing him a kiss, Anna left the kitchen.

Anna went to fetch her laptop and commandeered the dining room table as her work station. She had soon started to draw up an outline plan for her proposal to put in front of the board.

By the time they both fell into bed later that night a proposal had been drafted and only needed the facts and figures details to flesh it out. She would have to get onto them tomorrow when she got to work. Leon told her gently that it was time to switch off the business button in her brain and turn into his gorgeous wife again. Smiling, she happily turned into the circle of his waiting arms.

While Anna and Leon were dreaming happy dreams, Jo had already made her first decision and when the morning came she rang Jeni to put it before her. Jeni was surprised by such an early morning call from Jo, and even more so when Jo caught her up with all the latest news. Jo then gave her the explanation for the call.

"I want to find another way to increase my business profile and think that if I have a new van and driver I can kill two birds with one stone. A new van with a slightly bigger capacity would help accommodate the new orders we shall need to dispatch and deliver and the signage will increase awareness and deal with more advertising for me. "What do you think, Jeni?" She asked her friend.

"It makes great sense to me," Jeni was quick to tell her.

"Glad you like the idea, Jeni, as I could do with your help with the wording for my signage, please." Jo went on.

"Ok Jo, a couple of quick questions to give me a clue of which direction you want to go in and I'll try and come up with something for you to look over." Jeni promised. Then she picked up the pen from the notebook she had been writing in and fired off her questions in rapid succession. Having given her answers, Jo excused herself and rang off, as she had just seen the client she had an appointment with parking their car in the road in front of her cottage.

Jo flew along the garden path and managed to meet her visitor just as she was about to open the reception door.

Calling to Shona to let her know that Mrs. Drummond had arrived and asking her to put on the kettle, she ushered the middle aged and well preserved woman into her tiny office next to the Studio and seated her in a comfortable chair. Shona popped her head round the door to ask whether tea or coffee was required and then promptly left to fulfil their order. Jo then got herself organised to take Mrs. Drummond's order for a very special gift for her much loved grand-daughter's sixteenth birthday. By the time the coffee had been drunk, Jo, had learnt a lot about her client, her client's grand-daughter and managed to draw a rough sketch of what she hoped wold be a suitably unique piece of glass to make an heirloom gift to mark the special birthday. She proffered the sketch across the desk to Mrs. Drummond. Her surprised gasp and exclamations of joy were enough to convince her that she had nailed her commission, and to allow her to usher Mrs. Drummond out of the building moments later, a happy and contented woman. All Jo had to do now was make it!

Shona was quick to congratulate Jo, when she came in to clear the coffee tray and tell her that Drew was hoping to have a word with her. Jo followed her out to reception and warmly greeted Drew. "What can I do for you today, Drew?"

"Well I was just wondering how soon you might be needing that new van for the business." He asked. She then told him that she had only been asking herself that very question the previous night and had decided that it should be sooner rather than later.

"Och aye, that is good." He retorted.

"Why? Any particular reason, Drew?" Jo asked him.

"Well now, I heard that McCredie's Garage have had an order cancelled and now have a rather expensive bespoke van on their hands. I just wondered if it might suit us." He told her.

"Do you know anything more about it, Drew? Jo countered.

"Only that it's worth a wee looksee." Drew replied.

"Well, there's no time like the present, Drew. Shall we go give it that looksee you recommend?" Jo said. Drew's vigorous nod of assent had her set off to fetch her coat and bag and tell Shona that they wouldn't be back until after lunch.

The two chatted amiably as they rolled through the lanes to reach the nearby town and McCredie's Garage. Not a large firm, but well respected in the neighbourhood. It had graced the town for the past thirty five years. In fact, Jo's aunt had bought the very car that she was driving around in there some five years prior to her demise and it was still going strong. You couldn't say fairer than that, Jo thought to herself as she parked up on the customer part of the forecourt. Drew held the door for her with old world charm and led her into the office of old man McCredie. He introduced Jo and told him that they were there to see the white elephant lurking in the yard. Mr. McCredie's face brightened considerably at this news and was quick to usher them out into the yard, van keys clutched in his huge fist of a hand and extolling the van's virtues long before they had actually laid eyes on it.

Drew remained silent throughout the examination but managed to convey uncertainty while kicking the tyres and peering to search for invisible scratches. Old man McCredie was swift to assure him there would be no cause for complaint about any vehicle he supplied. Drew remained stubbornly silent. He only ventured to say a word when Jo asked him directly what he thought.

"Well I couldn't rightly say without a decent test drive." He told her.

"Would that be possible Mr. McCredie, please?" Jo asked. A nod of assent and Drew was given the keys and the vehicle was being put through its paces. Jo had decided that she liked it and before they turned around to return it had confirmed that Drew did too.

On the way back Drew told Jo that it would be better for Jo if he was allowed to negotiate the price to be paid; Mr. McCredie being known to be a hard man when it came to the shekels. Jo thought for a second and told Drew that she had been thinking more of a second hand vehicle and hence only thought of spending ten thousand pounds to get a decent one. Grateful that Anna's presentation had brought in the money she now needed to spend.

Drew's eyes twinkled as he asked meekly, "Was that with or without the new advertising paint job Miss Jo?"

Jo laughed as she realised that poor old Mr. McCredie would be very lucky to get one over on Drew. Therefore, it was no surprise to her when an hour later she became the proud owner of a business fleet consisting of two vehicles; one of which would be decorated with her new advertising – free of charge. All for the princely sum of ten thousand of the best Scottish pounds! Now all she needed was to advertise for a new driver. To that end she asked Drew for his advice. He pondered for a moment or two. You just couldn't rush him, but he was always worth waiting to hear from. In his considered opinion, she should advertise for someone with a clean licence and a proven track record of work as a courier all over the British Isles. Although Drew himself was quite happy to do the London run when needed, but it would be handy to have a back-up who could do that too. As for the rest, they could cover it between them. Jo took it all on board and returned to her office to draft a suitable advert. Shona could be relied upon to make sure it ran in both the local and national press tomorrow.

It was a very satisfied young woman who returned to the cottage that night for her trip to the cinema with Fernando. She had so much to tell him that they were talking nineteen to the dozen and so decided to stay in and make do with what they could whip up from the contents of Jo's fridge for supper while they caught up with events.

The next morning Jeni sent Jo the draft of her new signage for the new van by email and had a very excited and delighted Jo on the line by lunchtime. Jo was fairly buzzing with all the new marketing activities falling into place. She was enacting all of Anna's suggestions as fast as she possibly could and had even started to have some responses to the adverts that Anna had placed for her in select trade journals. Things were on the way up!

Jo's next job of the day was to forward her artwork and Jeni's signage email to McCredie's for them to get the van dressed in its new livery and ready for use. Drew was delivering his vehicle there at the end of his last run for its transformation into a fleet member too. Shona dropped by her desk to deliver a batch of emails with C.V. details of the applicants for the driver's job. "I've weeded them out a bit for you and these should meet your criteria, Jo." She told her. Jo thanked her and then began looking through them right away. As far as she could tell a fellow called, Xander Smith, seemed to be a perfect fit. He had all the things she was looking for; a clean driving licence and he was well-travelled with his previous job as a driver for Amazon. She asked Shona if she could set up an interview as soon as convenient. No sooner said than done with Shona on the case. She buzzed through mere minutes later to tell her that Mr. Smith was actually in the village that afternoon and could pop in straight away if that suited her? By all means, Shona was told. Get him to come along right away, we might as well see if he'll do as soon as possible.

About thirty minutes later a neatly turned out man, wearing a black blazer type jacket, blue shirt and tie, with pressed denim jeans and shiny black leather shoes was seen approaching the reception door. He was about mid-thirties in age and he looked both strong and competent. Mr. Smith had arrived.

Jo came out of her office to greet him and during the obligatory introductions she studied his face. His dark brown hair topped a strong face that by day's end would sport the start of a good beard. The heavily hooded eyes seemed almost black, but his smile appeared confident and his handshake was firm. She then asked him if he had previously ever been inside a glassmaking workshop.

"No, no, I haven't. But, I would be very interested to learn more." The man told her. Always eager to make a convert, Jo lost no time in giving him the guided tour. His intelligent questions and happy manner made for a favourable impression on both Jo, Shona and Drew. He'd done his homework well and by the time he had taken afternoon tea and shortbread with Jo in her office she was quite happy to offer him the post there and then. However, caution prevailed. There were still references to take up and the opinion of Shona and Drew to learn before making that commitment. After all they worked as a team; in reality, more like a family, at the workshop. She had to make sure that they too felt that he was a good fit. With a warm final handshake and a promise to be in touch by the following Monday at the latest, she then got Shona to see Xander Smith on his way. Jo quickly called Drew and Shona into the office to hear their thoughts on Mr. Smith. As they were both pleasantly surprised by his good manners and quiet charm and warmth, it didn't take long to confirm the decision to take him on.

Shona was asked to draw up a standard contract offer for the position of driver at a rate slightly less than Drew was getting and with a month's trial period built into it and was told to try and get it into that night's post. That way they might know by the weekend if he was willing to start work the next month. Jo breathed a contented sigh as she leant back in her chair and looked at her world around her. The famous words from a childhood favourite television programme floated into her mind. "I love it when a plan comes together!" They seemed to convey her exact state of mind. Her plans, brought into action by Anna's clever marketing strategy ideas, were fast becoming a reality and she couldn't be happier if she tried. Thank goodness the money had been made available via her bank manager. She did wonder just who had provided it but was assured that it was quite usual for there just to be the company's name on the contract and not that of the individuals involved. However, that little niggle could not dampen her enthusiasm for life one bit.

Chapter Twenty

WITH ALL THE exciting things going on, it had been three months before anyone realised that they had not had a group get together. It was then left to Jeni to organise a long weekend break for them all to have quality time, and hopefully, some fun!

Jeni put her thinking cap on and decided that perhaps a sailing trip to make the most of the last of the Indian Summer weather that the Highlands were experiencing might be a nice idea, if Fernando was able to fit it into his charter schedule. A phone call to him to ascertain when he had free and the date was set. A few calls, emails and orders placed and her plan had come together. Transport was even arranged. With the kind offices of Michael, his friend, Simon and their planes, everything was set for the final weekend of September. They would have a whole four days sailing round the Isles stopping where and when they felt like. It sounded blissful to the girls, and the guys were equally happy to be spending time out of the rat race with their girls.

It was therefore, a happy group of folk who met at the harbour to board Fernando's best yacht. With plenty of food and drink aboard courtesy of Jeni's order from her favourite caterer nothing more was needed. Other than some good sailing weather. As soon as the last bag had been stowed away safely Fernando had Jo cast off and they went sailing out of the Kyle and into the blue of open water. The kettle was soon on and chatting was prolific as they gathered round Fernando in the outside deck seating area and took turns to follow Fernando's clear instructions, to enable the neat craft to sail its way through the, sometimes difficult, waters off the Scottish coast. Today though, the sea was unusually calm and it was a wonderful late summer morning.

"Heavenly." Anna was heard to exclaim as she attempted to catch some sun on her up-risen face.

"It's just lovely to get away from all the pollution of London and the office paperwork and relax on the water." She told everyone.

"Hear, hear!" Came a chorus back at her from her friends. They all agreed that Jeni's idea of a sailing trip was a delightful one. Jeni blushed at all the praise being heaped upon her and was quick to direct the flow from herself and back onto Anna, simply by asking for the latest on how her fledgling Phoenix Consultancy business was doing.

Leon leapt in with, "Amazingly well!"

Anna quietly confirmed, that she had landed her old firm as her first large client and had even managed to add two smaller companies to her portfolio just that month. Congratulations were given all round and Anna passed the buck next to Jo. She asked if Jo's new driver was fitting in well?

Jo was happy to report that Xander Smith was proving a treasure. He seemed to carry out every delivery with ease and most importantly, no breakages. Did he get on well with the rest of her staff? Yes, he seemed to have a way with the ladies and fellows. He was just, perfect, according to Jo. Anna was pleased when Jeni asked how the order books were coming along and Jo now beamed.

"They are almost full to bursting." She told them. "I may even have to start looking for someone to help make my wares if this keeps up." Anna was happy. Her plans were fruiting nicely for Jo.

That night's anchorage saw them barbequing steaks and drinking red wine as they chilled out listening to music under the star filled skies. It had been a long happy day. Some had even swum in the sea, off an empty beach of golden sand watched only by the seabirds. They were all quiet, tired and contented, when Fernando suggested that they turned in for the night. This took a little while to arrange and goodnight kisses were of the long and lingering variety. However, silence finally reigned as peace descended on the "Mariella". All that could be heard was the sound of gentle and loud snores.

Woken early by the sun streaming through the portholes of the cabins meant that everyone got up together and breakfast was eaten round a campfire of driftwood on the beach. A not quite deserted beach, as the seabirds had swooped in to search around for any leftover barbeque titbits and a couple of seals had come to play and lounge on the rocks at the far end. The group of friends watched with amusement their various antics. A vigorous game of chase, some body-surfing when a bigger wave came in with the freshening onshore breeze. Best of all, how relaxed the seals looked when they hauled themselves up on a rock and closed their eyes and took a sun bath.

Tilly turned to Craig and said, "Perhaps you should take a leaf out of the seals' book and try for a little more relaxation, Craig."

"Yes, I know I haven't been around much lately. My last case was very full on and I wasn't sleeping well either. Sorry. I may have been short with you because of that, Tilly."

"It's a good job you have the most amazing girlfriend on the planet." She joked back. Craig leant over and gave her a gentle lingering kiss. When they surfaced it was to a round of applause from the gang. Tilly blushed royally, and Craig had the grace to look a little abashed too.

"It looks as though you two like making up." Jeni commented, before she asked Fernando where they were going to be heading that morning. He licked his forefinger and held it up high and then pointed westward. That's the way the wind is going to take us today. There was a ripple of light-hearted laughter at his decision making process, as they began to clear the breakfast things and prepare for sailing. With so many pairs of willing hands it was all carried out with ease and efficiency. Jo at the sink washing up was surprised to find that a shiver went down her spine and the hairs on her arm stood on end all of a sudden. She shivered again and Anna noticed and asked if she was feeling cold. No. no. Jo assured her, it was just someone taking a walk over her grave. Anna gave her a smile and carried on drying up; but Jo, looked up and thought she got a glimpse of the tail of another yacht as it passed the mouth of the cove they were moored in. A second glance revealed nothing there and she dismissed the vague feeling of being watched that had made her shiver. After all, no one knew where they were! She thought.

As the waves were sliced by the crisp prow of the "Mariella" and they all relaxed into sailing mode, a voice rose into the morning air to sing the chorus of a jolly sea shanty. Jackson led them from one song to another for the next hour or so. Sea shanties and country ballads, to songs made popular by the morning radio shows. When they had all sung their fill it was time to put the kettle on and break out the treat rations according to Jeni. Millionaires Shortbread and cuppas all round and chatting was in order. Fernando announced that he thought that they might like to do a spot of fishing next and catch their lunch. Jackson was duly sent below to fetch the necessary fishing gear from the locker and they decided to make it more interesting by dividing up into pairs to see who could catch the most fish in the following hour. The prize, to be allowed to sit and relax while the others prepared the lunch. A great incentive to give it a go. Fernando dropped the sea anchor to allow them all to take part. There was a short debate as to how they should pair up; as couples or same sex pairs, men versus women etc. However, once they had organised themselves each partnership took a stand at a different section of the yacht's sides and the competition commenced. At first glance, seriously. But after thirty minutes with Jackson being the only one to catch anything,

Craig's comment, "Well, that's not going to go far between eight of us!" Was enough to lighten the atmosphere and allow the fun side to emerge and with jokes flying back and forth there was suddenly a flurry of activity. The fish had begun biting. On several lines at once. Soon there were squeals of excitement as the girls hauled them in. The guys with landing nets in hand brought them onto the deck. No sooner were the hooks re-baited and lines redeployed than the process all began again. It was Fernando who had to remind them that the hour was up. The action having become so lively. When the counts were made and verified by Judge Jeni, the winning combo was Anna and Leon. Leon the Londoner had caught an astounding eleven fish!

"Good job we have a sizable freezer on board", announced Fernando, thirty three fish being far too many for lunch; they would save the rest for another day.

They set sail again and with those willing to gut and fillet the fish ready for cooking taking over the galley stove and the rest cleaning themselves up before lending a helping hand where needed to ready their repast. Fernando at the helm, chatted with Anna and Leon as they sipped an aperitif lounging nearby.

"This is the life, Anna" declared Leon grinning widely. "Waitress service for the drinks and chefs to prepare our lunch, we ought to do this more often."

"Just wait until it's your turn for cook duty and mine to drink all the gin!" Jeni told him popping her head out of the hatch. "Just letting you know that lunch will be served in about fifteen minutes, you lazy lot." She told them.

Delicious was the unanimous verdict. Fish fresh from the sea was now their favourite dish. The herrings had been served coated in oatmeal and fried lightly in butter and with some small new potatoes and a green salad. The lusciously creamy Lucas strawberry ice-cream had slid down easily when dished up with some summer fruits salad. With their appetites sated Fernando suggested that they might like to exercise by exploring a small island that had appeared off their port side. The others were all happy to agree and he had soon anchored their craft as close to the shoreline as possible. It took a few minutes to get the small inflatable craft seaworthy to ferry them all to land. Two trips and they were able to regroup. The inflatable secured high above the tideline, they were free to seek the hidden delights of their chosen isle.

They started off by stretching their sea legs out as they climbed up off the beach and onto the grassy slopes above. At someone's suggestion they made their way towards the high point and climbed again to reach the very top. The view was amazing! They could see the whole island laid out around them and far out over the rolling waves of the sea that went from pale turquoise to a deep slate blue. All finished off with flashes of white foam. It was a picture.

"I never realised that the sea here was so tropically colourful. We could almost be In Caribbean waters." Anna told them. They all agreed that it was a stunning spot. After they had sat for a while just enjoying it all, they elected to go off in different directions to explore some more. In reality, just to grab a little private time. The agreement being to return to the landing beach after thirty minutes or so.

"Any trouble, just give a yell." Fernando told them.

The next half hour was thoroughly enjoyed as they discovered the charms of this forgotten spot on the map. When they met up again they told of fascinating rock formations, rock pools full of starfish and Jackson even produced a handsome crab from behind his back to surprise them. Jo had found inspiration for a new project and Anna had gathered a small collection of shells. Everyone had something to share and as they returned to the yacht they were all very pleased with their afternoon as explorers. However, it was time to make a move if they were to find safe harbour for the night. All hands to the task and fortified by mugs of tea, they were underway and moving swiftly over the waters with a good following wind getting up.

Just as dusk was beginning to come down Jackson pointed out some lights ahead. As they sailed nearer they could make out more. Outlines of a harbour with colourful buildings behind that seemed to hover over it, gradually appeared as Fernando changed their course slightly to bring them safely within its stout stone walls.

"Where were they now? Could it be Tobermoray?" Anna questioned.

Their Captain smiled and said, "Not quite that far but a lovely place too. It's called Craignure, on the Isle of Mull. I thought that this would be a good place to have a night out in." The others looked dubiously at the sleepy fisherman's cottages that surrounded the harbour. A less likely place for a grand night out they had yet to see. However, after a freshen-up and a change into something a bit cosier, they were ready for anything. Fernando led the way along the harbour wall and up the small road through what had seemed like a gap between two cottages and into the heart of the village. A small square with a pub on one side and a church opposite. The other two sides comprising of a three or four small shops, one was a whisky specialist and drew the men's attention straight away. Opposite it, was a cottage sporting a blue lamp over the door stating, Police Station and a grander building with a Doctors shingle hanging outside.

"This way, follow me." Fernando exhorted them as he strode over to open door of the hostelry that had the rather grand name of "The Royal Arms". He opened an inner door and loudly called out over the hum of chattering voices to the landlord, "I'm here again Hector with another load of trouble!"

The large voice that gave a cheery welcome ushered from a somewhat smaller body. The man that emerged from behind the bar was both short and wiry slim and was soon followed by an equally petite lady. There was no other description that was more fitting for this landlady. She was already white haired but the face below the crowning bun of fulsome hair was almost unlined despite being well into her sixties. Her eyes were button black and alight with humour. She regally gave Fernando her hand to kiss and he pulled her quickly into a warm embrace, smacking a loud kiss on each of her, fast pinking cheeks. She scolded him roundly for taking advantage of her in front of his guests. The resounding cheer that went up from the regulars was one of approval. During the course of ordering some drinks and food, the group found themselves introduced to everyone present and were made to feel thoroughly welcome. They were assured that their orders would be forthcoming shortly and that they would be very welcome to stay on for the ceilidh that would be taking place from nine o'clock that evening, after they had stopped serving food.

They stood and chatted with the locals and there was much laughter over the language issues until they were told it was time to find a seat, so that their meal could be served before it got cold. Realising that the little sparrow would brook no argument, they were quick to take their places and after a quick grace were soon tucking in to the delicious fare that she had provided. Although the choice had been somewhat limited, to those who were more used to the large menus of city restaurants, the quality far exceeded their expectations.

"This food is amazing." Jeni was quick to exclaim.

"Absolutely out of this world" came from Anna.

The others too adding their recognition for the skills of the chef. Leon was quick to say that he had never expected to find such a first class chef in such an out of the way place. Fernando and Jackson were eager to sing their hostess' praises and to even let them in on a well-known local secret. Heather Glennie had even cooked for the Queen. "Really!" Fernando beckoned Heather over and asked her to tell them all about their summer visitors. With a very simple and modest manner, she proceeded to regale them with how a very damp and bedraggled group had come in one quiet, dark night.

The woman's headscarf was dripping everywhere as she took it off and shook out her damp dark hair. Her man equally wet but not the least put out by the foul weather. His well-tanned face was that of a man who enjoyed sailing the waters. The rest of the group appeared to be family members and he soon had them all organised and seated and was taking orders for their drinks. Mainly Dubonnet or Gin for the ladies and whisky and beers for the men. The younger element all wanted lemonades. Her husband had got busy with the orders and Heather had slipped into the back to fetch a couple of clean warm towels from the airing cupboard to offer them to finish up the mopping up process. The older lady in the group thanked her warmly for her kindness and quietly asked if they served food at their inn. Heather assured her that they could soon rustle something up for them if they weren't too particular as to what it was. She explained that their supply ship had been delayed due to the bad weather and they were a bit shorter than usual for some ingredients. The lady told her that they were good eaters but not a fussy lot, so whatever she could manage would be just fine by them. Leaving her husband to hold the fort, Heather had headed for her kitchen. She was almost hauled through the door by their daughter, Katriona, who was trying hard not to speak above a whisper but so excited that she could barely contain herself.

"Do you not ken who it is that you are serving Mither?" She had demanded of her mother.

"Yes, a poor family that's got caught in the shower and canna get back to their boat," Heather had told her daughter.

"No, no, Mither. That's the Queen herself and the rest of the royal family!" Katriona had blurted out.

"Don't be so ridiculous, Katriona, it never is Her Majesty," Heather had told her. "Now never you mind me, I have to get them all some dinner right away, they're all cold right through and in need of a good hot meal to warm them back up again." Heather went on to tell them all how she had bustled about getting the meal made while Katriona had kept popping her head round the kitchen door for another look at the family in the bar. By the time she had finished getting the meal on, Heather had had enough of Katriona's antics and had told her to mind the stove while she had a good look for herself. Katriona had promised that she would not leave her post again until her mother returned and Heather had sallied forth back into the bar.

Hector was firmly ensconced with a glass in hand; a rare event for him, and looked as though he was thoroughly enjoying his conversation with the older man of the group and his eldest son. As she listened a moment she learnt that they were debating the merits of the various islands and their beaches for picnicking on the next day. Heather looked closely. The tall man did have a look of Prince Phillip she had to admit, but the lad was far too scruffy and long haired to be Prince Charles surely. Heather took herself over to the table at which the lady she had spoken with earlier had migrated. "Excuse me, I thought that you might like to know that your meal will be served in about ten minutes and that if you would like to wash your hands, the facilities are through the blue door to your left" she informed her.

The woman thanked her again for her kindness and as she returned to the kitchen, Heather had heard her, admittedly refined tones, encouraging the younger element in no uncertain terms to get their hands washed and seated smartly if they wanted to be fed. Heather had smiled to herself, that wasn't the Queen. She was just another mother getting them licked into shape and ready to sit down to enjoy their supper. She had been taken aback to learn at the end of her scrumptious "banquet" that she had indeed been serving her monarch and family. Their empty plates were a testimony to the fact that they had rarely eaten a more splendid meal. Prince Phillip had then politely asked if they could take a photograph of her and their establishment. Of course! Heather then turned away and took down from the wall a framed photo of a very happy scene showing a very relaxed royal family on their "holidays in the Western Isles".

"What a wonderful, once in a lifetime experience, to have." Anna told her.

Heather smiled and said, "You'll not be wanting to see my album, then? They come back here whenever they can just to say hello and have a bite of my apple duff." Wonderment spread over their faces. They had dined at one of the Queens well-kept secret hideaways. How fortunate were they!

By the time they had finished their meal and story, it was time to clear the decks for the evening's entertainment.

It was to take the form of a ceilidh and every inch was needed for the dancing. The men were more than happy to lend a helping hand with the rearrangement of the tables and chairs while the ladies freshened up in the powder room. All were excited about the experience ahead. After the meal they had eaten they knew that it was bound to be good.

Indeed it was. The music of the local folk playing was superb, the rafters rang with singing of well-known folk songs by Robbie Burns and melodies sung by a popular local lass coerced into blessing them by her new husband, eager to show her off. Then pressed to sing again by the many voiced raised in encouragement. Others had then taken their turns to play, sing or recite and the time had flown by. In between it all, there had been reels. Strip the Willow, the Gay Gordon and even a first class display of the Highland Fling and some sword dancing. It seemed that everyone had a "party piece" to share and all were well received and endorsed by rounds of fervent applause from the group of friends in particular.

It was with laughter that the bell was rung for "time", for closing time had actually been at least two hours earlier when the local policeman stuck his head round the door and then had been urged to "come in and make yourself comfortable." The gang was almost the last to leave. They were profuse in their thanks for their wonderful meal and delightful evening. Hector and Heather warmly embraced each of them and telling them that they were welcome to come back any time they were passing. Replying that this was one invitation no-one would forget, they waved a final goodbye. As they made their way back to the harbour steps all had eagerly told Fernando that they had a fabulous time and could quite understand why he had so many return customers for his business if this was part of their experience.

The evening was about to change though, for when they reached the steep stairs down to the water, there was no inflatable jolly boat to be found.

Jackson produced a powerful torch from his jacket pocket and shone it around the area where they had tied up their small craft. There was no sign of it. Everyone was speculating what had happened to it. Were they sure that it was indeed the place it had been tethered? Could someone else have "borrowed" it? Perhaps mistaken it for their own craft? Could it have come loose and just drifted off on the tide? Jackson, Fernando and Leon decided that an organised search of the harbour area was needed. Someone may have just lifted it out of the water to ensure that it didn't get damaged by the incoming tide. There were lots of possible explanations.

Fernando asked to borrow Jackson and the torch for a moment and walked down the steps themselves, to the actual mooring ring that he had tied it up at and with heads together and backs hiding the ring from the view of the others they examined it. There was a short length of rope still attached to the ring that hadn't been visible from above. Jackson lifted it away from the slimy harbour wall and shone the beam of light directly onto the ends of the rope. Quietly he asked Fernando if he could see what he could see. Fernando nodded his assent. The rope had been cut cleanly with a very sharp knife. The jolly boat's disappearance was deliberate. Jokers? Fernando had queried.

"I think not, Jackson told him in a stern voice. I think we need to find some other craft and get out to the yacht and check it out. This doesn't feel right to me."

Chapter Twenty One

IN THE EXERCISE yard Mr. Big was letting off some steam. The recipient of his angst was actually cowering and trying to make himself as small as possible. Difficult for one who was all of six foot three and built like the side of a barn. His shaved head was bowed to catch every bitter word that Mr. Big was letting fly. Even though he knew that he was in no way responsible for the lack of news, he knew that his head would roll if things did not go the way Mr. Big wanted and he was running scared. A heavy bead of sweat was trickling downwards and as it gained speed, running down his nose. He was too scared to wipe it away and attract unwanted attention to himself. Frightened that it would drop and cause even more trouble for him, he turned slightly away and let it fall. It had been noticed. He shook. Mr. Big told him to get out of his sight. A second later, a grown man could be seen legging across the yard at breakneck speed wearing a look of relief as he scanned for a place to hide himself. He had been allowed to escape his "Sword of Damocles" and he was going to make the most of it.

When the next audio book message revealed that, despite having their man in Jo's business, Mr. Big was no further forward with a plan to wreck it. Nor was anything in place for the destruction of Fernando's yachts or Redman's car, as yet. Mr. Big looked like thunder and heads would roll. His permitted phone call would need to be very carefully worded but, it would be understood and obeyed. The next few hours were very busy as he ran various schemes and plans through is mind over and over again. Finally he crystalized them, wrote down his instructions and wrote down exactly what he would say during his phone call to his lawyer. Not the safest way to get the word out but beggars could not be choosers. His need was getting more urgent by the day. Once the call had been made there would be no going back and no time for regrets. He would be committed. His bed made, he would lie in it with enjoyment.

If someone had been alert on CCTV duty someone might have noticed a pattern emerging as one after another chose their moment to sidle over to Mr. Big and pledge their offer of help, and in return receive a promise of action on their behalf as recompense. It could have almost been a modern take on a scene from "The Godfather". Some were openly gleeful as they departed and others glum. However, Mr. Big grew quietly more confident with each offer, that he would be able to carry out everything that he had in store for those who had forced him to endure this degrading existence behind bars. By the time he re-entered his cell he was buoyant, sure of success, life was on the up again.

Over the following week several of the lowlife population suddenly found themselves the victims of a series of car accidents. Fights that left them with grievous bodily injuries. Or simply disappeared. The word had indeed got out and heads had rolled. Recruitment was more difficult but with higher rewards offered positions were filled and matters began to progress once again.

The gang assigned the task of destroying Fernando's livelihood were especially eager to please. They prepared the explosives they had decided were needed to make a good job of the office and even managed to plant them by having them delivered by a bona fide postman. As the parcel was marked PRIVATE and NOT TO BE OPENED OTHER THAN BY NAMED RECIPIENT, it had been carefully placed on Fernando's office desk to await his return. All that went smoothly. However, the burner phone bought via a chain of handlers proved to be another matter. As the gang would learn the hard way. In the meantime, they had elected to set fire to the yachts when they returned to dock in the harbour and were eagerly anticipating their success later that weekend. Their instructions had been to cause the downfall of the charter business with no loss of life. Unless, Fernando, Jackson or their friends were fortuitously on board when they went up! The cavalier attitude to life of Mr. Big was rubbing off on his employees. However, conscience was raising his head in one person's mind. He was quick to quash his disloyal thoughts. He was so scared of Mr. Big turning his hatred his way.

Meanwhile, the friends were enjoying another day of clear ice blue skies and some wonderful sailing. The Western Isles lay glorious in the light and everyone on board was having a lot of fun. The day was one where each couple had contrived to find a small space to be private and an apparently viable reason to occupy it with the object of their affection. How clever was that. Galley chores were done with lots of accidental bumping and kissing better. Giggles erupted from the shower room as it was being thoroughly cleaned by another pair.

Fernando and Jo were quite happy to sit together steering while they talked about future plans. Anna and Leon doing much of the same while they shelled peas and scrubbed potatoes. It was left to Jackson and Jeni to be more energetic as they carried out Fernando's occasional bellowed instructions about the sails needing trimming. In between the moments of intense activity, they told each other jokes and speculated who would be next to be married. The day passing pleasurably for all concerned much as the waves passed by the bows of their craft.

When they got to their safe harbour for the night it was time to check in for any messages from his staff and it was then Fernando received a very cryptic message that had been given to the Harbour Master to pass on to him as soon as possible. With no reference to a sender and a puzzle for a message, it was quickly dismissed as a hoax by him but dutifully passed round the others anyway.

Ring the cottage a.s.a.p. as world turned upside down.

Once they had read it out twice Tilly had worked out that the cottage meant her godmother, Cathy's cottage and Anna reckoned that perhaps there had been some sort of accident. Tilly had her questions about it. They were soon put to flight by a telephone call from Cathy, made to Fernando's office and the message sent on by his receptionist.

Please would Tilly give Cathy a call as soon as possible, as she had urgent news to tell her?

Immediately Tilly's mind was flooded with dread; had something happened to her parents. "I must get to a phone and call her in a place where I have better mobile reception." She told the others.

"You're getting married but not to Charles!" Tilly gasped out. Charles Kilwinnen was Cathy's devoted beau and it was the desire of their whole village that they would get married. Even Tilly had endorsed Charles in his proposal and encouraged Cathy to say, yes, so this was bewildering news. "Then who are you getting married to, Cathy?" She asked. Everyone present was already straining their ears eager to find out what could have caused such loud exclamations from Tilly.

The girls all shared a great affection for Cathy and over the years visited her themselves with Tilly often. Naturally the guys had been told all about Tilly's godmother and her adoption of Jeni and Anna into her circle too, as their friendship had developed. All were anxious to learn what the great upset was all about. As Tilly was silent listening to all the information that Cathy was imparting, they just had to impatiently wait for her to end her long phone-call. Tilly's loving goodbye and promise to return and visit immediately made them realise that whatever had happened, it was serious. Tilly's stunned face when she announced to them that her godmother was getting married, a.s.a.p., to a man called Percy Greystoke was like a bombshell landing in their midst. As the pieces impacted, the questions became rapid and all being fired at Tilly. She almost wanted to run and take cover behind Jackson's large frame. Instead, she held up her hands stating that she needed a stiff drink and Craig went to get her one from the emergency drinks locker. Tilly refused point blank to reveal more until she had swallowed a fair-sized mouthful. Then she told them just to be quiet until she had told them all she knew about the matter.

All she knew was not a lot. Really it was the bare facts. Cathy was not marrying Charles Kilwinnen. The nice man who had quietly and persistently wooed her and she had been casually dating for some time, only recently deciding that she would marry him during Tilly's last visit to Cathy's cottage. However, it seemed the wedding was off. Cathy was getting married and soon as it could be arranged, to a Percy Greystoke.

"Who is Percy Greystoke when he's at home?" Anna asked.

"Oh he is, apparently, her soulmate." Tilly told them.

"What do you know about him?" Jeni asked.

To be told, "Not a thing," by Tilly. "For as far as I as I can tell, they met by accident when Cathy went to town for the day to buy a new pair of sheets. They bumped into the same compartment of the revolving doors and when they emerged the other side she dropped the sheets. Mr. Greystoke retrieved them for her and then they parted. Only they met again as she was getting on the train to travel home. They shared a somewhat larger compartment this time and he bought her refreshments. By the time they took breath he had travelled past his stop and he decided to carry on and get off wherever Cathy did. Only, she didn't know about the passing of his stop until much later," Tilly added quickly before she ran out of breath.

"Then what happened?" Anna asked.

"Well they seemed to bump into each other everywhere Cathy went for the next week and ended up arranging to have lunch by the Wednesday and dinner the following Friday. On the Monday he took Cathy to town for a day out and theatre trip and the rest is obviously history, as he asked her to marry him on the train home from that, and she said, yes. Cathy had told Charles at their usual Wednesday lunch date. Percy bought her a ring yesterday and she has been trying to get hold of me to tell me ever since. The end!" Tilly finished in a rush.

Wow! That was fast work if you like! Good for Cathy. Hope Percy has lots of energy if he's going to keep up with the whirlwind. Were just some of the comments the gang came up with before Tilly could catch her breath again.

"Well" she had continued, "maybe it's more a case of Cathy being able to keep up with Percy, as he has completely swept her off her feet."

Tilly told them. "In fact, she sounds like a giddy teenager in the throes of her first massive crush." Tilly stated. "The outcome is that I, or should I say we girls, are required to assist in every possible way to put together a wedding for two weeks on Saturday."

"Two weeks!" Jeni had gasped.

Anna said, "It is do-able but it really depends what sort of wedding she wants."

Jo asked, "Did Cathy give you a clue?" Cathy had just told Tilly that she would leave her to make the arrangements and would email her a guest list as soon as she and Percy had put their heads together to create it.

Cathy had then concluded their phone call with an airy and I quote here folks, "I'm sure that it can all be done over the internet nowadays in no time at all." Tilly told them.

"Well," said Jeni, "I think that it's quite a tall order for the time frame."

The guys just looked totally bewildered by the idea of meeting someone and marrying them in less than a month. It's not that they didn't approve of marriage. They liked that part. It was just the speed at which it was to take place.

Jo offered to help in any way Tilly thought she could. Anna added that she could give her the website addresses for the companies she had used for their wedding and rounded it off with suggesting that Tilly's mother would perhaps like to bake the cake. Fernando offered one of his yachts for the honeymoon.

Craig and Jackson meantime had their heads together discussing what looked like some serious business. In fact, that's just what it was. Both suggesting a thorough background check on one Percy Greystoke. When Leon broke into their talk.

"Has anyone realised that Lord Greystoke was Tarzan's real name!" He said. They had all burst into laughter lightening the atmosphere considerably.

"Cathy must be having us on. What a great joke! We've been discussing this for at least an hour now. Phone her back, Tilly, and let her know that we have cottoned on to it now and give her ten out of ten from us," Jeni told her.

Tilly still chuckling picked up her phone and did just that, only to be told that it was no joke and asked how she was getting on with the planning! "Back to square one folks, the wedding of the year is definitely on." Tilly told them.

The wedding busyness going on around them, gave Jackson and Craig time to ring round and find out from their work colleagues just what this man called Percy Greystoke was all about. They put out their feelers and within minutes reports came trickling in. A snippet here and a snippet there was gradually adding up to a picture of the man. They had agreed to meet up again in the kitchen and pool their knowledge over a cup of coffee and after nearly an hour they did. Craig had checked Percy for a criminal record, involvement in underworld activities and known associates. Jackson had approached the matter through media sites, tax and other similar records.

Between them they had made a pretty comprehensive file of information on Mr. Percy Greystoke. Their conclusion was that he appeared to be the genuine article. The only secret he had was that he had chosen not to use, his title or the address of his main residence in any public place. He was not even listed in Who's Who! He was obviously an extremely private man. Why? They could find no logical reason for such secrecy, but both appreciated that some people are that way for reasons of their own.

Although this had alleviated their concerns somewhat, there was still a persistent niggle that refused to go away. However, they both agreed that it would have to do for now and that they would keep an eye out for any other signs that things were not what they appeared to be.

In the meantime, Tilly was gradually getting her act together and creating the perfect wedding for her beloved Godmother. She just hoped that Cathy would think that it was perfect too. In her own mind she was seeing it as a simple but elegant affair. No frills or fuss but pretty and sincere. Floral displays could do double duty for the church and then walked over to the hall. It could all be set up the afternoon or evening prior to prevent any last minute panics about it all being ready in time. With all in agreement, she ordered all the necessary items online. The next job was to see if Anna had managed to contact the minister. Yes. He was available and so was the village church on the specified date. Thank goodness!

Catering was another thing altogether. Gathered round with their teas and coffees they made their suggestions and gave their opinions. Most agreed that they preferred to choose what they wanted to eat but liked it to be placed on their plate rather than help themselves from a buffet selection. The men preferring hot food to cold. The ladies opting for lighter food with colourful salads. All however agreed that scrumptious, indulgent deserts were a must. Anna came up with the idea of an autumn feast. With a hearty coq au vin cassoulet or Beef Wellington as the hot options and a whole poached salmon and a couple of special quiches for the cold choices. With roast potatoes and a selection of hot green vegetables and jewelled couscous and bright salads to accompany them. Who would be able to produce all this food in a village hall was the question. Then Jeni started laughing. Everyone looked round at her.

She said, "Of course we know who would do this for Cathy." Puzzled looks were all she got back at her. "Who did we all work for in our holidays?" She asked the girls.

"Lafferty" they chorused back as the memories of waitressing at upmarket weddings, birthday bashes and other special events for James Lafferty to earn some extra cash during their university days flooded back. They all agreed that if James Lafferty couldn't rise to the challenge, then no-one could. Anna would have to be the one to call in this favour as she had always been his favourite. They all left Anna to it and she was soon back with James Lafferty's agreement in place. All he needed was the number of the village hall booking agent, so that he could just check what the facilities offered and Tilly had supplied that.

That's when Jackson asked "Have you remembered the drinks, Tilly?"

"Oh no, she exclaimed, how could I have forgotten that we would need drinks?"

Jackson said that the rest of them had all been discussing it and thought that it should be a "bring a bottle of wine" do. Perhaps have it written on the invitations and that way there wouldn't be any need for a license to have a bar or the faff of sale or return etc. The hall already had glasses they could use. Jackson had checked the hall booking website. Simple. Thank you so much for sorting that one out for me, Jackson, Tilly gushed. I would have never have thought of doing it that way, but it's a great idea she told him as they joined the others.

Everyone was relaxed now that the worst of the organising had been done. It was Anna's phone that rang next. It was Cathy again. Tilly's line had been so busy every time that Cathy had tried it so, she had decided to phone Anna instead. Cathy started to tell her the latest on the guest list when Anna interrupted to ask her to just hold on a minute while she put her on speaker so that they would all be able to hear her news. That done, Cathy told them that she thought that there were almost one hundred people that they would like to invite to the wedding. The list, complete with contact details would be emailed to Tilly after she came off the phone as Cathy's fiancé was just finishing entering the addresses from his list of contacts at that very moment. When Tilly came to report on how the wedding plans were advancing Cathy was delighted and more than happy with their choices.

"Do you want me to send the mock up that I've done of how it will all look for you to see and approve, Cathy?" Tilly asked.

"No, no Tilly I rather like the idea of it all being a surprise!" Was Cathy's response.

It was left there and Cathy was saying her goodbye and the group chorusing back their "See you soon, Bride-To-Be." Tilly was then encouraged to order the invitations to be printed right away when the email from Cathy arrived only seconds later. After a brief scan for any spelling mistakes etc. she had soon composed an email with attachments and fired it off to the printers. At last! They could all now switch off from wedding mania and chill out.

The late afternoon was long gone and the evening sun had gone down below the yard arm. No-one wanted to make any more effort that day. Fernando suggested that he ordered in a Chinese meal to be delivered to their mooring and they could watch a movie. Used by now to Fernando's treats being amazing, they all agreed. The order was placed and Fernando proceeded to show them how the main cabin could double up as a very comfortable cinema, complete with love seats and side tables for drinks and snacks. When all was in place the "Ahoy folks!" warned them of the arrival of their takeaway.

"Now that's what I call service." Leon told them.

In no time at all they had each selected their choice of food and were ready to eat it while they enjoyed the movie.

"What are we going to watch?" Asked Jackson.

"Well, this is Jo's recommendation and I'm hopeful it will suit. In fact, it turned out that it's based on the book that my nurse on board the Lady Luck was reading when she was supposed to be keeping an eye on me. It says in the blurb that it's a bit of a mystery, with some suspense and romance. Something for everyone, hopefully." Fernando told them. Jo, who had been looking at the DVD case cover notes, told them that it had a good cast and shouldn't be too bad, so they all settled down to enjoy the rest of their evening.

Two and a half hours later and the banquet of takeaway food demolished, the film came to a close. The last half hour had been watched in silence and now the lid was off, an explosion of chatter came out. They commented on the twists and turns and how they hadn't known who the villain of the piece had been until the end. Anna said that she wasn't sure even then! All agreed that it had been a nice way to end their day. No sex, no violence and refreshingly, no bad language. Very unusual in today's main stream films. It had just been a really good plot and very well directed and acted. What more could they ask for? A good night's sleep! A quick clear up and they were all ready for that.

Chapter Twenty Two

A FINAL DAY'S sailing would see them returned to their home port. An early breakfast and a clear away and they were off. A good stiff breeze behind and they were flying over the waves southwards once more. As noon approached Fernando had them change tack and then drop anchor in a rockier cove this time. With the tide going out there were lots of rock pools exposed and he had equipped them all with crabbing nets on poles and buckets and despatched them off to search them for some lunch. The guys tackled their task with enthusiasm and were soon yelling their joy as their quarries were cornered and launched into the buckets. The girls approached the matter of lunch a little slower and taking a lot more care. With the benefit of Jo's local knowledge they collected a selection of seaweeds and molluscs to cook and eke out the crabs. In a scant twenty minutes they were all ready to return to the yacht with their bounty. Fernando had a large pot of boiling water on the go for the crabs and the others were soon given their tasks to enable the lunch to be served a short twenty minutes later.

The crab was served on a bed of noodles with a garlic, fresh orange and ginger sauce with side dishes of mixed shellfish and seaweed. All being pronounced absolutely delicious when they finally declared that they could pick no more flesh out of the mountain of shells before them. Anna, Jeni and Tilly were all amazed that the seaweed that they had collected could taste so good. They had been thinking that it would just be too salty and disgusting. Now they were converts. The gentlemen were all good trenchermen by now and more than eager just to tuck in to whatever was put before them. However, all agreed that Fernando's on board recipes were first class. All too soon they had to set sail again and the weather was kind enough to continue to provide a following wind. They were soon seeing familiar coastal formations from their outward journey. The realisation that their all too brief idyll was coming to an end began to strike home. It was with mixed feelings that they sailed into the harbour at the Kyle of Drumcrae.

The girls were to spend their final night at Jeni's house before travelling south again. Discreetly, as thanks were being given, each young man drew his beloved aside and requested a quiet dinner for two that evening, pleading a lack of privacy aboard ship as their reason. Unbeknown to the others, each girl gave their assent, agreeing to have a word with their hostess about slipping away for dinner for two and letting their chap know when and where to meet them. Their hostess when approached in private was charmingly co-operative. Three phone calls were made and at timed intervals Tilly and Anna left Jeni's house to be picked up by their beaus.

"Alone at last!" Leon told Anna. "Oh I have missed having you to myself, Anna." He told her softly when they had been seated and their meal ordered at the bar of the village pub. "I think I prefer being married and spending time at home with you than going anywhere." He told her. Anna was touched that her quiet man had come up with such a romantic thing to say to her. It sounded just perfect to her ears.

"I love spending time with you too, Leon; but it was fun to go sailing with our friends too." She replied. The rest of the evening was spent discussing their experiences and the forthcoming wedding of Cathy and Percy. It was a mellow time softened by the quiet hum of the folk enjoying an end of day drink.

Fernando had been busy. He had found the number of the special restaurant and booked a table with candles, wine and food. It was an easy order since he now knew Jo's likes and dislikes so well after spending the last few days with her. He had also ordered flowers to be delivered to the table. He was determined to get this right. He had not had time to speak to Jackson about his plans but he was sure that he would approve. He had also managed to get to "Fiona's" jewellery shop to pick up the gift he had in mind to give Jo for Christmas. Fernando had left it there for cleaning on his way to the boat the day they had embarked for their sailing trip. However, he felt the timing was right now and he couldn't wait to see Jo's face when she opened the box. Right now though, he had to get himself cleaned up if he was to get to" The Mango Tree" before Jo did. It wouldn't look good if the host was to arrive later than his guest.

Craig had pulled up at the end of the lane from Jeni's house to wait for Tilly. Soon he saw her hurrying towards him. He thought she looked a picture. Skin all glowing from the wind and sun of their sailing trip and bright-eyed. She looked even more attractive, now that he knew her better than she did when she had first caught his attention while he was following the man who abducted her a few weeks later. Thankfully she had not been permanently damaged by her traumatic experience. It had been very nasty, but he had fortunately been able to rescue her before she had been physically brutalised. Tilly was a very lucky girl; or as she would say, blessed. He too, was eager for them to have some time on their own, after sharing her with her friends for the past few days. He was swift to jump out and open the passenger door of the car to let her in. He'd had to borrow Fernando's car for the evening and hoped that he had not put his host out too much but his need was great and Fernando seemed to have something of his own to do too. After he got into the driver's seat he took off towards the coast rather than inland, but before long he pulled off the road again at a quiet lay-by. He turned off the engine and turned towards Tilly's enquiring gaze.

"Sorry Tilly but I just couldn't wait any longer." He pulled her closer and planted a kiss on her warm lips. As Tilly drew him in, he deepened it and only when they were both sated did they come up for air. He carefully placed her back into her seat and buckled up. "Time for food now that the important business has been taken care of." He told her. Tilly nodded her assent and turned her rosy face to look out the window until she regained her usual composure.

Jeni was now quite alone in her house, but not for long. Jackson's car was soon to be seen rolling to a halt outside. She heard it draw up outside her garden gate and opened the door to watch him as he unloaded two paper carrier bags and locked the car up. Why? She didn't know, for no-one was liable to steal it when no-one lived along the lane except her. Habit, she supposed. Jeni watched Jackson as he strode up the garden path and admired his strong manly physique. Not handsome in the traditional mould but open featured and honest. A man of integrity. She knew that she could trust him with her life. Jackson would never let her down. As he approached, Jackson, transferred his load to one hand and reached his free arm around Jeni, drawing her in.

When she had been thoroughly kissed Jeni drew back saying with mock horror, "Jackson that's enough now. What will the neighbours think?"

"Good job you haven't got any ma girl, as I plan on doing a bit more of that tonight!" He answered. Jeni actually felt herself blushing as she backed away from the doorway to allow him to enter. Thinking all the while that it was rather a nice idea. Jackson followed her into the kitchen and unceremoniously dumped his two bags onto the nearest work surface. Then swiftly caught her back into another embrace. It was the smell of the curry permeating the air that made them once again aware that they were hungry. Jeni told Jackson to go and wash up and she would get the table laid so that they could eat. As she worked away between the kitchen and the dining room, Jeni found herself humming a well-known air. Jackson join in while he carried in the plates of food.

"The table looks lovely, Jeni lass." He told her. Jeni blushed again prettily at the compliment.

"Come away and sit down before the food gets cold," she said as she poured them both a glass of Gloria's homemade ginger beer to have with their chicken vindaloo. Jackson did not like to drink and drive. Another point in his favour, she thought to herself. For the following hour they concentrated more on their food than talking. Quietly content in each other's company. The meal over, they cleared away together and loaded the dishwasher. Then, coffees in hand, they made themselves comfortable on the sofa and looked out onto the cunningly lit back garden and the sea beyond.

For a while they quietly chatted about the surprises of the past few days. Slowly lapsing into silence as Jeni realised that Jackson seemed a bit pre-occupied.

"Anything the matter Jackson, she asked, you seem a trifle distracted this evening?"

He gently turned her face until Jeni was looking up at him and then very slowly and gently kissed her. His lips were firm but not demanding; more coaxing until she let him in. Intertwined, time passed accompanied only by the sound of the fire Jeni, had lit earlier that evening. It's hissing and popping muted into the background as Jackson eased Jeni away a little and told her that he had been doing some thinking earlier.

"Oh, what about?" She asked.

"You." Jackson replied.

"That's nice; I think about you too." She told him.

"I hope so." He quietly whispered. Then he took both her hands in his and pulled her to her feet. Looking straight into her beautiful eyes he made the bravest gamble of his life. "Jeni, will you marry me?" He asked softly. He saw her eyes widen and the surprise register in them and then the dawning of what he meant came to her. Then, he saw her smile start there and work its way down to her mouth as it curved upwards, before she flung her arms round his neck.

"Yes, yes, yes I absolutely will." She exclaimed joyfully.

He lifted her from her feet and gave her a smacking kiss that was brief but expressed all of the relief that he felt at her response. He had tussled with whether he should or shouldn't ask her. After all, she was independently wealthy from her books and would have more to offer financially than he did. However, he had reasoned with himself, he could bring other things to the marriage that might make the scales more even. Most important of all, he felt, was that he loved her deeply and would do all that he could to make their life together a happy one. The next couple of hours flew by as they discussed their plans for their future. Jackson wanted to know if she felt that she wanted to continue to live in Scotland after the work on her current book came to an end. Jeni was quick to assure him that it didn't matter to her where they lived as long as they were together. Just the answer he wanted to hear. He tried to explain that his work might involve him being away from home at times and even some travel further afield. He hadn't cleared his marriage plans with his superior and he was reluctant to go into detail about his actual job without permission. He knew that he would have to share that with her before they married. He knew that he couldn't possibly do his job, if he did not have his wife's full support. That would have to wait for another day. In the meantime, Jeni was all too preoccupied with how to let folk know and asking about setting a date for their wedding. Their wedding. It sounded wonderful every time she said it. Jeni couldn't help but pinch herself. Yes, she wasn't dreaming. She was getting married to Jackson. Wow! She couldn't wait until Anna and Tilly returned so that she could share her exciting news with them. Perhaps she should ring Jo so that she could be there too?

At that moment, Jo was sitting sipping her glass of lovely white wine and peeping over the rim at her handsome Latin dinner companion. The evening had been positively delightful so far and looked to be going on in the same vein, when she noticed the restaurant seemed to have suddenly gone very quiet. As if a hush had fallen over everyone. She turned to see what could have caused the moderately busy room to stop talking. She saw floating across the room, what appeared to be an enormous bouquet of lush, velvety, red roses. She remarked to Fernando, "What a lucky lady the recipient must be, to be so loved."

His quiet, "I hope so" got lost when the bouquet came to a halt right beside Jo and a head of shockingly blond hair peeped round it.

"Miss Jo?" The apparition queried.

"Yes." Jo answered slowly as the bouquet was laid in her arms.

"These are for you then, Miss." He cheekily told her before disappearing off in the direction of the reception once more as Jo looked down and buried her nose in the fragrant display.

"They are simply gorgeous, Fernando, thank you so much." She said as the room erupted into a spontaneous round of applause. Fernando had left his seat and was coming round to her side and taking her hand he knelt to ask her his question.

"Will you be my wife please dearest Jo?" He asked.

Tears came to Jo's eyes as she realised the thought and care he had taken to reach this point. Shyly she nodded her agreement to overcome for speech. Fernando reached into his jacket pocket and produced the blue velvet box that he had picked up from the jewellers. Opening it to reveal a beautiful antique diamond and ruby engagement ring.

Gently he asked, "May I?"

Jo again nodded, he placed it on her ring finger on her left hand, then kissed her. That done to the satisfaction of the entire cliental and staff, they were royally cheered and showered with the congratulations of their well-wishers. The management came out with a tray of champagne for everyone to raise a toast to the newly engaged couple. After that Fernando tugged Jo's hand and suggested that perhaps they should find a quieter spot to finish their special evening. Waving goodbye to the room and stopping only to thank the manager and staff for all their kindness they left "The Mango Tree" hand in hand to walk back to Jo's car. Fernando suggested that perhaps he should drive as Jo had drunk some wine and he had been too nervous to do more than have a little sip of the champagne. "Where to my wife-to-be?" He asked her as she handed him her car keys. Jo looked into his face and asked if they could go back to Jeni's house as she just wanted to share her joy with her friends first. Fernando was more than happy to oblige and off they set to do just that.

To those who had been listening at a nearby table this was the moment to put a plan into action. Waiting exactly one minute after the couple had exited, they had then dialled and pressed the only button needed. The explosion rocked the room as the sound wave blew in the restaurant door. For some strange reason the glass hadn't shattered with its impact. However, the fiery yellow of flames was easily visible in it.

The restaurant staff telephoned for the fire brigade at once and ran outside to see what they could do to help, not knowing what they would see. Their black silhouettes were outlined by the flames of Jo's burning car as they scrambled to stand upright and clinging to each other staggered towards the restaurant to search for help and safety.

Chapter Twenty Three

WHEN CRAIG AND Tilly had arrived at Jeni's, they were greeted by two very excited individuals each vying to share their news. Jackson and Jeni in turn had two very excited and voluble guests. To Anna and Leon who arrived very shortly afterwards, it sounded like a gaggle of very agitated geese had been let loose on the doorstep! Craig called for order and surprisingly was heard, everyone stopped talking. "Whatever the news is, it must be very important and far too special to be announced standing on the doorstep!" He stated as he steered them all in the direction of the sitting room.

"Right Jeni, it's your house and so you get to go first." He declared next. All faces turned eagerly to Jeni and she was suddenly struck dumb by shyness. Jackson couldn't let his beloved sink so, he stepped in to tell them all that he had proposed and Jeni had said, yes. Exclamations of joy resounded and there were hugs and kisses for them both. When Jackson coughed rather loudly it all calmed down as they prepared to listen to further news of their wedding. However, Jeni leapt in with the fact that she wanted to wait until Fernando and Jo arrived. Which was when the doorbell went once more.

It was Jo and Fernando alright, but the state of their scorched and blackened appearance behind the police officer who had pressed the doorbell, struck them all dumb. It was to be sometime later, after they had made Jo and Fernando feel a bit more human with drinks, food and the comfort of knowing they were safe and surrounded by their friends, that the shock of what had so nearly happened hit them all.

In the silence, after Anna asked the question, "Who could want to kill you Jo?" It had come to them that this was not a fortunate escape from a nasty accident; but rather a deliberate attempt on their lives.

Jackson decided there and then that he had to alert them to the possibility that even from behind prison walls, Mr. Big intended to redeem his promise to get his own back on them. He was indeed a man who hated any interference with his plans. Jackson didn't want to terrify his friends but nor did he want them to walk straight into danger unaware. This was no joking matter if the man didn't want to stop short of murder. Was the man even sane?

The exhaustion that was coming over them in waves was noted and Jackson suggested that they should have Fernando and Jo stay the night at Jeni's in order to keep an eye on them and as Craig was quick on the uptake, it was he who suggested to Jeni that they should all just camp out at her place as there wasn't much of the night left and the party for London would be leaving in the morning. Weariness led to tired assent and Jeni quickly found bedding and allocated sleeping quarters to those who needed them. All intending to crawl under the covers to fall into the abyss of sleep, but not before Fernando had been assured by Jackson that he would personally ensure that all the hatches were battened down securely. He had become a little too relaxed since Mr. Big had been put in prison. But, he had threatened them all with retribution as he had been led down to the cells.

The brides to be after such an emotional time were soon swiftly asleep. Anna too. Tilly, however, found sleep elusive. She realised that she was feeling very strange about the whole evening and she didn't know quite why. Perhaps it was a hangover from her abduction; this feeling of tension and things not quite adding up. She hadn't felt like this since Jeni was in trouble and had needed rescuing. She was just confused about it all. It could simply be that she was jealous of her two friends' obvious happiness. Perhaps, she admitted to herself. She found herself examining her own relationship with Craig. What would she have said if he had proposed to her that night and would she honestly have wanted to say yes? Was she unsure of him or just not ready for those sorts of questions? Anyway, who could want to harm her friends? She drifted off to sleep trying to answer them all.

Chapter Twenty Four

THE NEXT MORNING was bright, sunny and warm. The breeze blew away the night terrors and renewed optimism was in the air. Jeni could contain herself no longer and told Jo and Fernando the good news and in passing hoped that it would be helpful in taking their minds of their recent ordeal. Jo had turned to look at Fernando and with his nod of assent, began.

It was Jo's turn to tell their news and with gasps of astonishment from the guys and romantic sighs from the girls their engagement story was greeted with the same wild enthusiasm as that of Jeni and Jackson's.

Anna and Leon were the first to mention a double wedding. Though both couples took a minute or two to digest the suggestion, they did both agree that as they shared the same circle of friends it did seem a good idea.

It was Craig who said, "I thought that the bride would want it to be a day just for her?" Jeni looked at Jo and found that she was looking at her. Simultaneously they both told the group that they would love to share such a special day with such a special friend, it would just make it even more memorable. To make sure it would work, they could try it out with a joint engagement party later that month. If that worked out well, then they would go ahead with wedding plans.

"Now where will we hold it?" Asked Fernando.

"Why here of course, if Jo is agreeable?" Jeni offered. Jo was quick to accept as she knew that her little cottage could hardly house the number of folk that they would both like to invite.

"Well that is fine by me, Jeni, but on one condition. We must split the costs." Jo countered. With Jackson and Fernando nodding their agreement. A happy time was spent assisting the two couples compose their guest list for the special party with Jo saying she wanted her staff to be able to come too and Jeni declaring that Gloria, her housekeeper, must be a guest and enjoy a well-earned night off. The date was then agreed, after much consultation with calendars, for a month to the day.

Her questions of the night were still very much unanswered in Tilly's mind and got resolutely pushed down into her subconscious, while she concentrated on eating breakfast and getting herself packed up before the time came to go to the airport for their flight to London. By the time they'd had had a couple of cups of their favourite brew and eaten a veritable mountain of toast with various accompaniments, they were all looking a lot brighter. Except, that was for Craig. Craig had been teased about being the next one to succumb to the lures of marriage. He felt he had managed to deflect the barbs by re-direction and getting them all to focus on the travel arrangements for that day. It was probably entirely due to this that they arrived at the airport at Plockton to meet Martin and Simon with more than a few seconds to spare!

Martin Jamieson had landed some ten minutes earlier and was busy supervising the re-fuelling of his aircraft for the long flight south with his full load of passengers as Simon logged their flight plans with the staff in the airport office. He turned his head at the sounds of vehicles arriving at the small office block, doors opening and shutting as luggage was being unloaded. He recognised Tilly's voice and knew that he was needed and telling the pump man to carry on, he made his way over to the door into the passenger part of the building. The party waiting with their bags at their feet greeted him warmly and Tilly asked after his family. The men in the party were far more interested in admiring his plane and whether he had managed to do some sailing or off road biking whilst at home. Assured that his time had been well spent getting filthy with mud or salt spray, it was then time for fond farewells and the promise of a swift return a month later. A scant five minutes for Martin to complete his ground formalities and the four were being loaded luggage and all into the small crafts. Jeni was still nervous and unbelieving that such a small aircraft was perfectly safe to travel hundreds of miles. As she looked up, still waving, to see the speck of colour disappearing from view she was very glad of the company of her three companions to encourage her that all would be well with the friends.

For the others the flight was another opportunity to mull over the recent events and the journey literally flew by. They landed safely and thanked Simon once again for his kindness in flying them to and fro before he took off for home. They also thanked Martin and pressed on him an invitation to the engagement party. He had very happily accepted and told them that if they needed another plane to get them all back to Plockton, he might be able to arrange for another friend to help out.

At this Tilly flung her arms round his neck and exclaimed, "What a lovely friend you are to have, thank you so much, Martin." Then it was time to return to their respective cars and get back home to normality once more. As if it ever could go back to what it had been before all the dramas of the past days.

Once home again and on their own, Tilly was too exhausted to think and just put her suitcase to one side and quickly got herself ready for bed. Once her teeth were brushed she walked over to the bed and fell into it. With a flick of the light switch she was plunged into darkness and she shut her eyes firmly and fell swiftly asleep. She was dead to the world. It was as she slowly opened her eyes the next morning, Tilly realised that she was at home, in her own bed, safe, warm and life could be ordinary if she wanted it to be. What a relief, she thought. No more adventures for me!

Chapter Twenty Five

FOR THE OTHERS it was not quite so straight forward. Anna and Leon were glad to be home but now more appreciative than ever of the traumas that Tilly, Jeni and the others had experienced during their trying times. It was Leon who expressed their thoughts exactly when he turned to Anna and took her gently in his arms and told her that he was glad that they had been together during their adventure and would she mind terribly if they didn't have any more as he preferred their version of humdrum married bliss to that of her friends' singleness. Anna nodded and agreed that married life and ordinary days were just what she thought the doctor would order for them and that she was more than happy to take her medicine.

As for Jeni and Jo, they woke the next morning with the same thought, "I can't believe it. I'm going to get married!" The next hours being spent in a joyful haze of wedding euphoria.

Jackson and Fernando had quietly agreed to meet for a breakfast debrief at eight o'clock and took their time to get going as they organised their minds for that while they dressed for the day ahead.

Craig was another kettle of fish altogether as he was raring to go. He was a man with a mission. No sooner had he opened his eyes than his feet were over the side of the bed and touching the floor. Next stop a shower and shave, clean clothes and he would get on out. He didn't have time to waste. He had to get into work early to find out the latest on Mr. Big. He was convinced that he was the one targeting Fernando and Jo.

The time that day flew by for everyone. Calls and messages went between various parties as ideas for an engagement party kept occurring. Smaller, but important details, needed passing on to the police through Jackson. After his breakfast brunch in a private corner of the local hotel's dining room with Fernando, Jackson felt more alert and able to face the music when he reported in to his superior. Just as well; as it turned out to be some grilling he got. Right down to the minute detail he was questioned and everything recorded for transcription later.

His boss was alternately pleased and dismayed as the tale unfolded. His thoughts, of could they have done better if intervention had been possible earlier? Perhaps new measures for their staff's personal protection were needed. Better communication procedures to ensure that emergency response times were effective. These all buzzed around his head; he was going to be a busy man. In the meantime, he told Jackson, that once the formalities were dealt with that day he would be free to take the rest of the day off to regroup. Jackson conveyed his thanks and left the office later that afternoon as quietly as he had entered it. Few had even known that he had been in the building.

Fernando had more practical matters to attend to. He had a mountain of mail to sort through, a parcel to deal with, plus he had to make sure that the "Mariella" was returned to her usual pre-charter state of readiness and his business was brought back into its usual organised state. Assuming the parcel to be a part that had been ordered for one of the yachts he ignored it and ploughed through the correspondence which his receptionist had sorted into piles according to urgency. That done he took it through to her for her to follow up his instructions for it. He picked up the box to remove its outer wrapping when he noticed that it was making a noise. He gently and very carefully lowered it back down onto his desk. Picked up his phone and was about to dial the police when he thought better of that. He walked calmly out of the office and into the reception area. Without raising his voice he asked his receptionist if they had any visitors on the premises and was told, not today. He then confirmed this with, "We're the only ones in the building?" Her yes, gave him the urge to say then let's run for our lives. Instead he told her that he would like her to go next door and ask them to evacuate their building immediately to out past the harbour wall.

One look at his grave face had her up out of her seat and running out the door. Fernando was swiftly following her and once well clear he rang the police and asked for bomb disposal assistance. That got the operator right on to the case and sending officers to help ensure all persons and properties were evacuated to safety. The noise of sirens, flashing lights and appearance of so many emergency services was to fill the harbour area for the next few hours. While the bomb, for that was what it surely was, got safely taken away and disposed of, there were seemingly endless questions that needed to be answered to the satisfaction of the police. It was not until order had once more been restored and staff sent home to soothe their shattered nerves, that he had been able to follow Jackson into their local. Fernando had a long swig of the pint of draught beer placed before him, grateful for its slight bitterness to take the taste of fear from his mouth. Jackson gave him the space that he needed to come to terms with what could so easily been his last day on earth. As he had been present at the police interview of Fernando, he knew all the facts. It was Fernando's thoughts that he was after; what his instincts were telling him. Fernando took one last long swallow and then stated simply that he was sure that Mr. Big was at the bottom of the attempt on his life. Jackson simply nodded his agreement and drank his own pint before either spoke again.

The attractive harbour lying in the shelter of its ancient stone walls, Fernando's two yachts were moored having been searched, scrubbed, wood polished and brasses left gleaming. Ropes were stowed away and the fuel, water and galley re-stocked by the end of a very long morning's hard work. However, once that was done he told his receptionist that as nothing else was urgent, he would be off and would only be contactable for the next day or so by using his mobile number as he and his future wife had plans to make. That brought congratulations from all in earshot before he escaped out the door. Then he just pointed his car in the direction of Jo's home and drove there as quickly as the speed limit would allow. He needed to spend some time alone with her to put his world to rights and he was determined to have it.

When he arrived, it was to find her on the phone to Jeni discussing engagement party plans. He soon stopped that by kissing her. All thoughts of Jeni were dislodged immediately, he was able to take the phone from her hand, tell Jeni that she would be phoned back at a later date and say goodbye; all without one word of protest crossing Jo's lips. It was some time afterwards before they decided that they could perhaps sit down together on her sofa and discuss their future and how much they loved each other. Any talk that might lead them down other paths was banned, and the rest of their time very happily spent learning just what sort of life they would like to share. Much to their surprise they found themselves in agreement over all the suggestions they made to each other. Their conclusion, it was much easier to agree to be happy than to disagree and let sadness come into their lives. Waiting for the right person to share your life with was well worth the wait and a little more experience of life meant that they both understood that life is all about compromise on the little unimportant things and agreement on the major issues. They were both looking forward to their future together. They couldn't wait.

Domestic bliss was not what Mr. Big was contemplating. He found it hard to make compromises. He didn't want to make them, he wouldn't make them. What he wanted was gratification and he wanted it now. No more amateurish attempts. He would solve his need for revenge in one grand gesture and he would see for himself that it was carried out. That way he would know that he had not been thwarted for sure.

Jeni and Jo got together several times over the next week to thrash out the details of their joint engagement party. Both their beaus having agreed, that as they would be inviting most of the same guests it made sense to share the costs and workload, the girls had therefore laid out their plans. Each person was given their allotted task and times for completion. It was almost run like a military campaign. Jeni, being the writer was in charge of invitations and after everyone had submitted their own list of desired guests she cross-referenced them and as soon as Jo had agreed the design for them, they were dispatched to their friends and families. She then ticked the responses off her list daily as soon as they came in. One job done. Jo was placed in charge of decorating the marquee that they had settled on as it needed to hold everyone, after its erection on the side lawn in Jeni's garden. Her idea of fairy lights in the trees and down the walkways to illuminate the paths would make the whole scene look magical for their visitors. Gloria had come into her own as the Catering Manager. With help from her relations and friends in the nearby villages, she had been batch cooking for days filling the temporary freezers that Fernando had arranged to be put into Jo's garage, with delectable eats for the buffet. Jackson? Well he had the job of organising what drinks they would serve. The only arduous thing about which was the having to taste the wine suggestions. Tough job, but someone had to do it!

The day before the engagement event found Jeni and Jo in Glasgow choosing their outfits to wear. They had to complement their rings which were to be formally presented to them the following evening and their individual characters but also, not clash. When walking towards their preferred clothes shopping area from the station they happened to pass the window of a small boutique simply entitled Grace. One window and only one model displayed in all its elegant splendour. Its jewel colour a perfect match for Jo's ruby and diamond ring. Jeni was insistent that Jo would enter and ask to try it on. Jo was adamant that there was no way that she could possibly afford a dress like that. However, Jeni got her way and Jo agreed to at least ask if it was in her size. The shop's doorbell gave an attractive chime as they entered and almost silently a small but very smart assistant came from between some velvet curtains in the rear of the graceful and stylishly decorated silver and turquoise salon and came gliding towards them, already asking if she could be of any assistance. Jo, suddenly shy, turned to Jeni and nodded at her to encourage her to speak on her behalf.

With eagerness, Jeni, launched in to a question, to be one of many. "Do you have the dress on display in your window in a size twelve, please?"

"Well as it happens, that one is a size twelve." The lady replied.

"Wonderful! My friend here would love to try it on." Jeni continued.

Jo looked at her and mouthed. "No, no."

Jeni paid absolutely no attention to her frantic pleas. The lady introduced herself as Grace Carmichael, the proprietor and elicited their names and what occasion the dress was required for. After offering her congratulations to them both, she was more than happy to remove it from the window display and place it in the changing room for Jo to try on. In the meantime, she suggested that Jeni took a rather more comfortable seat and she would see if she had anything in the stockroom that might suit her too. Jeni was happy to comply and was even happier when she returned with a glass of fruit juice and one of water on a tray for Jeni to help herself to while she waited. How thoughtful. Jeni said to herself. Grace was swift to return again with her arms bedecked with two simply gorgeous gowns. With Jeni's dark, softly curling, tresses and deep violet eyes the swirling pattern in hues ranging from a soft dove grey through lilacs and lavenders to majestic purple and then indigos would look stunning. The other, a deep rich copper tone, too would look amazing. Jeni was just itching to try them on. However, just at that moment Jo drew back the changing room's grey crushed velvet curtain and emerged as if from a cocoon and for all the world, looking like a beautiful butterfly.

"Oh!" Jeni gasped out. "Jo you look ….. Absolutely perfect."

Then she was completely silent while Jo did a slow twirl to allow her to see the total effect. The front was a simple perfectly cut princess seamed shape with a modest boat shaped neckline; but the back was cut away cleverly and then the revealed space covered in an intricate panel of delicately embroidered lace. It was breath taking. The fit was as if it had been made for Jo. Perfection! The deep ruby red of the heavy satin brought a delicate glow to Jo's normally pale skin that made her eyes sparkle. When Jeni regained her composure, it was with tears in her eyes that she turned to Grace to simply say that they would be taking the dress.

"But we haven't even asked the price or looked anywhere else yet, Jeni!" Jo protested.

Jeni told her that there could not possibly be a better dress for her anywhere in the world that could make her look so special. At this, Grace wheeled out a large cheval mirror from somewhere behind another panel of curtaining, so that Jo could see for herself what Jeni meant.

"Is it really me?" She queried in amazement.

Jeni nodded vigorously and told her all over again how fabulous she looked. Jo turned to Grace and asked her how much it would cost. Grace asked her to wait a moment while she checked. Then she retreated beyond the salon curtains and left them admiring Jo's reflection in the mirror while she consulted her stock book. The price should have been five hundred pounds. She thought for a moment and took a peek through the gap in the drapes at Jo. She immediately took off one hundred pounds and walked back into the salon. She told them her price but saw the dismay in her client's eyes. It was still too expensive, she realised, for this modest woman. Jeni had already decided that she would buy it for Jo and indicated to Grace the same, but Grace saw Jo shaking her head.

So she said, "That does not include the reduction because it is a display model and therefore not bespoke. That will make the cost two hundred and fifty pounds."

Jo looked at Jeni and she gently nodded her agreement. "Then I would love to buy it, please." Jo quietly whispered. "I'd better go and take it off before I spoil it." She said before turning and making her dazed way back into the changing room.

Grace facing Jeni asked, if she would like to use the second changing room to try on her own selection of dresses. Jeni eagerly followed her lead and was soon stepping into the swirling confection and pulling it up to have its carefully concealed zip smoothly pulled into place. Jo was seated and drinking the glass of water when Jeni stepped out to view herself. Jo looked up from her daydreams and saw her friend looking gorgeously arrayed.

"I don't know what it is about your dresses, Grace, but they make us both look just as if we have walked off the pages of Vogue!" Jo declared. "Jeni you look so amazing that Jackson won't know what's hit him when he sees you in that dress tomorrow. You are going to buy it, aren't you?"

"Well, there's another one every bit as delicious, that I'm going to try on next and then we'll decide which we like best." Jeni told her. In no time Jeni was back and looking equally ravishing in the metallic copper toned robe. It was a little long to be standing barefoot in, but it moulded to her curves and Jo felt sure would leave Jackson feeling bedazzled and bewitched by Jeni's beauty.

"What do you think then?" Jeni asked her friend as she turned to look in the mirror. Before Jo could even formulate a reasonable reply, she came back with. "Oh, it's no good trying to decide between them now; I shall just have to buy them both and try to make up my mind tomorrow!"

With the important decisions made the girls could now kick back and relax while Grace wrapped their gowns in tissue paper and placed them in some stylishly simple, dove grey dress boxes and adorned only with bows of broad plain black satin and Grace in elegant copperplate script. Even the boxes looked too expensive to Jo. Could she really be taking home such a wonderful dress to wear at her own engagement party? It all seemed too impossible to be true.

After another two hours spent buying other vital accessories and with tired feet, they made their way to the train station to catch the train home. When they arrived at their destination they found not one but two eager suitors ready to carry their bags and carry them off to "The Mango Tree", for an early dinner. Perhaps just as well as they had forgotten all about lunch and were desperate for a cuppa too! The boys were happy to be told in only sketchy terms about the girls' good fortune in finding the small boutique. Telling them that they could look forward to seeing the results of their spending spree. When they took them home with their purchases a short time later it was to say reluctant goodbyes to two very tired young ladies. "Until tomorrow." They told them.

When the evening finally arrived and Gloria walked up to the house she saw Jackson was there to greet the guests as they walked up the garden path and direct them to follow the glowing orange pathway on and into the marquee. There they were made to feel welcome by Fernando and plied with the hospitality so typical of the Scots. While awaiting the entrance of the two ladies that they had come to see, there was time to start catching up with those they hadn't seen for a while or be introduced to the new members of the groups' families. Tilly and Anna and their partners were quick to rush over and greet Cathy and her soon to be husband, Percy Greystoke. This was their chance to get to know him when he was out of his comfort zone and off guard, thought Jackson and Craig; they still had not made up their minds about the man.

Jeni and Jo had decided to make a grand entrance worthy of their beautiful finery together and a hush descended on the place as folk the folk turned to look at what was going on. When Jackson and Fernando saw what had everyone silenced they were not surprised. They were stunning! An identical thought went through both of them. How could I have been so lucky as to find her; she's simply glorious. Not even excusing themselves from the present company, they flew across the space to join them and almost tumbled out the words of their delight at their appearance. The girls were more than happy to find their swains tongue-tied and blown away, it was just the effect that they had been hoping for, when preparing upstairs in Jeni's bedroom. In moments, it was time for the formal announcement of their forthcoming weddings and to receive their anticipated engagement rings. Next thing they knew they had rings placed on their fingers to a loud round of applause, wolf whistles and joy. Well pleased, they positively basked in the glow of the wonderful compliments their guests were quick to bestow on them as the two men proudly escorted them around the marquee under the fairy lights to show them off and chat with their well-wishers and receive their generous engagement gifts and cards.

Despite all the goings on, Jo took the time to especially welcome her staff, making sure that even her new van driver, Xander Smith, felt comfortable among a crowd of people that he didn't know. While she was doing so a young woman took the time to engage him and Fernando in a very flirtatious conversation that was witnessed by Jeni and a few others. Fernando seemed much taken by the glamorous woman who was making him laugh and almost snuggling into him as if by right. Jeni looked carefully at her but couldn't place her. She wasn't one of her friends or relations and so she assumed that she must be one of Jo's guests or family, or perhaps one of Fernando's own cousins. He did seem to have rather a lot of them. It was only a few minutes later that she found her own fiancé being amused by the mystery woman. She was certainly getting around the room and mixing well and looking very predatory, Jeni thought to herself. As the night wore on, that same thought was to go through the minds of quite a few of the ladies present causing them to enquire who she was and wonder quite which man she was after. It was later still when Tilly expressed it to Anna and they sought out Jeni and Jo to ask them about her. By the time they had disentangled themselves and captured the attention of Jeni and Jo the woman in question was nowhere in sight and they were then unable to point her out. However, both of them had noted her unsettling presence and turned to query the other about her. It was soon obvious, she was not an invited guest. Perhaps she was the partner of someone invited? No-one seemed able to answer that one. Then Jo said that she had seen her tucked behind some palm plants that the marquee had been decorated with talking to her new van driver, Xander Smith. Maybe she was his date for the evening?

No matter; the demands of their guests were what mattered now and they had a couple of speeches to make. Both Jackson and Fernando played their part in thanking their guests for joining them to celebrate their happiness and encouraging them to share their big day in the not too distant future. The cry of "when?" went up and the two men looked at their beautiful ladies and in unity came out with. "It can't be soon enough for us!" The girls were not so eager to appease their families and friends by committing to a definite date but smiled their joy and promised that they would be "the first to know." It was a crowd of very happy people who made their farewells in the early hours and four very happy couples who bade each other goodnight and went their weary way to bed smiling at all the happy memories they had made that night Anna, was the only one left with an uneasy feeling that they might not have seen the last of the mystery woman.

Chapter Twenty Six

LATE THE NEXT morning, Fernando was surprised to bump into the mystery woman from the party who had proved to be such fun, as he went for a run along the beach to clear his head from the after-effects of such a lively evening. She was jogging along the sand left damp by the outgoing tide and looking particularly attractive in her running outfit of sky blue, figure hugging Lycra. She soon had him jogging alongside her and kept him so happily entertained that he didn't even notice someone had entered the beach through the dunes and was standing staring over in their direction. In fact, Jackson had been standing there for some minutes watching the interplay between them before deciding that it was time to join them. Fernando finally dragged his attention from his companion when Jackson hollered "Woah there." She just smiled sweetly at Jackson's interruption. Neither guessed her deep annoyance at having her plans for the rest of the morning ruined. Making the best of her situation, she engaged them both with her humorous anecdotes about parties that she had attended and did her utmost to engage Fernando by friendly arm touching and leaning on him when her trainer got a small stone in it a short time later. She continued in a similar vein for another fifteen minutes hoping that Jackson would take himself off elsewhere. However, when he appeared to be settled in for the duration, she cut her losses and waved her goodbyes.

When she was safely out of earshot, Jackson, asked Fernando the burning question. "Who is she?"

"How should I know?" Fernando countered. "I thought that she must be one of the girls' friends."

"She probably is." Jackson told him. "Just one we haven't met before." Then dismissing her from his mind, he challenged Fernando to a race, with the winner to buy brunch at the beachside café. The words were barely out of his mouth before Fernando took to his heels. However, Jackson was in hot pursuit and both panting heavily they arrived together at the door of the café. It took a few moments to catch their breath and decide that it was a draw and then enter. Orders placed at the counter they found somewhere to sit down to go over the joys of the previous evening. By the time they had eaten they were concluding that there couldn't be two luckier chaps that morning than themselves. Gorgeous, strong, capable women who had their own careers and wanted to share their lives with them were not to be found hanging around on trees just waiting to be picked. An hour later they parted confirming that they would be present for the early dinner Jeni had planned for the families and closest friends before they left for home.

As Fernando walked back to his apartment he thought about the woman he had encountered on the beach and felt a little flattered that she had wanted his company. Then she was dismissed from his mind as his day got underway. If only he had been so easy to dismiss from hers. However, she knew that she would have to lay her plans even more carefully than she had thought, if she was to deliver what she had promised and deliver it on time.

In the space of the next few days Fernando was to bump into Candice, or Candy as she preferred him to call her, everywhere he went. In the shop where he bought his paper and fresh milk for his morning cereal, to the unisex hairdresser where he had his fortnightly trim. She was always impeccably groomed and utterly charming. She seemed to hang on his every word. Very flattering to his male ego. He realised that he found her quite fascinating, in a mysterious sort of way. In fact, by the end of the week he found himself actually looking to see her as he went about his daily tasks and was a little disappointed if he did not do so.

Jackson and Jeni, were not happy about hearing that Fernando had bumped into Candy, yet again. It was a case of "We are not amused" for them. Jeni even asked Jackson, if he thought that Candy was actually stalking Fernando. Her next comment being, that she was glad that Jo did not live in town to witness it all first hand, for it would surely lead her to questioning Fernando's devotion. If she could see them cosily having coffee together in the window of the Harbour Café, as they were at that very moment, Jeni felt sure it would ring alarm bells for Jo. Not wanting to express any opinion that might get back to Jo, Jackson held his tongue. However, he was wondering why this woman had latched onto his friend but did not appear anywhere else in the town or to have any work to do in the area. Why was she here he wondered? Far better to just get on with helping Jeni plan their wedding. It was more than enough to be going on with.

With the subject of weddings very much to the fore, he realised that it would be Cathy and Percy getting married next. He must ask Jeni what they should be getting them as a wedding present and as the opportunity came not two seconds later, he plunged straight in. Jeni told him that she did not have a clue but they had better get it soon as the wedding day was almost upon them. Discussions led them to look in the window of the local fine china store and to see a beautiful heavy crystal vase that Jeni thought would make a wonderful fruit bowl for Cathy's kitchen table. She knew that she had often moaned about buying far more fruit than her current wooden platter could comfortably hold. Jackson promptly opened the door and led her inside to seek the aid of the assistant. Ten minutes later they left with him carrying a beautifully boxed bowl of large proportions, that Jeni deemed the perfect gift.

In the meantime, Candy, was feeling very self-satisfied. She had over coffee, managed to manoeuvre Fernando into offering his help to move some furniture for her on Saturday. Now all she had to do was ensure that he didn't tell Jo, Jeni or Jackson about it and get Jo to witness him entering her flat when she was wearing something suggestive. She spent the intervening couple of days refining her plan and making sure that her timing would be perfect. She knew that Jo and Jeni had a regular date for Saturday mornings and had noted their routes and times in the previous weeks thinking that it might prove useful information. Now, all that hard work was about to pay off.

Sure enough, Saturday came round and when she looked out her window she could see that Fernando was on his way down her road. She just had time to get herself into position. As she opened the door to his ring, who should be driving past? Jo and Jeni got an eyeful of

Candy in her nightwear giving a kiss to an only slightly embarrassed looking Fernando.

"Why was Candy kissing him goodbye?" Jeni actually heard herself asking that very question and realised that she had done so out loud.

"So you saw that too." Jo stated.

"Well, I could hardly miss it, as we were driving right past them." Jeni replied rather abruptly. She just didn't know what to think of Fernando's behaviour; let alone what to say to his fiancée. Then she noticed the tear coursing down Jo's cheek. Seeing ahead a space at the roadside to pull into she gently told Jo to pull over. Jo did and promptly burst into floods of tears.

"How could he. We've only just got engaged." She blurted out between sobs.

Jeni searched for words as she tried to find some tissues to mop up the outflow of Jo's emotions. There was nothing she could say in Fernando's defence. She knew that he had been seeing Candy, but she had not realised that it had gone so far. She was sure that Jackson did not know either, what his friend was getting up to. What could she say? Nothing. Instead, she let her friend cry it out until she was a bit calmer and then suggested, very gently, that she should drive them both back to Jo's cottage. Perhaps, by the time they had got there, something suitable to comfort her friend with would have come to mind. She certainly hoped so.

For the next couple of hours Jo's emotions varied between burning anger and sheer misery at Fernando's betrayal of their relationship. They were due to meet for dinner that evening but she did not know if she could even face him, she told Jeni. Jeni murmured soothing noises while letting Jo get it all out. The rage and the silence. She knew that Jo really loved Fernando as she had never been quite this distressed when her previous boyfriend had broken off their long term relationship. This was far more serious. Jo was clearly heartbroken.

When Jo insisted that Jeni should return home, as she just wanted to be left alone now that she felt calmer, Jeni gave her a long hard stare. Seeing in her eyes immense sadness but no cause for real concern about what she might do next, she agreed to leave but with one caveat; Jo must ring her if she felt that it was all getting on top of her. Jo slowly answered that she would. Jeni gave her a big hug, squeezing her tightly and reiterated her love. Then she drove very slowly and carefully home to ensure that her inner rage would not compromise her own driving.

Never had Jeni been so pleased to walk into her kitchen and find Jackson, standing there calmly setting a table for two. She ran into his arms and felt so safe as her held her close. His gentleness, as he asked her what was troubling her, moved her to tears. His obvious concern for Jo and Jeni, when he knew the cause, even outweighed his concern for Fernando. It was only when he saw how seriously Jeni was taking the matter that he knew Fernando's engagement was in grave trouble.

Jo had come to that conclusion too. She just could not contemplate marriage to a man she could not trust. So, before she had time to change her mind, she picked up her phone and rang Fernando's number. He didn't answer. He must still be with her. She was so mad with him, that she left him a message. It read like a telegram as she spat the words from her mouth.

Fernando its Jo. The engagement is off! I just can't marry you. Goodbye!

It took only hours for the news to spread through the circle of their friends. Bad news travels fast. As Jo had turned off her phone the minute she had left her message for Fernando, she did not know that she had left Jeni to be besieged by concerned callers. Jeni had already called Tilly and Anna and reluctantly told them of the gravity of the morning, feeling they should hear from her rather than from the menfolk, Jo's engagement was off, after she had received a distressing call from Fernando. He wanted to know why Jo wasn't taking his calls and demanding to know what she meant by leaving him a message to say that their engagement was off. Jeni felt that it wasn't her place to tell him of his own bad behaviour. He should know that he must have been found out and so his protests fell on deaf ears. She merely handed the phone to Jackson. He told Fernando that he would come over and see him shortly at his flat if he was there. Fernando agreed with an "Of course" and then rang off. Jackson turned to Jeni and told that he would have to go and see what he could do to put things right. Jeni nodded her head in agreement and then Jackson left.

Heartbroken, Jo did what she often did when troubled. She locked up her cottage and walked to the studio to lose herself in creating something special. It soothed her spirit to create her unique pieces and made her feel worthwhile again, that she had a purpose in life. It did not, however, make her feel loved. Oh she knew that she was valued. Her parents and friends gave her that feeling of being valued and cared for. But only Fernando could make her feel really loved, only he could do that for her. Instead she poured it all out as she worked. Her phones rang silently in the house but it was not until very late that night when Jeni knocked at the studio window that she knew of the concern they all had for her well-being and happiness. The relief, at finding Jo at her work bench was written all over Jeni's face.

"Thank goodness I've found you!" Jeni almost shouted at her in her concern. "Why didn't you call me? I thought that you had done something silly when I couldn't find you. I was going to break the door down to see if you were alright!"

"I'm so sorry, Jeni, I just didn't realise the time!" Jo told her friend.

By the time they had closed up her workshop and walked into the cottage, Jo knew how much concern there was about her. Jeni had told that even her parents now knew about her broken engagement and phoned her when they couldn't reach Jo for themselves. Jeni had to promise them to come right over and find out what was going on. Then, Jeni had turned around and picked up the hall phone and handed it to Jo. She then told her in no uncertain terms, that she must phone her parents. Reluctantly Jo dialled her old home number and wasn't surprised when it was answered immediately by her mother. Or to hear her father's anxious query in the background. "Is she alright?"

It took a while to reassure them that she was fine and that yes, the news of her broken engagement was true.

"How had they heard so soon? She had asked them.

"Jeni had rung Tilly, who had rung Cathy and she had rung them, of course!" Her mother had said bluntly.

When she finally put the phone down a short while later it was with a sense of relief that at least now they knew. She was so drained that Jeni insisted on her sitting down while she got her a hot drink and warmed up some lasagne for her that she had found in the back of the fridge.

"But I don't feel like eating anything." Jo stated in a very flat voice.

"But you must eat, your body needs it even if you don't." Jeni told her firmly and stood over her until she had eaten half of the small portion.

"That's better, isn't?" Jeni said next. "But what I think you need most now is to sleep on the matter and see what the morning brings, so I'm going to leave you to do just that and I'll see you in the morning. I'll pick you up and we'll go to church together."

Jo just nodded her head in agreement and Jeni gave her a quick hug before she closed the door behind herself. Jo dragged herself up the stairs and went through her bedtime routine on autopilot as she tried not to think too much about the events of the day. Even her dreams conspired against her as she lived the scene where Candy and Fernando kissed over and over again all night. She knew she was very unhappy, even in her dreams. Someone was happy at news of the shattered engagement and it wasn't just Candy.

Mr. Big was in the library when he heard the news through his earphones. His chuckle was resounding off his walls so loud that the prison officer present commented, that the man seemed to be in an unusually good mood today.

His co-worker replied, "That makes a change, as he seems to have been in a foul one ever since he got here."

I love it when my plans are working out well, Mr. Big thought to himself. Maybe I'm getting somewhere at last? Phase two next, I think. The wheels were turning and they didn't even have a clue what was going to hit them. He would land his next hit via Cathy just to throw them all off guard and then sweep in for the coup de grace. By the time he was finished with them their lives would all be wrecked. He found himself chuckling off and on as he plodded through the rest of prison day.

Candy took the beautiful meat pie that she had bought from the bakery next door to the butchers in her street and carefully stowed it in her picnic basket along with the bottle of red wine and one of beer. She was prepared. She slipped on her coat and shoes and walked smartly down the road towards the harbour. Soon she was ringing the bell of Fernando's apartment above the ship's chandlers. It was a couple of minutes before she heard his feet as he trod heavily down the stairs. When Fernando finally pulled the door open, even she was shocked at how drawn he looked, but she didn't stop. She pushed past him and headed up the stairway. Fernando, outmanoeuvred, could only close it again and follow her. It was this little scene that Jackson witnessed and had him do an abrupt one hundred and eighty degree about turn and head back the way he came. He was puzzled. Why was his friend acting so strangely? Didn't he care about Jo? What was he up to? The questions kept flying round his head as he walked away. But he had no answers.

He wasn't to get any in the following days either. Fernando's laissez-faire attitude seemed so out of character that Jackson began to think that Fernando must be under the influence.

"Under the influence of what?" Jeni asked him.

"Drink?" Jackson proffered.

"Don't be ridiculous! You told me yourself that he hasn't been seen in the pub since Saturday when it happened." Jeni told him.

"Drugs, then?" Jackson persisted. Then immediately retracted. After all he had never known his friend to take anything. Not even the proverbial aspirin for a headache, but something was making him act so oddly. It just didn't gel with the man he knew. Jackson felt himself siding with Jeni and Jo and thinking that perhaps Fernando wasn't as trustworthy as he had once thought.

It was Jeni who saw Candy next, when Candy took to the pavement to carry her basket to Fernando's flat. As Jeni was on her way to Fernando's herself to try and confront him and find out what exactly Fernando was doing with Candy, she followed her. Sure enough, she saw Candy knock on Fernando's door. Jeni saw him answer it, but wasn't near enough to hear what they said. What she could see was his smile of welcome and how easily she was invited in. Seething, Jeni made her way back to where she had left her car and drove straight home. Debating with herself the whole way, whether to tell her friend what she had seen or not. Meanwhile, Candy had been acting the part of sympathetic friend so well, that she had usurped Jackson and she now found it much easier to keep Fernando's attention focussed on her, especially with her daily visits. He was proving much more manageable. Her manipulative machinations were isolating him and making his friendships virtually impossible to maintain. He had become reliant on her without realising why and she fed him with the lies that she wanted him to believe and he believed them. Fernando felt let down, bewildered and confused. Why was his world crumbling around him? How had it happened? He just couldn't understand what was going on and was fast losing the will to try and work it all out.

Chapter Twenty Seven

THAT'S WHAT JACKSON was thinking too. With Jeni so concerned about her friend and tied up on the phone to others all the time, she hardly seemed to have any time for him or them. Even their wedding plans were being neglected. However, it was Cathy and Percy who were getting married on Saturday and they were still going to it together so, he hoped that they would get some quality time while they were away and restore some balance to their relationship. Then, Jeni told him that they were taking Jo with them, as she didn't think that she should be going on her own. As she had already discussed this with Jo it was a fait accompli. Jackson acknowledged her information and told her that he would pick her up as planned and then they would collect Jo and be off on Friday morning.

When Jeni spoke to her three dearest friends that night about the preparations for Cathy's wedding it was clear that the matter was well in hand. The individual skills that they had all brought to the table to accomplish this miracle were formidable and complemented each other perfectly. The wedding would be everything Cathy could want and then some. Outfits discussed and worked out to avoid clashes and all that could be done was done until late Friday afternoon. That's when all hands would be needed on deck to get the church and village hall decorated and the catering needs arranged satisfactorily. Until then, Jeni would focus on her own work and keeping an eye on Jo. Both Tilly and Anna were concerned about Jo too and had asked if she would still feel able to come to the wedding. Jeni had told them that Jo planned to, but it would really depend on how strong she felt on Friday morning. However, Jeni felt that it would do Jo good to get away for the weekend as she had hardly been out of her workshop since she had made her dramatic announcement. Not a good sign. As for Fernando? His behaviour was getting stranger and stranger. Even his staff had approached Jackson to express their concerns. Fortunately, the charter season was practically over and the others had been able to cover for the lack of their main man. However, if this continued the business may well fail; for they freely admitted that it was Fernando's charm and great skill as a captain that it thrived on. Without that they may all end up out of a job. Jackson took it all to heart and tried to talk to Fernando but found him very distracted and unable to focus on the urgency of the matter in hand. What was going on in his head? Whatever it was, Jackson hoped that he would snap out of it soon, otherwise he could see him losing everything that he had worked so very hard to achieve in one fell swoop.

He then asked him about the wedding on Saturday.

"Who wants to get married, I don't!" Was Fernando's nonsensical sing song reply.

All Jackson could conclude was that he wasn't intending to go to Cathy and Percy' wedding that Saturday after all. Perhaps just as well in view of the awkwardness of having Jo there too!

It did make him think to ask Jeni a plain and simple question the next time they met up. Did she want to marry him and if so, when?

"Yes, yes, yes of course I do! As to when? Are we in a hurry?" she replied.

"Yes. At least I am." Jackson told her. "I want to marry you before you change your mind about me."

"I wouldn't do that ever. I'm a woman of my word, Jackson, you know that." Jeni responded.

"Right then let's get married before Christmas." He countered.

"I was planning to make it next summer anyway." Jeni retorted.

"No, not next Christmas. I mean the one coming up shortly." Jackson explained.

"It's only six weeks away. I haven't got a dress yet. Where would we have it? How?" Flooded from Jeni's lips.

"At least you're not telling me it's impossible!" Jackson laughed.

Jeni looked at him with love in her eyes and told him that she would marry him whenever and wherever he wanted, but that she would rather like to have some friends and family there to witness their momentous event.

After another hour they had a date, venue, had asked the bridesmaids and the parents had been told. "You've only got to ask the best man to play his part now and I will need to get a caterer and florist organised." Jeni stated and then went on to ask. "Do you have any food preferences or shall I just surprise you, Jackson?" Her eyes twinkling with merriment. She seemed to be finding his surprise rather stimulating and exciting. Jackson answered that he would be happy with anything she chose.

"Carte blanche! Just what I like to hear." Jeni exclaimed while she gave him a big hug.

As he looked down at his woman and couldn't help but smile broadly she was definitely the one for him. However, he was wondering if Fernando was the one to be his best man. His behaviour lately had Jackson questioning his choice. Fernando had asked him to be his best man but that was before his engagement had been called off. He avoided the issue by asking Jeni what she had around to eat.

"All this excitement has made me really ravenous and if you don't watch out I'll be eating you up, you look so scrumptious!" He told her making a mock lunge for her person.

Jeni was soon happily placing an array of dishes in front of him and he was a happy man with a full stomach.

Chapter Twenty Eight

It was the eve of Cathy's wedding to Percy and the girls were all working away arranging the floral displays in the village church, followed by those in the village hall. Which scarcely resembled its former utilitarian appearance. Its ceiling had been draped with yards of tulle in glowing colours to match the flowers and looked more like a Bedouin Sheik's harem tent, according to Jeni and Anna. The plain white pendant lampshades had been similarly altered to cast a colourful glow. Now the hall looked warm and welcoming. Jo was putting the last touches to the gift table by arranging her wedding gift of a beautiful guest book held open at the second page with a suitably elegant pen. She had already got the "wedding crew" to enter their names and good wishes, so that they would not be forgotten. However, she had left the front page for Cathy to fill in the details herself. A job Jo would have loved to do herself for her own special day, she knew. It made her so sad to think that would never happen now. She would never marry now and would end her days as an old spinster unwanted and unloved, as she couldn't conceive of finding another person to love like she loved Fernando. Her maudlin thoughts were interrupted when Anna's voice announced that she felt that they had done all they could tonight, it was time for them all to get off to bed. After all, bridesmaids were meant to look beautiful not hag-ridden.

The next morning they reconvened at nine o'clock to assist the caterers in with their vast mountains of food while the menfolk made sure that fridges etc. were brought in and connected to the electrical supply. Once all that had been checked, they all left to get dressed for the big day.

Tilly's mother was in charge of getting Cathy organised and dressed and her father had the job of escorting her to the church on time, so Tilly was free to join Anna and Jeni and don her bridesmaid dress. Jo had kindly offered to act as their hair and make-up girl and would ensure that they too made it to the church door to welcome the bride. All went well and looking good enough to eat, they arrived in time to see the men going in to take their seats having ushered in all the guests. Her mother was in the church porch and Tilly went forward and gave her mum a big hug. She wanted to check that all was well with the bride.

"Oh yes, Cathy is fine. We just want to know what has happened to the groom." Her mother whispered in her ear.

"What? We've no groom." Tilly whispered back.

"No groom, no best man and no one at all from the Greystoke side. I asked your young men to sit that side as the church looked so empty there." Her mother continued whispering.

By now the other girls had sensed that something was up and drawn closer. What was wrong they wanted to know? Could they help? Tilly was bemused. She took a deep breath and made the decision to phone her father to ask him to delay Cathy's arrival at the church by ten minutes. Her excuse, it's traditional for the bride to be late. Then she explained to the other three girls what the situation was.

"Well" said Jeni, "has anyone tried to contact him?"

Tilly turned to her mother. Apparently not! Jo was dispatched to obtain Jackson and his phone so that he could make the call as he had Percy's number. The call was made and a very anxious group huddled in the church porch awaiting the response. There was none; it just rang and rang before it cut off completely. All was not lost though. Tilly had George Crowther's number somewhere on her phone, she thought. She had asked him for it to keep him in the loop about the wedding preparations when she and Craig had met up with Cathy, Percy and George for a pub lunch the previous weekend. It had been a getting to know you session so that they wouldn't meet as strangers on the day of the wedding. They had rather liked George. He seemed genuinely fond of Percy and they obviously went way back. When Tilly had filled Anna, Leon, Jeni and Jackson in on the meeting it had done much to allay their doubts about Percy Greystoke's haste to get married. However, now it their qualms were all back again as it took, George Crowther, a few minutes to pick up the call. A very long couple of minutes.

Percy had been all for calling the whole thing off and George had had to been very firm with him. However, he had soon realised that Percy was not getting cold feet because he didn't want to get married to Cathy. What he saw in Percy' eyes was fear. What on earth was he afraid of he couldn't imagine? He'd met Cathy and thought her perfectly delightful. What could the answer be? He wondered. Then he said. "What's bothering you Percy? I know it's not Cathy, I've seen the way you look at her!"

Percy took his time to answer and when he did, it was to shock his old friend, George to the core. "You've got mixed up with gangsters and they are threatening you into marriage with Cathy for their own ends! If I hadn't known you for thirty years Percy Greystoke, I would never have believed this ridiculous tale. However, I know that you would never lie to me, or look so worried, if it wasn't the truth." George told Percy.

Percy had plonked himself down and wearily held his head in his hands. Then slowly explained to his best man how he had been persuaded by a new friend to go to a classy gentlemen's club and ended up gambling away a fortune. When had they found out that he could not pay it immediately he had given them an I.O.U. and that had been sold on for a favour instead of the cash he owed. All he had to do was entertain a lady and fix her interest on him. That hadn't seemed so bad. Then it had escalated into leading her to the altar and ditching her either at it or at the door of the church. It had seemed such a simple thing to do when he hadn't known Cathy, or fallen in love with her, he told George. It would have cleared his debt and he would as such have been able to get on with his life again. Now, he wanted to marry Cathy and he would still be in debt as he wouldn't have kept his side of the bargain. All he could see was that he would never be free of this millstone round his neck.

George thought a moment and then suggested to Percy that he ought to tell Cathy everything and trust her love for him to allow the wedding to go ahead. He then asked exactly how much the I.O.U. was for.

"Eighty thousand!" Percy blurted out. George blanched and then told him that he would loan him the money to pay off the debt right away. That way he could be free of the cloud hanging over him. Percy looked up into his friend's face and George could see the struggle he was having with himself. Percy desperately wanted to say yes and ease his mind but, he knew that George must be offering him every penny he had in savings to do it with. What a friend he was.

"George, thank you my dear, dear, friend but I can't take your life savings. What if you need them?" Percy had countered.

George responded with. "Well, I have a good friend who would always help me out if I need it."

Percy again looked full into George's eyes and saw only compassion, kindness and friendship.

"I will pay you back as soon as I can sell off some of my assets. I had already put things in motion but they just wouldn't wait." Percy stated.

"What are you going to do? Marry Cathy anyway because you want to or come clean and risk losing her?" George asked.

"Marry her." Percy told him.

"Then let's not worry about that now, let's just get you to the church on time." George chivvying Percy to get him out of the hotel and see if they could salvage this wedding after all. Then his phone had rung. He confirmed to Tilly that he had Percy and that they would be on their way tout suite. The rest would have to wait until the ceremony itself was over. Sufficient unto the day and all that.

Their arrival at the church was greeted with sighs of relief, as by now even Cathy was aware that Percy and George were the only ones missing from her wedding. With a quick kiss on her cheek and a promise to explain all later, the two men then galloped down the aisle to their places and the organist once again took his seat, the signal for the wedding march was given and finally, the wedding itself was underway.

As they stood at the church door an hour later having photos taken George whispered in Percy' ear that he should get the deed over and done with a.s.a.p. so, he would slip off for a few minutes to transfer the funds into Percy' bank account, and then he should get it all off his chest by telling Cathy all about the matter. "It's not good for a man to keep secrets from his wife." George had said simply.

Percy' reply was equally simple. "Will do."

It was to be a couple of hours later, after the food was eaten and the speeches delivered and received with much laughter, that Percy was able to slip away into a small room just off the main village hall with his bride for his quiet chat.

"Cathy, my darling, you do know that I love you?" He asked.

"Of course I do, silly, otherwise I wouldn't have married you today." Cathy promptly replied.

When she looked into his face Cathy could see that wasn't all that was bothering her new husband.

"What is it Percy? What has you so upset?" She questioned.

Percy pulled her down onto a small settee and took hold of her left hand and unconsciously rubbed her shiny new wedding ring as he began his confession. "Cathy, I have to tell you that I am in a bit of trouble and I was at my wit's end and was going to call the wedding off until George stepped in to rescue me." He went on.

At the words "recue me", Cathy's heart seemed to stop in her chest. The need for rescue held terrible memories for her, of days of not knowing if those she loved were alive or would be found dead. They were not one's she wanted to hear in conjunction with Percy. Her face paled and she gave an involuntary shiver. "I think the sooner you tell me everything, the better Percy." She quietly stated.

"I'm a gambler. No, no. I mean I was a gambler. I've given it up." He told her emphatically. Before continuing to tell her how he had found himself deep in debt and that the debt was to be cleared by him doing a favour.

"What favour?" Cathy was quick to ask.

"I know you won't like this, but please bear in mind that when I agreed to do it, I hadn't met you." Percy pleaded. Then the rest came out in a rush. "I was to meet a lady and get to know her, flatter her and enchant her into spending time with me. At least that's what it started out as. Then they wanted me to get her to agree to marry me and for me to drop her at the altar." He reluctantly came out with.

As the reality of the situation hit, all Cathy could think of was, why her? She barely heard Percy tell her that what he had actually done was fall in love with her. Her ears had taken in the information but her mind was baffled. Why would anyone want her heartbroken as payment for a debt?

"It doesn't make sense. It just doesn't make sense, Percy." She exclaimed. "Besides which we are married now, so how are we going to settle your debt now?" She asked.

Percy was heartened by her use of the word "we" and told her that George was loaning him the necessary to repay the money he owed as soon as the banks opened on Monday morning.

"What about paying George back?" Cathy asked.

"I've already arranged to sell off some off my assets to do that. It will take a couple of weeks but George is willing to wait for me to get it to him." Percy admitted.

"Well, you certainly have a good friend in him." Cathy stated feelingly before adding, "Are there any more surprises that I should know about, Mr. Percy Greystoke?"

Percy assured her that there were no more secrets between them. Then he blushed and rather sheepishly told her that he had forgotten to mention that he had a title. He was, in fact, Lord Percival Marmaduke Greystoke and she as a result would now be Lady Greystoke.

"Well, at least that is something I can live with!" She assured him.

Percy was very relieved to hear that as he couldn't bear to think of losing Cathy. She meant so much to him and he was so lucky to have found love this late in his life.

When Anna was sent to look for them some thirty minutes later, it was a very subdued couple that assured her that they would be along shortly, not the bubbly bride and groom who had emerged from the church into the autumn sunshine. When she returned to the village hall Anna did her best not to show the others her concern and told them that the bride and groom would be along momentarily. Sure enough five minutes later, they were. The evening continued with dancing and congratulatory hugs from all as they gradually slipped away to return to their homes. Soon it was only the bridal party themselves that remained, the caterers having packed up their things and left too.

Jackson turned and surveyed the colourful but empty space and asked, "Shall we clear away now or in the morning?"

Anna clearly said, "This will all wait until then but we will not be leaving until we find out what is wrong with you and Percy, Cathy."

Cathy looked at Percy as the others all focussed their attention on the couple. What's up written all over their faces? At Cathy's gentle smile of encouragement, Percy nodded his consent, so she started. "I didn't think that we could fool you that all was well. You girls have always been able to tell when something was bothering me, I think that it is best if we get this over and done with now. I've never been able to keep secrets for long and I have a feeling that this one will be better out than in."

The others gathered round a table and sat themselves down ready to learn what this one was.

Cathy gave them a carefully edited version of what had transpired and Percy told them that George had kindly loaned him the funds to put things right again and that it would all be fine now. Jackson found Craig's eyes and they exchanged a nod of understanding. They had been right all along about Mr. Percy Greystoke being a funny one.

Anna was outraged. "Did you not think that you should have given Cathy the option of deciding whether she wanted to marry a gambler or not before she walked down the aisle today?" She almost shouted across the table at Percy, who had at least had the grace to blush, before Cathy leapt to his defence.

Cathy told the girls in no uncertain terms that she would have married Percy anyway, "But I am glad that he decided to tell me today." She followed up with.

The others in the circle nodded their own agreement with that. Jackson sensed that there was actually more to the story than they were being given and wondered just how deeply Percy had been sucked into such a mess. Maybe some follow up enquiries might be a good move.

Whereas Jeni was concerned to ask; "Would it all be behind them before they left for their honeymoon?"

"Yes, yes." Said Percy. "I will take the money transfer to the man concerned first thing on Monday on our way to the airport and all will be well."

Anna sharply interjected, "Just don't forget to get your I.O.U. back and a receipt for the money you give him. In fact, write one out before you go and then all he has to do is sign it."

"That's sound advice, Percy. Just mind you heed it." Jackson was quick to add.

Nodding vigorously, Percy assured them all that he would.

It was then that Leon suggested that they all ought to be packing up the wedding presents now and putting them in the designated cars to be transported to Cathy's cottage. The next fifteen minutes were hustling and bustling as they followed the plan. Then it was good nights all round as the bride and groom left for the bridal suite at the local hotel and the others to see the rest of the night out in their various accommodations before meeting early the next morning to finish the rest of the clearing up together.

It was a sunny and bright morning with a residue of summer in the air when they joined up and after eating a hearty breakfast to keep their sugar levels up for the task ahead. They went to work throughout the hall and kitchen restoring everything to its former pristine state. The chatter was of the revelations of the previous day. Craig and Jackson had agreed that they would each pursue their individual enquiries and see if they could learn more about the difficulties that Percy had plunged into. The girls were far more concerned about Cathy and Percy's relationship. Would it grow stronger or had this set their feet on a very rocky path? Anna knew that Cathy had fallen for Percy hard and could understand that she would still want to go ahead with her marriage. Jo, however, thought that she should have decided to have it annulled immediately. Jeni's was the voice of reason; as she told them all as they gathered ready to make their move back to the cottage, there was nothing that they could or should do.

"This is their marriage and they love each other and we must not interfere." Anna said. The group reluctantly agreed that what she said was true and that they would abide by it. The weekend was over and they had all to return to their normal lives and leave the new Mr. and Mrs. Greystoke to start theirs.

Devon Chance was not happy to have to deliver his report that evening. He knew that it would not go down well with his boss. He knew no other way round the matter and so just bit the bullet and told it as it was and got out of range as fast he possibly could. A lesson that others would have done well to adopt when doing their reports. That the man could hardly refuse the full payment of the debt from the new Mrs. Greystoke when Cathy was determined to see for herself this job through to the end. Her insistence that she should retain the I.O.U., rather than accepting his offer to burn it later was only agreed to with reluctance. The receipt for the monies paid being signed under duress too. As for Mr. Big? He was definitely not amused. His plan for chaos and harm being thwarted once again by honesty and goodness. It couldn't go on. All this incompetence. He needed to act. There was going to be an almighty show down.

Chapter Twenty Nine

JENI JUST COULDN'T understand why Jackson was being so secretive. After the debacle with Percy, she thought that he would have known better than to try and keep anything hidden from her. But she knew that he was up to something and doing his best to cover his tracks. Jeni had discussed it with her girlfriends but they had no help to offer her. They only wanted to know one thing.

"Have you found The Dress yet?" No, she hadn't. The date was now set and she still hadn't got what she had always dreamt of, but there was really not enough time to have a dress made even if someone could follow her rambled description of what she wanted.

"What was she going to do?" Anna had asked her.

"Hopefully find the perfect dress by the end of my shopping trip to Edinburgh with Jo next Saturday," her friend replied. Last Saturday had been spent in Glasgow scouring every place they could find but they had returned home footsore and weary, despite having worn trainers all day, but with no wedding dress. The bridesmaids all had their dresses and had even managed to have the necessary alterations completed by now. Tension was mounting but Jeni was convinced that she would find the very thing in the wonders of the capital city.

Anna wasn't so sure, but Anna had enough issues of her own to deal with. She had a business trip to Spain to go on that week and she put down the phone on Jeni after their usual farewell and climbed the stairs to their bedroom to pack her suitcase for the week ahead.

Leon told her over their dinner that night that he was going to take her to the airport before going into work the next morning. His boss had been forewarned and wasn't expecting him until half ten and it would make it easier for Anna than having to take the tube into London to catch the Gatwick Express out to the airport. Anna smiled and thanked him for his consideration.

"You really do look after me very well husband dear." She told him.

"I aim to please." He grinned his reply as he cleared the dinner plates off the table.

"I think I'll just have to keep you then." She quipped back as he took them off to the kitchen. Anna smiled again as she realised that it was this light hearted banter that they shared she would miss most during their few days apart. Married life had certainly brought its joys.

Spain was still enjoying a long summer and the weather was very pleasant when Anna landed. She might even manage to top up her tan a little while she was here. Right now though there was work to be done. It wasn't until two whole days had passed before she was able to give herself a two hour break for lunch and perhaps a little shopping, she thought, at the end of a successful morning of meetings. She quickly packed away her "props" and made her way down to reception and asked for somewhere she could get a quick bite before hitting the shopping sector of the city. Following the instructions given she found the small bistro not too far from the hotel and her appetite assuaged she quickened her pace to hit the main shops. Just before she reached Barcelona's version of Oxford Street or Rodeo Drive her peripheral vision caught sight of a young woman rushing across the road towards her. Almost as soon as she did she crashed into her. In her arms was a white, dustcover wrapped, garment which promptly dropped to the ground. They both scrambled to pick it up and bumped again.

This time Anna said. "Just catch your breath a minute and I'll pick it up for you."

The young woman was halted in her tracks by Anna's impeccable Spanish and Anna was able to retrieve the garment bag without further risk to life and limb. She gave it a little shake to resettle the contents and noticed some rather fine lace through the clear window in the top of the bag. It looked gorgeous. She wouldn't mind a proper look at the contents. It might even be a wedding dress. She thought to herself. She was surprised to learn that she had expressed herself out loud, when the young woman responded with, "In that case, you'll just have to come in here with me and see it in all its glory." While she opened the heavy plate glass door and encouraged Anna to step into the air-conditioned entrance hall, still carrying the garment bag.

From the elegant navy blue and white tiled floor to the pristine white paintwork and colourful paintings on white eggshell walls everything shrieked expensive and tasteful. Anna wondered where she could possibly be. The décor could be anything from a private house to a chic boutique hotel or the private offices of a multimillion pound company there was just nothing to say which. The young woman introduced herself as Margarita Consuela Fortunata but my English friends call me Maggie and welcome to my home, as she stretched out her hand to take Anna's. Anna had to give herself a mental shake as she appreciated what a wealthy background Maggie must have to live in such a fabulous place. Anna reciprocated with her own credentials.

"Do you live here in Barcelona, Anna?" Maggie asked her.

"I'm just here for a few days to conduct some business for a client and then I'll be returning to London's grey skies." Anna told her. Maggie then complimented her on her excellent Spanish accent and speech before asking her what line of business she was in. Anna filled her in briefly on her new role and Maggie surprised her by suggesting that she could possibly be of some help to her if she was looking for any new clients in Barcelona. Not one to look a gift horse in the mouth, Anna produced her business card to give to her. Maggie carefully placed it on a low table beside the smart sofa that she had laid the garment bag out on. Then she started to open up the bag itself and remove its contents.

Anna couldn't help a gasp as Maggie revealed a beautiful wedding gown made of exquisite lace over a shimmering, oyster white, heavy satin under-dress. The cut was simple but fabulous. The lace pattern crusted with swirls of pearls. It was stunning! Maggie turned the garment around to reveal the back view. It was equally or perhaps even more beautiful than the front. The under-dress being cut to show some of the shoulder but the lace not so. Tiny pearl buttons fastened the dress at the side to allow ease of access for putting it on. The dress then flowed to the floor in a demi-train or maybe it was called a fishtail. Anna couldn't remember which. She was just too bemused by its beauty. All she could think was how wonderful Jeni would look in it.

Maggie loved the way Anna was looking at her dress. It was just how she imagined the guests at a wedding would look when they saw the bride come in wearing the dress. Feeling very self-satisfied she asked Anna. "Do you like it?"

Anna was so under its spell that she could barely croak out that she thought it was absolutely stunning. Maggie was more than pleased with that. She knew now that she had fulfilled her brief and created a truly amazing design. Anna quietly asked if she could take a closer look. With a nod of assent from Maggie she approached closer still. In close up, Anna, could see the workmanship of some very talented seamstress and the cleverness of the cut, for shaping the garment to its wearer. She turned to Maggie and told her. "It's a work of art, Maggie. As beautiful in its own way as any Old Master. Can I ask who the designer is please? I have a friend looking for the perfect dress for her big day and I think that I've just found it for her."

Maggie appeared to grow taller in front of Anna's eyes as she held her head proudly and said. "I designed it."

Anna was astonished that someone who looked so young could have made such a wondrous garment. She was obviously very gifted. Anna asked if she had been designing wedding dresses very long whilst realising that that was hardly possible given her youthful appearance. Maggie still managed to surprise her again when she told her that this was her very first creation and only just completed that very morning.

"All I can say Maggie, is that you are going to be a force to be reckoned with in the field of Wedding Fashion if this is anything to go by. My company would love to be able to have such unique gowns to offer in their bridal boutique." Anna told her.

At this, all the sophistication that Maggie had been projecting fell away and the emotions of her race came through when she burst into tears, while all the time saying how much she appreciated all the compliments. Anna quickly whipped out a clean tissue and mopped up her tear stained face just as a distinguished looking older man appeared on the scene. He immediately demanded to know what Maggie was making such a noise for and a verbal torrent came forth from Maggie's lips in rapid response.

"Margarita Consuela De Fortunata Cristobel, please remember where you are and compose yourself before your guest flees the building thinking that she has entered a madhouse." He told her in a stern and stiff tone.

When silence reigned again, he asked her to kindly introduce her guest. Maggie once again produced her sophisticated self and made the formal introductions.

"Anna Lewis, may I present to you Don Juan Manuel De Fortunata Cristobel." Maggie intoned clearly and with warmth. Almost in an aside she said. "He's my grandfather too."

Don Juan Manuel held out his hand and shook Anna's firmly. This was no frail and feeble old man. He was a man in command of others and more importantly, in command of himself.

"Now Anna Lewis, what brings you to our lovely city?" He asked her.

Anna told him succinctly and only added that she had met Maggie in the street outside when they had bumped into each other and Maggie had dropped her garment bag. At this point a twinkle appeared in the man's eye. He was obviously used to his grand-daughters escapades. What he was not used to however, was her inviting a stranger to come into her home with her on first meeting. At this point it was Maggie's turn to leap in with the story of how she had finally finished her gown and was bringing it over to show him it. She stood back and let him see the wedding dress draped over the sofa. He looked carefully. Not rushing but as if savouring a well presented delectable plate of the finest food. Then he asked her to hold it up and then to turn it around that he might see the back view. Not once did he allow himself to be distracted by the girls in his presence.

"Well?" Maggie asked.

His reply. "Yes. Very well." Said all that needed to be said as far as Margarita Consuela Fortunata was concerned. He approved!

At the silence that followed Anna felt compelled to add her penny's worth. "I for one, think that it is the most beautiful and beautifully made dress that I have ever seen. The design is absolutely exquisite."

Don Juan drew himself up to his full height of five foot ten inches and proudly said. "But of course, it is designed by Margarita Consuela De Fortunata Cristobel of the new House of Fortunata."

At which the dress found itself unceremoniously dropped back onto the sofa and the old man was hugged and smothered in kisses by a rather excitable, large, jumping bean. After tolerating it for a couple of minutes he held her gently away from him and reminded Maggie again about Anna's presence. Maggie was quick to assure him that Anna would understand her excitement at having her very own fashion house to design for. Anna looked at Maggie and saw only a girl whose dream had just come true. It was at that moment that the gown decided to slip gracefully from the sofa and down onto the floor.

"Oh no." Anna exclaimed as she tried fruitlessly to stop its fall. "Your beautiful dress, Maggie!"

"Don't worry about it, Anna. In fact, why don't you have it to take to your friend who's getting married; a little gift from your new Spanish friend."

Anna protested that she couldn't possible accept such an expensive gift, even on her friend Jeni's behalf. Maggie half turned to her grandfather and imperiously demanded, that he should make Anna take it. Don Juan was laughing as he looked beseechingly at Anna and asked her to please accept the gift as otherwise how could he ever hope to regain any authority over his grand-daughter if he could not even arrange such a simple matter for her, whilst shrugging his shoulders eloquently.

Anna couldn't believe it. She had been given the perfect dress for her perfectly lovely friend, Jeni. How incredible was that? She knew that she couldn't possibly afford to pay for the gown but perhaps she could repay Maggie in kind by ensuring that she would have one of the best bridal boutiques in London exclusively market and sell her designer wedding gowns. The suggestion was greeted with enthusiasm by both Maggie and her grandfather, subject to contract, of course.

When she returned to London two days later it was having made at least two new friends in Barcelona, in Maggie and Don Juan. Plus, a new supplier for the company. In addition, over dinner on her last evening with them in a very swanky restaurant, she had been introduced to a couple of potential new clients for her new business. Things were on the up. When Tilly rang shortly after Anna got in from the airport that night to ask if she had anything that she wanted taken up to Jeni that weekend Anna was able to say yes. A special box.

Tilly said that she would swing by in an hour to pick it up on her way to the airport.

"Is Martin giving you a ride?" Anna asked her.

"Yes, it's a bit last minute as he only just told me that he has a space free in his plane and Jeni wants me to come up and help her hunt down the perfect dress. Three sets of eyes being better than two!"

Anna chuckled and said, "I may have something to say about that one."

"What do you mean Mrs. Anna Lewis?" Tilly quizzed her.

"Just you wait and see, Tilly Brown." She replied mysteriously. A cheery "bye for now" and Anna was able to rush upstairs and get the box tied up securely for transporting and write a hasty note for Tilly to give to Jeni with very strict instructions not to open it until Tilly and Jo were there with her and one was on loudspeaker on an open line to Anna while the other used her camera phone to video it all.

She had only just managed to get it all done before the doorbell rang. But it was only Leon not Tilly, so she swiftly pulled him in the door and gave him a long kiss. All thought to ask why Anna had left him locked out of his own house flew from the poor man's mind with that one.

"Well, I think you should go away a bit more often if that's the effect it has on you." He told her. "I rather like it."

Before she could utter a retort, the doorbell rang again. This time it was Tilly, and she was in a tearing hurry.

"I must fly, Anna. Oh, hi Leon. Sorry but Martin is waiting for the off and I got delayed in traffic. Must go. Bye!" All said as she grabbed the box and note proffered out of Anna's hands and flew back down the path and into the impatiently waiting car which sped off into the early evening light.

"Well that was definitely a flying visit, if you like." Leon concluded.

His wife just chuckled and told him. "All to the good, as I have plans for you!"

Leon seeing the twinkle in her eye and replied. "Oh yes, She Who Must Be Obeyed."

Jackson moaned again. His feet were killing him and there was still another twenty minutes to go. To think that he had thought that he was reasonably fit. He had never realised how fit you had to be to make the grade as a professional dancer. It was certainly a lot harder than he thought it would be. However, Madame Nijinsky came highly recommended and he did seem to be making progress despite all her head shaking and tut tutting. All he had wanted was a few lessons to enable him to lead Jeni confidently in the first dance of their marriage. He didn't want his clumsiness on the dance floor to embarrass Jeni on their big day.

Madame Nijinsky stamped her foot once more for the pianist to play and once again and he was off again twirling with her round the floor. Then she stopped in her tracks and called for quiet before asking the pianist to fetch Kirsty into the room to dance with Jackson. Instantly Jackson felt very hot under the collar. He wasn't at all sure that he was up to dancing with a complete stranger. It had taken him long enough to get used to Madame. However, he would just have to suck it up and see how it went.

After fifteen minutes of being drilled about his posture, his hold and his heel leads he was both mentally and physically at the end of his tether. No one was more relieved than Jackson Redman when Madame Nijinsky called a halt. They changed and he returned to say his good byes. Madame Nijinsky beckoned him over and finally gave him a word of praise and encouragement.

"Mr. Redman, I am happy to announce that you have, at last, made progress. In another year I can perhaps enter you into a dance competition with your waltz. However, I feel confident now that you will not embarrass me with your dancing at your wedding. BUT! You may only dance the waltz and the salsa. Do not under any circumstances attempt any other dances. That way you can be assured of success."

With that, she saluted him on both cheeks and with a wave from her presence, dismissed him. With such high praise, Jackson left the building on cloud nine. He could dance; or he could at least dance a waltz and a salsa. Just to be on the safe side, he had downloaded the music they used in class so that it could be played at the reception. He felt that he had cracked the first dance with the bride and could now afford to relax a little. He got out his phone and called Fernando's number. It rang for some time before he answered.

"Yes Jackson. What's up?" He was asked. Jackson told him that he felt like celebrating and wondered if he was doing anything.

"Not at the moment." Came with an edge of reluctance down the line. "Tell you what, shall we meet at the pub in fifteen minutes?" He asked Jackson.

Jackson had agreed rapidly before Fernando changed his mind. He had been doing that a lot lately. Cancelling their plans at a moment's notice or not even ringing to explain his non-arrival. It was baffling. His behaviour was so unlike the Fernando he had known for most of his life. In fact, he didn't look much like him either, Jackson thought, as he watched Fernando come through the pub door with Candy clutching his arm. It was Jackson's good manners that prevented him from asking what she was doing there with Fernando.

Instead he greeted her with a "Nice to see you tonight Candy, I had thought that Fernando was on his own this evening." Jackson noticed that she didn't even bat an eyelid when he continued with, "Did you bump into each other on the way in?"

Fernando had a slightly awkward look about him.

"Actually, she was with me when I took your call and it seemed a good idea for her to come along too."

Not as far as Jackson was concerned. He had hardly had a private chat with Fernando since the night of his engagement party. Candy either interrupted in person or by cutting it short in some other way. It was as if she was trying to separate Fernando from his friends deliberately. He thought. Well two can play at that game.

The evening turned out to be battle of wills as they each tried to hold Fernando's attention on themselves and oust the other from Fernando's side. But Jackson had all the tenacity of a Scottish terrier whose bone was about to be filched from under his nose. His persistent charm of manner finally wore her down and she announced prettily for the room to hear, that she really ought to be getting home as she had an early start planned for the morning.

"Are you coming Fernando?" Candy had asked in a final fling.

Jackson looked at his friend and saw wariness in his eyes and then, as if with the flick of a switch, eagerness.

"Yes. We'll be off now, Jackson." What Jackson hadn't seen was the discreet signal Candy had given Fernando which called him to heel just like a well-trained dog.

No sooner said than done. Jackson found himself alone again and wondering just how she'd managed to do it.

When Mr. Big learnt the very next afternoon during prison visiting that Jackson and Fernando were estranged, he was delighted and insisted on a re-run of the tale. His plans were on track again and another nail had been banged into the coffin of Redman and his friendships and grinned all the way back to his cell.

His grin however was no match for the one that Anna saw when she took part in the conference call as Jeni opened her surprise box with Tilly and Jo. The shrieks of wonder and amazement were very satisfying. When they had got it out and seen the wedding gown in all its splendour, Jeni had ended up speechless. It was Tilly who told her that it was absolutely "The One" for her. Anna could only agree. The story of the dress was briefly told and Jeni's joy at being given it expressed. Her only question was. "Would it fit?"

When Tilly phoned Anna back some fifteen minutes later it was to show her the view of Jeni wearing it. It was Anna's turn to be speechless. Jeni looked magnificent in it. Like every bride should look and feel when wearing their wedding dress. It was quite simply perfection. Jeni and Tilly could only agree. When Jeni wanted to pay for the dress realising that it was couture and way beyond Anna's means, Anna had a suggestion. As this was a gift, could she pass it on to Jo when she was finished with it, if Jo ever had need of a wedding dress in the future?

"What a lovely idea, Anna." That taken care of Tilly rang off and the rest of the weekend was spent with Jo and Jeni finalising the wedding arrangements. It flew by and Tilly was being waved bye shortly after tea on Sunday evening sure in the knowledge that Jeni was a very happy bride to be now.

Chapter Thirty

THE MAN DID a mental check of what he would need that morning. The van with a full tank of petrol. Two large thick blankets. A roll of gaffer tape. An eye mask. A bottle of water. A packet of sandwiches. A packet of biscuits. An apple. A bucket plus a packet of wet wipes and a spade. Yes, that was the lot. A glance at his watch showed him that the time was now five o'clock. Time for the off. As he drove through the narrow roads to reach his destination he reviewed his instructions. He had to abduct Jo Lawson. He had to make sure that she didn't see him or have a chance to raise the alarm either. Once in his van, he had to drive her to a small croft. Its thick, rough stone walls and darkened by age thatch meant that it merged well into the surrounding landscape. It sat well off the beaten track in the hills some twenty odd miles away from Tillymurie. He was to unload her there with all the items from the van. The spade was to be left outside the croft. He was to put her in the windowless room. Then he was to free one of her hands only, to enable her to eat and drink etc. before leaving her to fend for herself. He had to lock the door of the room and double check that nothing had been left unlocked before he went to work at his normal time and from his usual direction. All this to be accomplished without saying a word or being seen by anyone.

He switched off his headlights as he approached Jo's cottage and turned off his engine to coast to a halt without disturbing her neighbour or Jo herself. Then he rummaged in his glove compartment for his full face ski mask to put on. Once he was sure that no hair or revealing feature was showing he quietly unlocked and opened the van door, making sure to leave it open and the side door open too. Another check round and as all was quiet he carried on up to the little house and round to the rear. He quietly let himself in with a copy of the back door key he had made when left for a moment alone in the office one day last week. She really ought to keep her spare house keys in the safe, he thought to himself. He crept up the stairs holding the bannister with his gloved hand and his "tools" in his free one. He knew which way to turn when he reached the top of the narrow steps and then stood like a silent ghost listening for any sounds of stirring. Nothing. He took a moment to envisage his next moves. Ready. He turned the handle slowly, glad to note that it didn't squeak. Two strides and he was at the bedside but there was no body lying in it! A flustered moment went by before he noticed the thin strip of light coming from under the ensuite bathroom door. He had only a second to get across the room and hidden in the darkness behind it as it started to push open. His heart was thumping with all the tension his body was under. He'd made it by a whisker. As Jo emerged from the small room he could see in its light that she was already dressed warmly for the working day ahead. Then he launched himself on her. He knocked her flat to the floor and all the wind out of her body. Jo never knew what hit her. He snapped a large plastic electrical tie over her wrists and pulled it tight before she could open her mouth to protest and as swiftly covered her mouth with one hand to prevent her screaming for rescue while he masked her eyes. That done, with the other he got his roll of tape out of his bag and efficiently fastened one end to one side of her mouth. Next thing Jo knew she was unable to make more than a mumble. Jo then found herself roughly stood on her feet and a blanket over her head. She tried to struggle and kicked out as hard as she could but he agilely dodged her violent kicks. His next move was to knock her down onto the bed. Once there he rapidly trapped her legs and bound both together at the ankles with the gaffer tape. Then he proceeded to do the same just below her knees. Now the blanket was taped round her hips. Not so tightly this time, she would need some access for air! It all took less than two minutes. The bag repacked, he then put it on his back and picked up her body. She got tossed over his shoulder and carried down the rickety narrow staircase as fast as he could safely carry her. It's a good job she doesn't weight much, he thought to himself.

All the while, Jo was screaming her panic in her head and doing her best to dislodge herself from his grip. Why was this happening to her? Who on earth was he? What was he going to do with her? All that went when she realised that she was outside now. It felt colder and damper. She was hot in the confines of the blanket but could feel the cold morning air on her lower body. Next she was lowered down onto something soft and she heard the soft click of a door being quietly being closed. Silence. Blackness. Fear. What was going on?

The silent man swiftly raced back up the path and into the house. He flew up the stairs once again and turned out the ensuite light. Then he gently drew back the bedroom curtains and pulled up the bed tidily before racing back down the staircase. He pulled the front door quietly shut behind himself and calmly walked swiftly back to his vehicle and got into the driver's seat and took off the ski mask. Door shut, seatbelt on. Another check all round to ensure no-one was looking out a window at him and then he let the handbrake off and rolled on down the lane before he engaged his engine and lights to get away and get away he did.

He drove on at a steady but rapid pace until he reached his destination. With no heed to the speed at which he took the many twists and turns in the roads he took, Jo was soon being rolled around the interior of the van. She whimpered every time she banged into something and as they were all harder than she was, it really hurt. She knew that she would be covered in heavy bruising if they didn't stop soon. It was with tears of relief when that happened and she heard the doors opening a few minutes later. They had arrived; but arrived where? The man had made his preparations well and he was now ready to transfer her into the only room in the cottage without a window. He'd thrown an old mattress onto the floor and put the bucket and foodstuffs into a corner. Jo was not going to lose this opportunity to make her presence known. She tried her best to shout through the tape over her mouth, kicking and doing all she could to draw attention to her plight. All in vain. She was carried once more over his shoulder and downwards into coldness. Once in the room and thrown roughly down onto the mattress, she found herself shivering as fear overtook her anger. Still the man hadn't said a word. He rolled her over onto her tummy and snipped the tie cutting into the soft flesh of her wrists. She started to lash out immediately and managed to land a hard punch right into what she thought might be an eye socket. Then he grabbed one arm and bound it behind her back again. The second he left free. Why? Jo puzzled. Then she felt him turn round and go away from her. She was being left alone. In the distance she heard the engine burst into life and the man drove off again. She knew that she was totally on her own now and she felt it.

Xander Smith drove swiftly back towards the glass studio knowing that he must arrive on time as they had not one but two very big orders to go out today. As he pulled up outside in his usual parking bay he could see through the office window that Shona and Drew were looking very anxious indeed. He casually walked up the path and opened the door into the reception area calling out his usual chirpy "Good morning folks."

Shona and Drew looked up eagerly when they heard the door go, but disappointment clouded their faces when they realised that it was only Xander making his presence known. He asked them what was up and they had to admit that they did not know what had happened to Jo. Shona started by telling him that the studio had not been unlocked when she arrived for work that morning but Xander pointed out, that wasn't such an unusual occurrence. What had raised the alarm was that Jo had left no message as to her whereabouts or instructions for the day. When Drew had arrived he had gone to the cottage to see if she was just running late while Shona had handled the incoming calls. His return with no news on Jo's whereabouts had them both baffled and concerned as it was so unlike her. More so, because they had a big order to get out that day. Shona quickly and with her usual decisiveness delegated the day's tasks to Drew and Xander and sent them to get on with them. Then she carefully closed the office door behind herself and sat down at Jo's desk. She dialled both the cottage phone and Jo's mobile again. Still no answer! After a seconds reflection she swiftly dialled Jeni's home number. She was worried.

Gloria answered the phone's persistent ring, correctly surmising that Jeni was in her study working on her latest book. When she realised that it was Shona from the studio calling she became much less cautious and told her that it was far too long since they had spoken and asked her how she was getting on with their new employee.

When Shona abruptly cut her off with, "I really must speak to Jeni urgently please, Gloria."

Gloria knew something must be up. Shona was such a laid back and chatty soul normally, it must be very serious. She assured Shona that she would put her through right away and asked her to hold the line. When Gloria explained why she was having to interrupt Jeni at her most productive time, Jeni became anxious too. The infection of fear was spreading.

Shona soon brought Jeni up to speed on the mysterious disappearance of her boss. Jeni asked immediately if they had tried Jo's phones and checked the cottage. Shona assured her that they had indeed done both.

"Are you sure that she hasn't had a fall and is lying on the floor upstairs or something?" Jeni asked. Shona told her that although they had looked into the cottage on the ground floor and found all well, they hadn't liked to use Jo's spare keys and enter her home without having her friend there to witness what they found. At once Jeni told her that she was leaving right away and would be with them as fast as she could and promptly rang off.

Jeni didn't have to go and look for Gloria as she just opened the study door to find her waiting outside. Gloria could see from her face that the call from Shona had not brought good news and asked, "Is there anything I can do to help?"

Jeni explained that she was leaving for Jo's cottage without delay as Jo was missing and they needed to find out if she had taken a fall upstairs before taking matters any further. Seeking to reassure Jeni, Gloria suggested that perhaps she had seen Fernando the previous evening and had not returned home yet. Jeni's face lightened for a moment at that thought, but then she soon shook her head. She knew her friend could not have kept a reconciliation to herself and certainly would not have stayed overnight at Fernando's place. They had made it a rule to wait for their weddings before spending the night with their men. They wanted to come to their marriages unsullied by baggage. It was something that they found that they had in common not long after they had met and their beliefs and views being so similar had encouraged the rapid growth of their friendship and that of those Jo had formed with Jeni's best friends Tilly and Anna. They were quite a quartet. However, right now she needed to find out what had happened to Jo and was soon racing along the roads to reach Jo's cottage.

As she drew up at the garden gate Jeni could see that not only was Shona waiting for her, but Drew and Xander were too. All looking very pinch-faced with care.

Her first question was, "Have you got Jo's spare keys, Shona?"

"Right in my hand, Jeni." Shona replied as she handed them over to Jeni.

Jeni had the door opened in a flash and they all trooped in as she called out Jo's name. Jeni looking round to check that all had been left as it should be. The ground floor was quickly checked as there was no response and then it was time to go upstairs. It's very quick to search a small cottage and none of them were surprised when they found no sign of Jo. They would have heard her call for help easily and there was no evidence of an accident or incident. It was baffling. The bedroom was neat and tidy with the bed already made but showing signs of having been slept in.

"Could she simply have gone for a walk?" Shona asked.

Jeni opened the wardrobe door to check for the outfit and footwear that was Jo's usual dress when she went for one of her rambles.

"No folks, her walking clothes are still here." She told them. Then she checked to see if Jo's overnight bag was missing. It may be that Jo had been called away to a family emergency. Gloom descended on them all when it was found to be in its usual spot too.

By now Jeni had a sinking feeling in the pit of her stomach. She was more than worried now. She could feel the fear flowing through her veins. She had a dreadful sense of déjà vu. However, she didn't want Jo's staff to be worried too and so she brightly suggested that she would give a few of Jo's friends a call to see if they knew where she might be while they carried on their work as usual. "After all, isn't it today that your biggest shipment yet is going out?" She queried.

Drew hastened to assure Jeni that it was and they would get right on to it now. He and Xander turned and left to do just that.

Shona, not fooled by the bright smile Jeni had put on, quietly asked her, "What's your plan now?" Jeni held out her hands palms upwards and shrugged her shoulders. It was eloquent enough for Shona to carry on with the suggestion she had just thought of.

"Do you think that it might be an idea to give your very helpful fiancé a call?"

Jeni thought it just the right thing to do. Even the thought of Jackson Redman made her feel calmer and stronger. Shona took herself out of the cottage and back to the reception again. If nothing else, she could be useful by carrying out her normal duties and keeping on top of the telephone enquiries, which were getting a bigger issue day by day as Anna's new advertising promotion was reaching a larger audience every week it seemed.

In the meantime, Jeni was dialling Jackson's number. When she told him where she was and what was concerning her he promised that he would be with her very shortly and tried to reassure her that Jo would be fine.

On the drive to Jo's cottage Jackson tried to assimilate all the information that had tumbled from Jeni's trembling lips. He too thought that Jo's disappearance was totally out of character with the girl he knew and had grown very fond of over the past months. However, his practical nature would not allow him to jump to any conclusions without any hard evidence to back them up. After fifteen minutes examining Jo's cottage and even taking a walk over to the studio too, he was no further forward as to an explanation for her sudden disappearance. Drew and Xander had already left to do their deliveries but he had questioned Shona carefully about Jo's demeanour over the previous couple of days. Other than the lingering air to quiet sadness that seemed to hang over Jo ever since her broken engagement, Shona could not think of anything untoward in Jo's behaviour. As Jeni couldn't either his recourse was to suggest that Jeni contact Jo's parents, carefully sounding them out as to her whereabouts without alerting them to her disappearance. Shona was delegated the task of double checking Jo's office for any overlooked appointment or mail that could enlighten them further. He left them going about these tasks while he decided that he ought to try Fernando, even if it was just to eliminate that avenue from their enquiries.

Fernando heard his mobile phone ring and turned it over to check the Caller ID. It was Jackson. He decided that he didn't want to speak to him. He would want explanations and Fernando knew he didn't have any. However, when a text followed seconds later he was curious enough to want to know what it said. What he read had him reaching for his jacket and telling his receptionist that he had to go out urgently but that he could be reached on his mobile, if necessary. All sign of sluggishness was gone as the adrenaline flooded through his body at the thought that his Jo was missing and she didn't even know how much he really loved her. He rushed to get his car and sped recklessly along the familiar route to Jo's cottage. He couldn't get there quick enough. After almost colliding with a tractor emerging from the field gateway onto the road he realised that it wouldn't help Jo's cause any if managed to get himself killed on the way.

Jackson's hope for Fernando's return to normality, soared when he saw his car screeching to a halt at Jo's gate. This was the Fernando he knew and loved. His concern for Jo obvious to the world with every worry line on his handsome face. Jackson felt the tension in his body relax fractionally. Now they would work together and find her. The thought that this wasn't the first time Jo had gone missing popped into his head. Fear chilled him as he flung the door open to let Fernando enter. He found himself being hugged and questioned all at the same time.

"Any more news?" "Who discovered that she was missing?" "Does Jeni know where she is?" Fernando fired at him.

"No I don't! I only wish that I did! I'm so worried and afraid after what happened last time." Jeni told him.

Jackson and Fernando both turned to her and asked why she thought that Jo's disappearance could have anything to do with Mr. Big when he was banged up in prison hundreds of miles away?

"How do I know? All I know as this doesn't feel right and as he is the only bad man we've ever run across, I just know that it has to be his fault!" She said tearfully.

She had tried not to let herself get worked up but now sheer terror was getting a grip as her, always vivid, imagination created scenario after scenario for her to be frightened by on Jo's behalf. Jackson quietly took her hand and pulled her close. Time for a hug. Quietly he tried to reassure her, Fernando and himself that there would be a simple explanation for Jo's absence and they would all be laughing about it before the day was out. He just wished he had believed it himself, for then he might have sounded more convincing. However, now was not the time for doing nothing! He asked Jeni if Jo's parents had given them any clues. Her shaking head told him otherwise. What to do next became the priority.

It was time to call in a few favours and get Jo found.

The call to Commander Angus Guthrie of the Kyle of Drumcrae Constabulary, was put through immediately

Jackson gave his name to the Duty Officer, such was the respect shown for his previous work with them. Angus Guthrie was surprised though to learn that his first call for the day and an early one at that, was to be from Jackson Redman, but not overly concerned. He knew that his team had done a good job in rounding up all those concerned in the abduction of Jackson's friends and such a major case had brought them some well-deserved recognition. However, he was curious as to what he needed help with this time and so his greeting was warm but cautious.

"Well good morning to you Mr. Redman, I thought that you would be too busy catching up with your paperwork to be needing our services again so soon. Lost your dog or something?" He chuckled down the line.

Jackson skipped the formalities and rushed straight into his dire need.

"I'll fill you in with as much as I know but this one will need to take priority over everything today, Sir."

As concisely as he could Jackson told him what the morning light had revealed. Angus Guthrie then asked if he thought that this could be linked to their previous case together.

When told that there may well be a connection; but the motive for Jo's disappearance was not at all clear, Guthrie was quick to ask Jackson, "What ground have you covered so far?"

Having ascertained that the results of the initial enquiries made had been totally negative, he remarked to Jackson.

"This does look like an abduction after all and a professional one at that." He promised Jackson that he would re-direct the forces at his command to pursue all the usual procedures in these cases at once. He was not going to delay until the normal period for a missing person case to be opened in this situation. The risk to Jo Lawson's safety was too great. He excused himself to commence action with one last request. "Can you confirm that the contact details we have for the various parties are still operational, please?"

Jackson confirmed the same and told him that he would be obtaining further assistance from his own superiors to ensure enough manpower would be available to them and their conversation was swiftly ended to allow them both to carry on with the search.

Once he had done all that he could for now, he went in search of Jeni and found her at the studio, sitting a Jo's desk and with the phone to her ear. He realised that she must be talking to Tilly or Anna from her end of her conversation, but at her shake of her head that there was nothing to be gained by interrupting her. He turned round and walked back out to the reception desk and addressed himself to Shona Adams. He gave her a heads up as to the imminent arrival of the police from Drumcrae and asked her to let the other staff to know and ask for their full co-operation.

"Of course Mr. Redman! I'll give both Drew and Xander a call and get them to return straight after they have made their deliveries. They should only be about another hour as we just had the two major clients to deal with today and they are as anxious about Jo as we are." She assured him.

Jackson thanked her and in a more casual tone asked how Xander Smith was settling in. She told him that though it was only a couple of months that he had been with them it felt like longer, as he had fitted into the dynamics of the business so quickly and well.

"Nothing seems like too much trouble for him and he has proved a very willing worker for Jo." She told him.

"How did Jo find such a treasure in this day and age?" Jackson probed. Having been filled in on the details, Jackson quickly closed down the conversation with the excuse that he thought that Jeni had finished her call and he needed a word with her to bring her up to speed. In actual fact, he needed to inform Angus Guthrie of this new possible line of enquiry a.s.a.p.

Jeni had ended her call to Tilly a few minutes before but had no sooner put it down than Anna had come on the line. Having assured them both that everything possible was being done to find Jo and fielded all the questions she could she had used Jackson and Fernando's appearance in the office as an excuse to end her call far more abruptly than usual, but with the assurance that she would let them know the moment any news was forthcoming.

Fernando was the one who had met the police officers assigned to the case on the garden path and when his identity had been checked out offered to let two into the cottage to carry out their investigation, directed another to the neighbour's front door and was taking Michael Graeme, the plain clothes officer from the Kyle of Drumcrae Police Station who had been assigned to Jackson as his assistant to help find Jeni, straight to the studio in search of them. The relief at seeing a familiar face helped Jeni to feel a bit more confident that the police would be able to help them find Jo quickly. She knew that Michael had worked alongside Jackson last time and proved useful and prayed that he would be so again. His firm handshakes all round gave them all more confidence in a happy outcome that had been lacking when they had been living in the bubble of their own fears. It felt as though progress could and would be made now. An illogical perception given the dearth of clues to Jo's whereabouts perhaps, but a glimpse of light at the end of a very dark tunnel nevertheless.

Jackson slipped out and asked Shona if she could provide them all with a cup of coffee before re-joining the three to bring Michael up to speed. Jeni had completed her part of the tale when Shona brought in the tray of coffee and biscuits. When she left it was his turn to expand the details of the enquiries that had been made. Michael made notes of it all and asked questions as they went through it all, but it was Fernando who summed the situation up. "This was no accidental happening." He told the room. "Jo has deliberately been targeted but I cannot for the life of me see why."

Michael told them that he agreed. "This is definitely a professional job, if your initial assessment of the care taken at the cottage to make it look as normal as possible was to delay any useful enquiries being carried out for as long as possible." He stated. "However, having such a loyal staff and circle of friends has meant that we now have a quicker start on the road to her recovery!" "I have just a few more questions for you Jackson, if you two don't mind if we let you carry on with drinking your coffee for a minute or so, while we walk over to the cottage." He said as he led Jackson out of the room. Jeni and Fernando nodded their assent and returned to their own silent contemplation of their coffee cups.

As Jackson and Michael covered the ground to the cottage door Michael told Jackson what measures had been put into place by Commander Guthrie and told him what steps he would take next. By now they were inside and the two men that Michael had allocated the job of examining the cottage came together to give him their report. It was a simple one. There were no obvious signs of a struggle or damage to the property. No blood or other forensic evidence at all. The cottage only showed its normal usage as far as they could discover. In one way this was disappointing; but it confirmed for Jackson, the professionalism of the kidnapping and showed the planning and care that had been taken. However, it would not help them to find Jo. What they needed was some sort of a clue as to how someone could have taken her.

It came when the younger of the two policemen said that he had examined the locks on both doors into the cottage and found nothing on the front door or the back door to indicate a break in by an intruder. What he had found though, were some minute pieces of metal in the rear door lock itself. He thought that they may just have come from a newly cut key being used for the first time. Michael turned to Jackson to ask if he knew whether Jo had a new key cut recently. Jackson shook his head. It hadn't been mentioned; but they could soon ask Shona to find out the answer to that question. Michael delegated the task to the young man and asked the older one to remove the lock carefully from the door and bag it up and send it off to the lab for a more detailed analysis.

The sound of another arrival at the front of the house had them walking into the hallway to find the policeman dispatched to talk to the closest neighbours coming in to make his report. At the go ahead from Michael, he gave a quick rundown on what he had learnt from his investigations. Most of the neighbours in the three houses in the road had been asleep in their beds and neither heard or saw anything. The nearest neighbour, a

Mrs. Shelley Green, was however, a lighter sleeper. She had been having a disturbed night and decided to come downstairs to make herself a cup of tea. Having made it she had taken it into her lounge to sit and drink it. Not feeling like reading or anything she hadn't put a light on but just sat down in her favourite window seat to sip it while enjoying the view of her garden in the peace and quiet of the pre-dawn moonlight. Although she had heard no sounds of a vehicle or even seen any lights she thought she had seen a vehicle going down the lane towards the main road.

"How certain did she seem about what she had seen?" Michael asked the young man.

"Oh, quite positive, Sir." Was his eager reply.

"Was there anything else she said that might be of help?" Michael continued.

"No sir." He replied. "Mrs. Green had dismissed it when it moved out of sight and had taken herself back to her bed and knew nothing of Miss Lawson's disappearance until I arrived on the scene, Sir." He stated. His report now finished he stood quietly to attention awaiting further instructions.

Michael told him to return to Mrs. Green and ask if she would mind accompanying him to Jo's office at the studio. Then he and Jackson returned there while the lady was fetched.

Michael then asked Jeni if she would be kind enough to look more carefully at Jo's clothes and see if she could work out what she might be wearing for him and if her handbag was missing. He asked Fernando to check with Shona if any money had been removed from the safe or petty cash from the office just as Mrs. Green made her appearance.

Jackson stood behind Michael while he sat in Jo's chair at her desk and Mrs. Green was settled on the visitor seat opposite it. Michael introduced himself and Jackson to her. Shelley Green told him that she had met Jackson briefly before when he had been visiting Jo with his fiancée, Jeni, one day. Jackson acknowledged this information with a quick nod. Now that she was settled in her chair, Michael felt that he could get on with his job and begin to question her as to the facts of the previous night and try and find out if she knew anything more helpful that she might not have mentioned to the police constable. Sadly, nothing else turned up. However, when Jackson casually asked how she thought Jo's new van driver was fitting in? That did illicit a different response to what he was expecting.

Shelly Green had a very different opinion on the man to Shona and Drew. In her view Xander Smith was not a very nice or considerate man at all. Jackson was eager to learn why the man should provoke such diverse opinions as to his character and Mrs. Green was nothing loath to tell him why. It turned out that it all stemmed from earlier than his starting to work at the glassworks studio. He had apparently annoyed Mrs. Green by throwing rubbish into her garden when he parked right by her hedge when visiting the lane.

Michael wanted to know if she could remember what day that was and the date, if possible and even if she knew what the rubbish was that he had tossed over her hedge.

Of course she did, she'd had to pick it up. It had been a Monday and he hadn't started working for Jo until a week later, on the following Monday. Jo had come in that weekend on the Sunday evening to let her know that she would be seeing a new face around as she had hired a new driver to work alongside Drew. Shelley told the two men that Jo had always been a considerate neighbour that way so, she was quite sure of her facts. Her indignation was apparent, as she went on to tell them that she had seen the man throw the paper bag containing the leftover food from a well-known fast food chain over her hedge. She had gone out to remonstrate with him but when he had seen her coming he had high-tailed it off down the lane at a rate of knots.

She then commented, "I was a bit surprised when Jo told me he was the man she had hired. However, I thought that it must just have been a one off and gave him the benefit of the doubt." She then hesitated for a moment; as if wondering or arguing with herself over whether to tell them more. The two men waited patiently. Having won her argument with herself, she then told them what had made her more doubtful about Xander Smith. "It was what he did next that made me think that he was a strange one." She continued. "He came back on the Tuesday morning the following week a-knocking at my front door with a bunch of flowers to apologise for being a litter lout. They were from a local garage and not very expensive at that. She told them. He just thrust them into my hand and said his sorry and strode off." She put her head on one side and after another moment's thought added. "It was almost as if he resented having to do it, as if someone else had told him to and he didn't want to." she came out with, as if she had only just thought of the idea.

The two men's gazes met. This was more like it. They now had a suspect. A rotten apple had turned up in the barrel. After a further minute or two Michael was able to wrap up his interview and send Shelley Green back home with his sincere assurance that she had been of great help to the search for Jo. A quick conflab with Jackson and a way forward was mapped out. The first step was to bring Xander Smith in for questioning without arousing his suspicion. Jackson went to learn if Shona had got hold of Drew and Xander. Yes, she had. They were on their way back to base.

When did she think they would arrive, he had asked her next.

Shona looked up and out of the adjacent window before answering. "Well, this looks like Xander arriving now and Drew will be here in about five more minutes. Does that suit?"

Jackson thanked her and swiftly returned to the office to tell Michael to expect Xander Smith momentarily. He then went back into reception and propped himself up on Shona's counter as if he was waiting around to be told what he could do next and getting rather fed up with it all. Or so Xander Smith thought, when he saw him seconds later as he came through the outside door. He greeted them both with a good display of anxious concern and asked immediately if there was any news of Jo.

Shona's sad "Not a word."

It was music to his ears but none of that was reflected in his face or demeanour. Jackson was now convinced that he was their kidnapper and more than grateful that Shelley Green was a keen observer and judge of character for without her help they would have been stuck in limbo for goodness knows how long.

Shona went on to tell Xander that the police were here now and would want to speak to him, and Drew on his return too.

At that moment, as if on cue, Michael stuck his head round the office door and asked, "Have any of the drivers come back yet?"

Shona was able to tell him that Xander Smith had just returned that minute. Michael came out then and asked Xander into the office for a chat. Jackson saw the door shut firmly and asked Shona if she would mind popping over to the cottage to take a message to Jeni for him.

"Not at all, I'll just switch the phone to automatic messaging and go right away." She told him. Jackson explained what he wanted and off she went. Jackson felt happier when she was safely out of harms reach and positioned himself outside the office door to run interception if Mr. Smith should make a run for it. In the meantime, he rang Angus Guthrie and updated him swiftly and asked him to pass the latest onto his own boss for him.

"Certainly. That's no problem and well done. Let me know the outcome as soon as you can, I'll be waiting for your call." Commander Guthrie told him.

Jackson could now hear the scraping back of chairs and the office door opened. All seemed calm so, Jackson stayed put seated and waited to see what happened next. Michael was shaking Xander's hand and thanking him for his co-operation. The man appeared to be very relaxed and not at all wary. All well and good there then, Jackson thought.

After Xander had returned to the warehouse part of the building Jackson quietly asked for Michael's impressions of the man. Michael told him that his instinct was that they had found their man but that he was merely a hired hand. Professional true; but not the one in charge, not the one who knew the reason behind what had happened, just the tool for a job. He had decided that it was better not to alert him to their suspicions, but instead to have him watched and followed in the hopes that he would give away Jo's whereabouts. Jackson nodded his approval of this plan of action just as Shona returned with Jeni hard on her heels. The next few minutes saw Jeni give Michael a very detailed description of Jo's clothing that was missing and the news that she must not be wearing any shoes. "How do you know that, Miss?" Michael asked.

"Well, I checked all her footwear and everything was there down to her wellies. Shona helped and agreed nothing was gone too." She informed him.

"Bare feet or socks only, is confirmation that we are dealing with an abduction. I shall have to make a full report to my boss right away so, if you'll excuse me I'll do that in the office and join you in reception momentarily." He told them.

Jackson took Jeni's arm and led her back into Shona's domain and turned to them both as the door shut behind Michael Graeme. He had decided that he would brief them both together to save time and hence, started how he meant to go on before he got distracted from the task in hand. He told them that the police would want them not to reveal to anyone that they were interested in Xander Smith. Not even Drew was to be alerted for fear of scaring Mr. Smith into running before they had been able to find out where he had hidden Jo away or who was behind it all. Both women vigorously nodded their agreement but didn't interrupt his flow. He asked them to continue as normally as they possibly could, but not to place themselves in any danger and the rest would be dealt with by the police or himself. At this point Fernando appeared again. Jackson had almost forgotten that Fernando had been on the scene earlier and now wondered what his friend had been up to all this time. He was to find out soon enough.

Fernando had gone and asked Shona about the state of Jo's finances and was almost relieved to learn that all was just as Shona had left it the previous evening. Robbery having been ruled out he had gone to check the workshop and warehouse for any further leads. None there, he had been about to re-join the others when Drew had returned. Taking matters into his own hands he had asked him to hold on a minute and caught up to ask the man where he had been and where the other driver was. Drew had got used to Jo having Fernando around and was delighted for them when they had announced their engagement. Mystified by the breakup, he had respected Jo's privacy and left matters well alone but had she asked his opinion, he would have told her that he thought that she had made a big mistake breaking the engagement off. He was, therefore, glad to see that Fernando wanted to be a part of the search for Jo. He was more than happy to answer any and all of Fernando's questions but had no clue to offer as to her whereabouts. When asked if Jo had been acting strangely lately or made any sudden changes, he just shrugged and said that the only thing that he could think of different was the arrival of the new van and driver. When he realised that Fernando was waiting for more he told him about their rapid acquisition and the part he had played. Fernando mentally dismissed the van as that seemed all above board but did latch on to the rapid hiring of Xander Smith. It didn't sound like Jo to offer the man the job on the spot; she was normally far more cautious in his experience. It surely warranted a deeper investigation. He had called the police station himself and spoken to Angus Guthrie about it. He was assured that the matter would receive their immediate attention. He was waiting for his call back when he returned to the reception to hear Jackson's cautionary tale. He waited until it was over before telling them that the police were now checking into the background of Mr. Xander Smith even as they spoke.

Jackson's mobile rang and he put his finger to his lips for quiet as he answered Angus Guthrie's call.

Guthrie was asking, "Was Xander Smith still on the premises?"

A prompt, yes, from Jackson and he told him that a warrant had now been issued against him and that he could now be brought into custody. The investigation into his background had revealed that Xander Smith was in fact an alias. A trawl around local agencies had brought to light rental agreements both in the name of Xander Smith and that of Damon Rigsby, his real name. The isolated nature of the second rental property making it a very likely place to stash Jo Lawson while he remained in plain sight.

Jackson's sigh of relief was patent and his question, "Are we going there now to mount a rescue?" This served to bring much needed hope into the eager listeners' hearts. Guthrie's assurance that a task force was being brought together as they spoke was met with, "Give me the co-ordinates and we'll meet you there." When the conversation was over he was besieged with impatient questions. It took only seconds to arrange who would do what and to leave Shona in charge of the studio. While Jackson went to fill in Michael with need to arrest Damon Rigsby alias Xander Smith, Fernando went to feed the co-ordinates into the sophisticated navigation system in Jackson's car ready for the off. He and Jeni would travel with Jackson as neither of them had held any sway with her over being left behind, she was determined to go with them no matter how dangerous it might be. Rather than waste precious time, Jackson had nodded his assent. Five minutes later they were gone.

The journey of twenty or so miles seemed to take forever. In the meantime, Jeni had texted Anna and Tilly with the latest update and ask them to pray that they would find Jo safe and well, very soon. Then the trip was punctuated at intervals with text messages from the girls, an instruction update from Commander Guthrie and a confirmatory one from Michael Graeme that Damon Rigsby was now in custody and on his way to the police station for further questioning. Michael also noted that Rigsby was not admitting to knowing where Jo was. In fact, he was claiming that it was all a case of mistaken identity.

Chapter Thirty One

EVERY PRECAUTION HAD been taken by the police to avoid being seen as they approached the isolated cottage. A general sigh of relief went up when no vehicles were spotted outside the lonely dwelling hidden in the hills. It could mean less people inside to deal with. However, with their previous experience to go by, no rash moves were to be made, so taking care to avoid being visible from the windows the police officers made their cautious approach from both the front and the rear of the property simultaneously. Once in place, the instruction was given for the Sergeant at the front door to try to gain access in the normal manner of a visitor and ascertain who was within.

When there was no response or noise heard by now, it was time to look in the windows to see if there was any sign of life within. The report of nothing unusual or out of place being fed back, it seemed unlikely that this could be the hiding place after all. It was all securely locked up and no obvious reason to suspect that it was the place they needed to find, made breaking in to enter and conduct a more thorough search seem unnecessary. It was a young constable who pointed out that the spade propped up outside against the cottage wall did seem a bit odd when the rest was all tidily locked away, made them think again. They were ordered to enter with caution.

Front and back doors were forced open simultaneously and the officers had soon searched every room in the ground floored dwelling. Each room being pronounced clear as they progressed through. Still no sign of Jo.

By now the three sitting in the car waiting were on tender hooks. Why had they not found Jo?

Jeni's mind flew to the dread that was haunting her. Was Jo already dead?

Fernando turned to Jackson desperate for reassurance. Jackson, looking straight at the cottage front door could not see the anxiety and dread on Fernando's face, but he could feel it. He was aware of his own growing the longer the search went on. The seconds went by like minutes and the minutes seemed like hours.

Inside the cottage every inch was being inspected for any trace of Jo. Surely she must be here somewhere or at least a clue to where they should search next. It was the sergeant who noticed a scrape on the well-worn kitchen flags. A faint but quite clean mark in a vaguely arc shape. It led from the middle of the room towards the heavy oak dresser on the outer wall. All eyes were now focussed on the wall and eager hands were dragging the heavy piece of furniture away from it and further into the centre of the room. At the first glimpse of the section of wall revealed a stout wooden door recessed into it. The knob rattled but the door was very securely locked. The search for a key to fit its strong black lock was instigated. The young constable knelt and tried to look through the sizeable keyhole but could only see blackness behind the door. However, his imagination was a vivid one and knowing that he would want to know that help was at hand he shouted loudly through it that the police were here now and rescue would be soon.

That was to be the first hope that Jo had of being restored to the real world outside her prison walls. All she could do was raise a hoarse cry of "help". Her voice had long since been worn out by her shouts, despite realising that the centuries old and three foot thick walls of the small bothy would thwart her desperate pleas for rescue. Someone was out there and they must get her out of this dank misery. It was to be sooner said than done.

The place had been built to hide well its treasures and no modern ram was going to make much of an impression on it but time was moving on and they needed to find Jo before her abductors returned. It was the spade, the one that had stood outside that was to enable her escape. With its help the old iron hinges were able to be freed from the corrosion that held the hinge pins and then its leverage allowed the door to be opened while the lock was still intact. Young Constable Harris was held back at the top of the flight of steps that lead down into the cold dark depth of a root cellar. It was not until Jo moved that they knew anyone was within. The torch beams centred on the origin of the noise and blinded Jo completely but brought a cry of relief from her rescuers. She had been found alive and well.

An even greater cry of pure joy was to be heard when Jo emerged from the bothy door bedraggled, injured, footsore and weary but safe once again. When Jo looked up and saw Fernando she just forgot all and remembered only that she loved him while she ran straight into his wide open rapidly advancing arms. All he did was hold her, as she sobbed away her terror and then to whisper in her ear that he loved her and was never going to let her go again. She was home where she belonged at last. The ordeal had taught Fernando a valuable lesson. They were much better together than apart. A reconciliation had taken place without a word being said. They and Jackson and Jeni knew it. All was well once more in their world. Jeni, her phone in her hand pressed send and all that the text said was "SAFE." It was all Jo's parents and the girls would need to know for now; explanations could wait.

Jackson swiftly cleared it with the Commander to take the party back to Jeni's home after the First Aider had ascertained that Jo's condition was sound. It was Jeni who had also been given the job of first breaking it gently to Jo's parents that what Jo needed now was the quiet of her own home and sleep to help her come to terms with what had happened to her. Their subdued agreement reflected their profound concern and their willingness to put their own desperate need for physical reassurance that Jo was well aside for her good. The drive back was a quiet but happy one with Jo and Fernando sharing the back seat wrapped in each other's arms. Shona and Drew were waiting outside to greet them by the time Jackson had put his handbrake on. Tears in their eyes, they welcomed Jo home again and said their own silent prayers of thankfulness that she had been returned to them safe and sound.

Later on, as the day faded into evening and all the police questions had been answered from the safety of Fernando's arms and Jeni's sitting room sofa, Jo found that there was still one more question she had to face. Fernando simply asked her, "Is our engagement back on?"

"Yes. Oh yes please." Was Jo's eager response. Jeni could see that he had more in mind than just an engagement. She turned to her own man and asked and received confirmation of his agreement without a word being spoken. Fernando's wasn't to be the last question of the night.

"Then shall we make it a double wedding?" she asked.

Fernando said, "That's fine by me." Jo following him almost instantly with, "Yes please, if you're sure you don't mind sharing?"

"That's all settled then!" Was Jackson's response. "We'll be each other's best man and still be the grooms." On that happy note it was time to leave. They would get together for breakfast at Jeni's in the morning as the police would still be working at Jo's place for at one more day according to Michael Graeme.

Jeni's mission was to facilitate a rapid climb up the stairs to the guest room's comfortable bed and she was more than content with her lot. Her friend Jo had been restored to her and there was a double wedding to look forward to, perfect.

All Jo needed to do herself when she woke the next morning, was to give her parents a call to let them know the wedding was back on and would be a double one to be held at Christmas. That should be enough to stop them in their tracks and any questions about her trials of the previous days would be forgotten.

Their response, "Thank goodness for that!"

It was a very tired but relieved quartet that allowed Gloria to wait on them hand and foot at the breakfast table. Jeni perhaps looked the worst of the lot for wear for she had been on the phone long into the night reliving the eventful day for both Anna, Tilly and Cathy. Jo actually seemed fine apart from the dressings on her wrists and the marks on her face where the tape had been torn from it, Jackson thought. As for Fernando, he was like a different man altogether! His mind seemed clearer and sharper than it had in ages. His beaming smile showed his happiness and his clear eyes shone with an eagerness for life that had been sorely missed. His friend was back. He was to look back and realise that he had been too quick with his judgements.

The following weeks were very difficult despite being kept busy with wedding arrangements. The question of a dress for Jo being just one. It was Anna who had suggested trying Grace and it was a good job that Grace Carmichael had come up trumps. It would be a triumph on the day her mother had told Jo. She also told her that she needed to get some proper sleep before she got married. The dark circles under Jo's eyes were matched by those round Jeni's. Nightmares and poor sleep were common among the four girls. They reflected their underlying fear of something else going wrong. It had become a permanent cloud hanging over them. Especially, as the news from Jackson was that Damon Rigsby was proving a hard nut to crack. Also, when the enquiries into her whereabouts were made Candy had disappeared off the face of the earth. After her quick departure, which had been explained by her landlady, as due the severe illness of a relative; the forwarding address that the landlady had been given proved to be a dead end, as did any other pointers to Candy's past. A mystery woman indeed.

The fact that there was no news or any other incidences made the girls only a little more confident that the matter was put behind them for good. Even Jackson had a twitchy feeling that all was not well that he couldn't explain away. He had contacted his aide, Tom Bruce, that very useful fellow who had brought Jeni back to them safely from her brush with Mr. Big, to see if he could come up with any other leads while Jackson was so pre-occupied. The underlying tension remained until the reality of the wedding upon them swept all else from their minds.

It was the actual week of the wedding now and Anna and Tilly had driven up to Scotland together midweek to help with the final running around errands. Leon and Craig would fly up on Thursday afternoon to join them and the rest of the wedding party. It was a good job the girls were staying at Jeni's house and the men folk with Fernando as every B & B or hotel nearby was fully booked with the guests for the weekend that were coming from far and near to join in the celebrations. The next two days dashed by with check lists crossed off and the marquee and florists to keep happy, let alone the jittery brides. It took all of Anna's quiet assurance that all would be well on the day to prevent them crashing from one melt down to another as minor hiccups kept cropping up. By Friday when Jackson was dispatched to go to the airport to pick up folk, he was quite glad to get away from it all for a few hours. Poor Fernando had had to stay behind because he was needed to run messages and ferry folk from the rail station to their accommodations. Craig had been left in charge of looking out for the girls. Both Jackson and Fernando felt happier knowing that they had their own police officer to guard them.

Once all were re-united again over dinner together after the late afternoon rehearsal in the church they all relaxed a bit in the knowledge that everything for the wedding had now been slotted into place. Though their thoughts then turned once more to Jo's abduction and the latest on what had been behind it. All seven pairs of eyes turned to Jackson as the font of all knowledge on the subject. He told them what had been learnt, but also telling them that little of their findings could be proven. Yes, they knew that Damon Rigsby was responsible for taking Jo; but as he had not said a word since his arrest, they had not confirmed the perpetrator of such wickedness. The police and Jackson himself, were sure that it was the workmanship of Mr. Big; but they had not been able to find any direct link between the two. However, an unexpected nugget had come to light when looking for the link.

"What?" Went up the cry.

Mr. Big had had a visitor one afternoon in prison. Jackson told them. She answered to a general description of Candy but she was an unknown quantity as far as police records were concerned. She had vanished from sight no sooner had she left the prison confines. The trail had gone very cold. However, Jackson assured them that something would come to light if the police dug deep enough, it always did!

The day of the wedding had arrived. The girls were laughing and giggling as they went from bathrooms to bedrooms half-dressed and hair half done. Cathy had arrived and was trying her best to calm them all down, but it was much harder to do that now than it had been when they were all much younger. Just then Jo arrived, at Anna's suggestion, to have her hair and make-up done with them. She was soon glad she did; as it was much more fun than on her own at home. She just hoped her Mum understood. Her mother would see her in her dress before she went to the church, when she dropped her Dad off and picked up Gloria to take her to the church with her. In the meantime, there were a lot of laughs to be shared and happy memories to be made as they sipped Buck's Fizz and did each other's nails.

It was while they all took turns to take photos of themselves getting ready, and it was the ones that Anna took of them laughing and giggling at the memories of their student days or funny events that would bring the most pleasure and were the photos that made their day. With Jeni and Jo as the brides that had left Anna and Tilly as the bridesmaids. Cathy was given the role of Matron of Honour and Jo's best friend from childhood, Lucy, was to be a flower girl with her seven year old daughter, Suzy. As Lucy was barely five foot it didn't look odd at all. In fact, she looked more like her daughter's big sister than anything! As both Jo and Jeni loved the colour, turquoise, all the girls had been allowed to choose to have their dresses made up in a shade of it that they liked best. The result, a rainbow of hues from the palest aqua to sea jade. They looked stunning. Jo's mother, Maihrie, told them so when she arrived to drop off her husband. Rory was looking fine too. He was resplendent in full Highland dress. The colourful Lawson tartan complemented by his co-ordination of jacket and matching hand knitted knee-high socks. His sporran was highly polished and brushed and his lace jabot carefully ironed to cascade beautifully.

"Oh Da. You look grand." Jo told him as he hugged her and asked, if she really expected him to walk her down the aisle of the kirk wearing that tatty looking wrapper that she had had since she was fifteen or sixteen. She hastened to reassure him that she would put her dress on any moment now, but that she also hadn't wanted to wait until her make-up was finished to give him a hug. Rory was then shooed out of Jeni's bedroom which they had taken over as it had the best mirrors for doing their make-up and told to make himself at home downstairs while the brides got their gowns on.

Fifteen minutes later he was to watch his daughter descend the lovely curved staircase with his mouth wide open and unable to stop himself shedding a tear.

Maihrie could only keep repeating, "Jo, Jo you look beautiful, simply beautiful." As Jo gave her mother a farewell hug to send her on her way to the kirk, her mother whispered in her ear that she looked as beautiful on the outside as she was on the inside. Happiness had given her a wonderful glow and that was what she had always wanted for her darling girl, to be happy.

They all turned as the bridesmaids trooped down to join them, followed by the flower girls and then finally, Jeni the bride. She had not come down before Jo had had her special moment with her parents, but knew that her own parents would be equally wanting to see her too before going to the kirk. Cathy came behind to ensure she didn't trip on her slight train as she descended. Her parents had only seen Jeni briefly the day before when they had arrived after their long flight from Australia. Wanting to be fresh for the big day, they had decided to have a quiet time resting at their hotel. Now feeling refreshed, they were able to appreciate how wonderful their daughter looked on this her wedding day. Marion was full of how fabulous her dress was. "Where did you find it?" There wasn't time for a full explanation as they all had to make a move, but she did tell her that it was all down to Anna and that it had come all the way from Spain. One look at the clock and Rory was ushering the ladies of the party out of the house and into the cars to set off for the kirk. Five minutes later there were only four of them left. Two gorgeous brides and their two very smartly dressed fathers. Tim too had scrubbed up very nicely and looked very dapper in his silver grey trousers and tail coat. He was even prepared with a matching top hat and umbrella. Just in case!

Anna was on the phone for a final word with the caterers while they waited in the church porch. Nothing too dire, thank goodness she told her anxious spectators.

The dad's gave their daughters a brief pep talks and then they were ready to get into the dark navy blue limousine for the last trip for the brides to be as single women.

While all this girly stuff had been going on no-one had been watching the news. It was only a small matter. Quite low key. Reporters had been told to keep a lid on the matter until the escaped prisoner was back in custody in return for a more detailed explanation at a press conference to be held later. However, his name would have been enough to alert any of them to imminent danger and at least made them more conscious of what was going on around them. Instead, they were all totally oblivious and Mr. Big was able to slip over the border into Scotland unnoticed and unchecked. His plan to escape prison to see Jackson and his friends get their comeuppance for himself may have been a late idea and very swiftly executed but it had gone amazingly smoothly. He had been whisked northwards in a style and comfort that he had missed dearly during his enforced incarceration. He had even had time for the Turkish wet shave that he favoured and of course, a change into a Saville Row suit. It felt so good to be back to his normal dress. In consequence he was much more like his old self; in command and ruthless with it! He was ready for Plan Revenge to begin.

Candy's parting words came floating unwanted to mind. "If you don't get this right you will never taste freedom again in your lifetime."

A daunting thought after his experience of the past months but then he laughed and the menace he emanated was palpable.

Chapter Thirty Two

JACKSON WAS JITTERY and he didn't know why? Fernando looking at his friend was so surprised. Normally it would be him having an anxiety attack but this time, he felt quite calm.

He asked Jackson if there was anything he could get him or do for him to help.

"Help with what?" Jackson asked him.

"Well, you are pacing up and down wearing my rug out and have been for the past hour. What's up? Fernando asked him. Are you thinking that Jeni's going to get cold feet?" He asked him.

"No, of course not. Jeni wouldn't do that to me!" Jackson retorted.

"Are you getting cold feet then?" Fernando continued in his efforts to get Jackson to release his agitation.

However, Jackson had decided that he needed to slow down and put everything that was niggling at the back of his mind away. This was his wedding day and he didn't want to miss another minute of it.

He looked at his best friend and told him how grateful he was that they had decided to have a double wedding. It was definitely easier to go through this experience with someone in the same boat as himself. That led them to thinking and sharing about some of the other adventures that they had together over the many years of their friendship. That in turn led to laughter and hilarity at the recalling of some close scrapes. They decided that they ought to mark this occasion with a selfie so that they would remember their last hour as free men. Once taken, it was time to don their wedding finery and make their way to the kirk.

Half an hour later and both were dressed very smartly in their chosen garb and looking pretty grand; even if they did say so themselves. As they set out on their short walk together they were both smiling and sharing the same thoughts – how lucky they were to find such wonderful women to love and be loved by. It may have taken them a little time to get to this point in their lives, but it was well worth the wait to be so blessed.

As the two walked through the kirk-yard and up the path to the open doors they were greeted by another of their companions in their previous adventure. Kevin greeted them, in his usher's role, with a cheery grin and a slap on the back.

"Well guys it's too late to change your minds now; I've just heard that the girls are on their way and you need to make your ways to your posts!" Taking the hint, they did just as he instructed.

They walked down the central aisle to smiles, greetings and good wishes from the friends and family they passed and found their allotted places at the front. They were ready. Unfortunately, so was someone else!

Chapter Thirty Three

HE WAS WELL placed to see but not be seen. Arrangements had been made to enable him to hear every word. It had taken a lot to find a useful electrician to do his bidding to cut off the church electricity supply, but it would be worth every penny, he felt sure. Even the thought of what was about to happen that afternoon was enough to make him feel like breaking open some champagne. Turning to look over his shoulder and finding his quarry he signalled that he wanted the large picnic hamper residing on a beautifully dressed table opened. Adjacent to it, was a stand complete with bucket, ice and a magnum of fine vintage Dom Perignon champagne. The virtually invisible manservant now popped its cork and poured half a glass full into the Edinburgh Crystal champagne flute laid out for that very purpose. He then placed it on a gold salver containing a small crystal dish of caviar on its own bed of ice along with another of crackers and a small gold butter knife. Once satisfied that all was perfect he offered the tray to his master who spread a generous helping of the seafood onto a cracker and ate it whole. Orlov was careful not to betray his thoughts by even the twitch of a muscle, as he knew how dangerous that could be. Still he could not stop himself from thinking what an uncouth man he worked for. Several heavily loaded crackers later and his hunger satisfied, Mr. Big returned his attention to the window to watch the events of the afternoon unfold.

By now everyone had made their way inside Drumcrae Kirk and been seated by the ushers and an expectant hush had come over the ancient building. The candles everywhere had softened its harsh stones and the floral garlands and displays had made the air within its walls smell almost tropical with their sweetness. The scene looked stunning in its simplicity and beauty. Nothing could spoil this day Fernando thought. Then he looked at Jackson standing beside him. He looked so tense; as if he would snap if you so much as breathed on him and what was he scanning the guests so intently for? Fernando glanced around quickly but all appeared to be fine.

"Pssst. Pssst." A little louder he said sharply, "Jackson. Got your attention at last! What on earth is the matter with you now?"

Jackson started and realised just what he had been doing and for want of anything better told Fernando just what it was that he had been doing too.

"Scanning for strangers." He replied.

"At our wedding! Don't be silly. Why would a stranger want to come to our wedding?" Fernando scoffed.

"Jackson's response, "How should I know why? But, I can't help that something is wrong and that's all I could come up with!"

Fernando was just about to mock his friend as being overly sensitive and full of wedding jitters when the organist burst into the Wedding March and the kirks enormous wooden doors were flung open. There was a second or two of stunned silence as the two men and all the wedding guests caught their first glimpse of the two brides to be. Then spontaneous thunderous applause drowned out the music. The organist stopped playing and waited a moment or two until he would once again be heard before re-commencing and the bridal party did the same. That way everyone had time to take in the spectacle and appreciate the beauty on display. By the time Jeni and Jo arrived at the altar and took their places all thoughts of trouble had vanished from Jackson's mind and he was very much in the moment. Then the service began.

The organist was most encouraged by the enthusiasm of the congregation for the first of the hymns selected. Their singing was powerful and if not perfectly in tune, at least joyous. Even Mr. Big enjoyed it as he listened in to the service. As he saw it as one more step nearer to his goal. Then the minister asked them all to be seated and got the couples to turn to face each other ready to take their vows. He then made his address about the gravity of marriage and its joys before asking if anyone here present had any objection to the marriage. All in the congregation went into a shocked silence when not one but two people stood and called out "I have."

Out of the corner of his eye Jackson had caught the movement of them rising to their feet and turned his face towards the people sitting down but was totally bemused by what he was hearing. Jo looked horrified when it dawned on her that it was Candy who had spoken. But who was the man? The ripple of whispers behind hands grew louder as questions about what was going on were aired. The minister had never experienced anything like this at any of his weddings before and was at somewhat of a loss as to know how to proceed. However, Candy and her partner in crime knew just what to do and did it.

As she walked swiftly down the central aisle Candy was expounding that Fernando had promised her marriage and was now holding aloft what looked very much like an ultrasound of a baby in the womb. Jo promptly burst into tears and ran straight past her out of the church with her mother, father and Anna swiftly bringing up the rear. Fernando stood rooted to the spot unable to believe what he was hearing. Just then the man who had raced down the aisle after Candy broke ranks and started pulling on Jeni's arm and telling her that she was coming home with him.

Jackson's, "And why might I ask would she want to do that?" boomed into the crowd but only caused a slight hesitation on the man's part. "Get your hands off her right now!" Came out of Jackson's mouth next but this was accompanied by his dragging the man practically off his feet and away from Jeni. Jeni's bewilderment was obvious to all. Jackson held onto the man and demanded an explanation for his actions.

His, "She's already married so she can't marry you can she?" Caused the involuntarily release of Jackson's captive and the man swiftly stepped aside to join Candy and pursue his dropping of bombshells. By now everyone was bemused and bewildered and accusations were rife. Jeni was now livid. Her family too. It took the minister some seconds to reduce the noise level to some sort of chaotic order.

It needed Jackson's boom of "Will you weesht folk and give the minister a chance to speak", for all to remember whose house they were in.

To the minister's invitation for Candy and the man to accompany him into the vestry to allow this serious matter to be resolved, there was point blank refusal by all parties.

Fernando was adamant and said so. "If they chose to make public accusations, then they should be prepared to have a public response." Jackson too chose to stand his ground. He gently manoeuvred Jeni close to his side so they presented a united front to the congregation. All the while thinking, *he protests too much.*

It was Jeni who burst forth next with, "If I'm supposed to be married, then who am I married to, for I've never seen you before in my life!"

The man immediately retorted with. "My brother of course."

Jeni fired back without a thought, "Then where is this so called brother of yours?"

Equally rapidly the stranger responded with, "In the hospital where you left him."

Every person there was avidly following every salvo of their guns. Jackson chose that moment to intervene, as Jeni was practically toe to toe with the man to give as good as she got. Only, Candy got there first by drawing attention to herself by bursting into loud sobbing. All eyes were now upon her. Some of the older and more distant aunts and cousins began to make sympathetic murmurings. "Och, the poor thing and expecting a bairn too."

Jackson looked over her head at Fernando and mouthed, *set up.* At his friend's nod of agreement. He took charge of the situation and looked over the heads until his eyes met those of Tom Bruce, his friend and work colleague. Seeing understanding dawn in them, he discreetly signalled him to position himself behind the man and Fernando nodded assent to his implied role.

Jackson then said, "We'll be taking this out to the vestry after all folks; just keep to your seats and we'll be right back."

Just as Jeni was about to add her protest to their protagonists' she felt the pressure of Jackson's hand squeezing her forearm. As sharp as ever she took the hint and made to tug Cindy towards the vestry door which the minister was helpfully opening wide. Fernando closed the gap to be right on Cindy's heels and give her no room for turning. With Jackson and Tom on his case the stranger was also trapped into doing their bidding. Once the solid oak door had shut on them, Jackson and Tom were checking the room for escape routes. None found, it was time to put an end to whatever charade Candy and her cohort were up to.

The minister was even more alarmed by what happened next. Jackson and Tom had the odd couple speedily seated in the only two chairs in the small room and trusted up in seconds. Their protests being loud and vigorous at their treatment. Then Jackson had Tom quietly telephone through to the police station to arrange for their collection. Jackson meanwhile was telling Jeni in no uncertain terms of his belief in her innocence and in an undertone, his certainty that this was all due to Mr. Big. He then instructed Tom to try and slip out of the vestry's outer door to try and locate where Mr. Big could be hiding. For by now, Jackson was also convinced that he would have come to see for himself the havoc his actions had wrought.

Mr. Big could not understand what was taking so long. When he heard the vigorous protests he was reassured. He hadn't realised that he was listening to his own minions through the thickness of the ancient wood. He was very happy to think that he had wrecked their plans for a lifetime of happiness. However, he had his finale to think of now!

Tom Bruce was using all the training and the experience of the past few months so that he could try and spot anything that might be the clue to the whereabouts of Mr. Big. He quietly slipped along under the cover of the thick hedge and stone wall that surrounded the kirk-yard. Quickly calculating the maximum distance any transmitting device could be from the church. His caution had covered the sky too for any drone activity. For he assumed, quite rightly, that there would be cameras to enable Mr. Big to have eyes on what chaos was going on inside and therefore no need for anything but rudimentary measures on the building's exterior. As he covered each side of the church searching for a discreet but close observation post and dismissing the most unlikely as he went; Tom became surer of his quarry's actual location.

In the meantime, Jeni was carrying out her own interrogation of Candy and her partner in crime. Jeni's responses to her own accusations were increasingly loud and provided all the cover Jackson needed to ensure that Mr. Big would not be encouraged to flee the scene any time soon. He pulled the minister to one side and whispered to him what he thought was going on and begged his indulgence for a while longer while he got outside assistance and deployed it when his scout reported back. No sooner was Jackson off the phone to his boss making his need for help than Tom was reporting in. Jackson instructed him to pass on his findings directly to the police and then told the minister that it would be about fifteen minutes before the situation would be under control and asked him if he could perhaps go stir up more noise in the church to hold the perpetrator's attention.

"How?" The poor bewildered man protested.

Jackson told him that perhaps he could merely suggest that they could pray together for the couples to come to a happy resolution of their issues. That should cause enough of a speculation outburst to keep Mr. Big from thinking that the game was up. The minister felt happier with his role as an instigator of prayer than as part of some sort of conspiracy and went out the door quickly, but not before Jackson had provoked another loud outburst to be heard by all and sundry. However, Jackson was very aware that they were not out of the woods yet!

Tom had hastily phoned Anna to return to the church as he needed her to get a distraction going to liven up the talk in the church itself to hold the attention of Mr. Big and his crew. Anna had put on her thinking cap, as Tom had emphasized his need for her to convey his need without alerting the unwelcome listeners to the plan to capture them. She had arrived back at the church with arms waving and overly loud voice. Demanding to talk to the bridal party instantly. Telling her tale of Jo's anguish and demand that Fernando renounce this other relationship if there was ever to be a wedding.

Fernando's response of, "If Jo wants to be so demanding, I won't," meant speculation and suggestions were launched at him from all sides. Anna slipped the news that she been had sent by her parents to fetch the cavalry into the melee along with, Cathy was needed to sort Jo out.

The cavalry's discreet arrival did not catch the attention of Mr. Big and his minions at all. It was Anna who held their attention outside with all her goings on that ended in her departure with Cathy to see Jo. They were also so absorbed in the soap opera being played out at the church that they had all been focussing on via a monitor and listening to the transmission of all the shouting too. When they found the upstairs room being stealthily entered by the fully armed Rapid Response Unit they were taken completely by surprise. But Mr. Big was still scrambling to reach the table at his side as he kicked and struggled to be free of his captors. He was even trying to throw himself onto it! It was not until he was safely restrained and the minions removed from the room to another to be held, until the removal force arrived to take charge of them all, that they were able to check out the table and find out just what he wanted so badly. To their horror, it was a remote control device. Had he been trying to set it off or stop it? They speculated as they realised what the yellow flashing light being all that was visible on a small black remote control meant. They just couldn't be sure. What was clear was their Commander's quiet call to Jackson. It was simple and to the point. "Bomb Alert Code Red Immediate Evacuation!"

At that Jackson went instantly into action and had Jeni and Fernando out of the room and on their way down the aisle telling everyone to leave the building immediately as a fire had broken out. Although panicky the wedding party was obedient and all were out and well away under Tom's guidance in no time. The last to emerge was Jackson with his two prisoners who were discreetly taken to a waiting car and whisked away. Fernando had the bright idea of herding the crowd across the green and into the nearest pub by announcing that the first round was on him!

"Well done for that one. It was positively genius, old man." Jackson told him as he caught him up still encouraging everyone swiftly out of the danger zone. Then ten minutes later someone noticed that there were no fire engines, just a bomb disposal vehicle, then there was panic in the air. However, it was the minister's turn to shine as he assured them that everything was under control and they were all safely away from the scene. The entrance of a very well-padded up officer in his bomb disposal suit, who loudly announced that it was a false alarm and that they could resume normal service as soon as his men had left the scene, was greeted with a sigh of relief all round. Which was swiftly replaced by pointed stares at the three men standing close together by the door. Under their scrutiny, Jackson was able to diffuse the situation with is explanation of a workmate's wedding hoax and that the actors employed to carry it out went a little over the top carrying out. The hearty chuckles that raised lightened considerably the heavy atmosphere that had been created, the free drinks did the rest and it was a merry crowd – now with the addition of a few of the pub regulars who escorted the bridal party back into the church. Only one matter remained to be resolved. That of the missing bride.

It was Anna who managed to get through to Jo that it was all a genuine misunderstanding and that she should return to the church and speak to Fernando herself before she called the wedding off. When Anna saw everyone trooping into the church all smiling and happy, she encouraged a still very confused, but a little more reassured Jo, in that direction. When face to face in the church porch, Fernando, with Jackson's backing, briefly explained what Mr. Big had been up to. Jo, was all apologetic for not believing Fernando instantly and for abandoning him when he, and all their family and friends could have been blown to smithereens. It was so shocking that Jo collapsed into his arms. How could she ever make it up to him?

All went very quiet as the enormity of the danger finally hit home. Anna saw the colour blench from Jackson's face and knew it must mirror the reaction in her own. They had all had a very close call indeed. It was the sight of such sombreness that made Fernando certain that, if he wanted to marry Jo today, he had to change the current mood of horror and angst to one of excitement and hopefully, joy.

Fernando's cheeky, "Well you'll just have to marry me and spend the rest of your life making it up to me."

That made her take stock; decide what her priority in life was. She made up her mind that marriage was just what she was more than willing to agree to.

The happy people who followed the brides and grooms down the aisle and out onto the greensward in front of the kirk made for some wonderful photographic memories of a very eventful day. Though it was the photo of four happy couples giving each other a group hug that was the one that held pride of place in the homes of the girls. It could have ended so differently. There would often be times when "the horror of the might have been" would catch them unaware sometimes. It would help them to count their many blessings. Each girl had gained even more people to love and friendships that would never fade. Would that we all could say that in life.

Lightning Source UK Ltd.
Milton Keynes UK
UKHW010752180822
407492UK00002B/323